When René moves into hi[...] come with roommates. T[wo handsome] roommates, to be precise. Too bad they're ghosts.

The fact that they're dead doesn't stop them from running their fingers through René's hair or tackling him onto the bed. It's not long before things escalate and René finds himself with two ghost lovers that treat him better than any living partner ever has.

However, they can't eat, can't go far from the house where they died, and their fingers feel like icicles against René's skin. The longer René is with them, the more he can sense them, but nothing can reduce the chill of their bodies against his. Still, it might be worth the hypothermia.

COLD LIKE SNOW

Sita Bethel

A NineStar Press Publication

Published by NineStar Press
P.O. Box 91792,
Albuquerque, New Mexico, 87199 USA.
www.ninestarpress.com

Cold like Snow

Printed in the USA
First Edition
July, 2018

Print ISBN: 978-1-949340-25-9

Also available in eBook, ISBN: 978-1-949340-21-1

John, you plucked your wings to make sure mine had enough feathers. "My life for you."

Chapter One

RENÉ STOOD IN front of the doorway and ran his finger over the outline of the key's metallic surface before wedging it into the lock and stepping inside his new house. The cold air puckered the skin of his arms and neck. He rubbed his shoulders to keep them warm as he looked around. The flooring throughout the house was black-and-white linoleum. A wide living area faced him—to his left was a fireplace, straight ahead stood double glass doors leading to a small garden, and to his right a half bathroom, dining area, and kitchen. Between the dining room and the glass door, a staircase with a thick cherrywood banister curved up to the three bedrooms and a full bathroom.

René walked to the staircase and stopped short of the first step. He examined the black-and-white squares. They looked clean at first glance, but since he was searching, René noticed the thin rust-colored lines between the tiles. It was why he had bought the house. He'd heard the two previous owners had died after falling down the stairs. Afterward, the old building fell victim to exaggerated ghost stories. True, it did make the building more affordable, but the real reason it appealed to René was because he loved ghost stories and all things macabre. Ever since he was a child, tales that made others grimace had made René smile. He squatted to the floor and reached out to graze his fingertips against the tiles.

A long sigh escaped from between René's lips. He stood and headed to his moving truck. After several hours of carrying boxes in, he decided to save the larger furniture for the next day. René lit a fire; orange light crawled across the floor and walls. He unrolled his sleeping bag near the hearth and slipped inside. The old house creaked. The silence in the house amplified every other noise, which echoed like a lullaby and soothed René into a hard sleep.

At dawn, before René was fully awake, he dreamed someone dragged their fingers through his hair. He rolled on his side, muttering, "It's too cold to get up." The next time he opened his eyes, sunlight brightened the room through the garden doors. He sat up, rubbed his face, and remembered the odd dream of being petted. He smiled at the dream as he stretched and moaned. René slipped out of the sleeping bag and shuffled toward the kitchen to make coffee.

The day labored on as René set upon the tedious mission of dragging his furniture inside his house by himself. Most items—the bed, the office desk, his baker's rack—he had dissembled before loading into the rental truck, but a few pieces—the washer, dryer, and sofa—he had to strap to a dolly with bungee cords, making it slow to get them inside the house. There was nothing better to do during the constant back and forth than think. He'd spent most of his thirty-four years of existence rushing past his own life. He'd sped through junior high and high school as fast as he could, desperate to get away from the small-minded town where his aunt and uncle had raised him after his parents died of heat exhaustion during a camping trip. After he graduated, René fled to the nearest city, waiting tables to scrape up enough cash for a small apartment while he earned his associate degree. He jumped into a relationship with the first guy who openly pursued him, infatuated by the bold, flirtatious attitude that René never experienced from any of the guys back home. Even after his heart broke, René hurried straight to the next boyfriend, who ended up being much worse than the first.

He learned his lesson after that one, sticking to casual hookups as he focused on work and his studies. Once he finished school, René was desperate to find a job where he could afford more than ramen noodles and dollar-store socks. Now he was at a point in his life where he wanted nothing more than to appreciate everything he obtained and accomplished over the years. He escaped the small town. He made enough money to pay his bills. He finally bought a house. René wanted a chance to breathe and enjoy it. Perhaps find a decent partner who wanted to settle down, or at least get a dog.

He went through an entire box of granola bars and a pot of coffee before he decided to go to the store for groceries.

When he returned, René made a sandwich for lunch and then continued to set everything in order. By the end of the day, each stack of boxes sat in the correct room and the furniture was more or less placed where he intended to keep it. Too exhausted to assemble the bed, René spent another night in his sleeping bag near the fireplace, feeling like a strange post-modern male Cinderella.

In the early gray dawn, he had the same dream. Fingers, barely felt, ran through his hair and gingerly touched his cheeks and collarbone. René exhaled with content at the soft, misty caresses, and he wished ghosts were real before sinking into a deeper sleep.

In the morning, he started unpacking in the kitchen until he found the toaster and a skillet. After eating breakfast and unpacking the kitchen, he assembled the bed. Two nights on the floor had his shoulders stiff. René cursed as he balanced the sideboard of his bed frame in his lap and worked the first screw in one turn at a time. For the cost of a six-pack of beer and some pizza, May would have been more than happy to help René both move his furniture and set up the bed, but René relied on his best friend too much already. The next time May visited, René wanted to go out and have fun, not unpack a mountain of boxes, so he finished tightening the first screw and wondered where his bag of extras had disappeared. René groaned when he saw them on the other side of the room. He would have sworn he'd set them beside his lap when he started, but apparently he hadn't. By the time he pushed the box spring and mattress onto the completed frame, René was worn out. He dropped onto the bed and made snow angel motions with his arms and legs before resting.

"Forget unpacking. I should just go to sleep," René spoke to the bed, having no one else to talk to.

His muscles ached from carrying boxes and furniture, and the bed was firm but soft enough for him to sink a little. René shut his eyes and pulled a deep, intentional breath into his lungs. Daydreams played out behind his closed eyelids. It'd been awhile since anyone else had been in his bed with him, and he imagined a mystery lover sneaking to his bedside, sitting beside him, and kissing his stomach as he unzipped René's pants. His fantasy spun out of control. The mattress felt like it really did shift with the weight of another person sitting close. René sat up and shook his head to rid himself of the ridiculous daydream. He made the bed before going downstairs to finish unpacking the living room.

By the third night, the house resembled a home. René examined his progress in the living room and nodded his head in satisfaction. As he stood in place, René's hair slid against his shoulders, as if someone had brushed the long strands away from his face. He froze a moment, wondering if his imagination played tricks with his mind again, but the distinct pressure of a hand lighted on his shoulder and fingers ran down his cheek. He blinked, trying to process the strange sensation of being touched by invisible hands.

"Hello." René's voice sounded loud in the visibly empty living room.

The touching stopped after he spoke.

"Wait, don't leave," René said, afraid he'd somehow startled whatever had interacted with him. René's gaze darted across the living room, searching for any indication that he wasn't alone. Nothing was out of place. René sighed, his shoulders slumping forward. "I didn't imagine that," he whispered, to convince himself he hadn't daydreamed the experience.

An idea drifted into René's head. He spoke to the air in a bashful tone. "If you can hear me, would you follow me. Please?"

He walked up the stairs and opened the door to his office. Stacks of boxes lined the walls and surrounded the desk like strange cardboard obelisks. René pilfered through the boxes until he found one labeled *office odds and ends.*

He pulled the tape from the top of the box and set aside small statues of gargoyles, skeletons, and imps. With both hands, René removed the old Ouija board from the cardboard box. He'd never used it before and only owned it for the aesthetic, but now he sat on the tiled floor with the board in his lap and the heart-shaped planchette under his fingertips.

"I know this is dumb," he said. "I know this is a stupid toy, but why not use it? Crap, I hope I'm not talking to myself. I just want to—" A breath hitched in René's throat as the planchette scrawled across the wooden surface of the board.

"Oh good! I was hoping you'd want to talk. Hold on. Let me get a pen." René rummaged through another box until he found a pack of pens and a notebook. He held the paper in his lap so he could write down the letters. "What's your name?" René asked, but to his disappointment, the planchette only swerved in between the *yes* and *no* options at the top of the board. He frowned, thinking of what he might be doing wrong. Another question came to mind. "How many of you are here?"

The pointer swerved to the number two on the board.

"What are your names?" The planchette moved without him touching it, freeing up his hands to write each letter.

Marcus.

Bastion.

"Really?" René raised an eyebrow. It was a rhetorical question, but the heart planchette spelled another sentence.

You have a problem with our names?

"No." René smiled. "My name's Rembrandt. Our mothers should be slapped. Call me René, though." A nervous chuckle slipped past René's lips. "Not that I can hear you say my name."

Invisible fingers ran through his hair. René leaned toward the sensation.

"Why do you keep petting me? It's not scary in the slightest." He laughed again, conscious that he laughed too much. The way he chuckled reminded René of how he acted during his first date, but he couldn't stop the nervous reflex.

It made everyone else run away.

"Not me," René said.

You're cold like snow.

Your hair feels like sleet.

It's fun to touch it.

Sometimes the planchette darted to each letter in quick bursts of movements, while other times it curved around the board, almost dancing from letter to letter. René's gaze stayed locked on the board, mind guessing who moved it based on *how* it moved.

Does it bother you? The planchette swung in smooth little arcs.

"The petting?" René's voice was more breathy than he'd prefer. "No. Talking to you is exciting."

What if we want you out of our house? That time the words were spelled out in of rush of straight to the point movements.

"Couldn't I stay? You don't want an annoying, large family with kids moving in, do you? Even if you run everyone off, this place would fall into disrepair. Wouldn't it be better to have someone look after it? I'm quiet and good at dusting." René winked.

All right. A-L-L-pause-R-I-G-H-T, all quick dashes, like Morse code with letters instead of telegraph taps *You can be our pet.*

Our tenant. Drawling, easy movement of the planchette, like the ghost only used two fingers to move it instead of both his hands.

René smiled. "I think I prefer the term 'roommate.' I'll put this board near my bed. If you need my help with anything—not that I'd be much help, or that ghosts ever need anything—but if there's anything I can do, let me know." René looked at the board. He didn't want to end the conversation, but his lids hung low over his eyes. Exhaustion from assembling furniture and unpacking boxes washed over him. A palm cupped the side of René's face. He held the hand in place. Pulling it away, René gripped both the ghost's hands. They were ethereal to the touch, not *quite* fully there. Despite the strange sensation of only *mostly* existing, René could feel the callouses on each finger and the broad coarse palm. His chest rose and sank as his breathing sped up.

"This is amazing," he whispered. "Who am I touching now?"

Marcus

He was still holding both Marcus's hands, which meant the curvy, easy movement of the planchette belonged to Bastion. René reached out above the planchette until he his fingertips brushed against another set of hands, smoother skin, longer fingers. René switched from Bastion to Marcus and then to Bastion again, memorizing the differences between them. They both reached out for René. Each of them ran a hand down one side of René's face, his arms, his chest. René's cheeks warmed as they kneaded his body, reminding him just how long it'd been since he'd brought a guy home.

"Um, I need to go to sleep. Good night." René stood to break their contact with his body

The planchette swung across the "goodbye" at the bottom of the board. René carried the toy Ouija board to his room and set it down on his nightstand.

"So much better than the floor." He slipped out of his pants and sunk into his pillow-top mattress. He exhaled and nuzzled deeper into the goose-down comforter.

René missed the light from the fireplace, but a weathered blackjack tree grew outside his bedroom window, and the twisted branches cast thin, gnarled shadows resembling long fingers against the bedroom walls. René stared at their writhing forms and felt a thrill deep in his chest.

He slept well, and on the fourth morning, when the slight caresses shifted him out of sleep, he didn't have to wish the sensation was something more than a dream. René lay in bed and enjoyed the cool, tickling, cloud-soft touches of his new friends—an indescribable but pleasant experience, like the flicker of candlelight, only chilled instead of warm. The touches matched the way the planchette would glide across the board. One set of fingers danced up René's arm and through his hair. Meanwhile another set of fingers ran through his hair in rapid strokes. Bastion—he knew it was Bastion from touching their hands the night before—smoothed a fingertip over René's bottom lip and the sensation pulled a deep moan from René. His eyes snapped open at the sound he'd made. It was much, much too loud, and he was embarrassed. René sat up, rubbing his face to hide the obvious blush.

"You guys are ridiculous." He tried to laugh off his own embarrassment and stood. Walking toward the shower, René pulled his shirt low so the spirits didn't notice the beginning erection creeping down his thigh.

He kept the shower water a little cool, so it would sober him up. René splashed water over his face until his cheeks no longer burned and then gave his skin a thorough scrubbing with a washcloth. An ice-cold finger dragged up René's spine and he jerked forward.

"Oh come on, you two. Not in the shower." René made a shooing gesture with his right hand. "Leave me alone for fifteen minutes, and I'll talk to you with the board when I'm done."

He waited thirty long seconds before giving up and turning the shower water a little colder. The *watched* feeling made René's heartbeat quicken. The chill in the air gave them away. They were both still in the bathroom, but René couldn't blame them. If he were a ghost, he'd mess with people in the shower too. He was sure they found the whole situation hilarious, but the main reason he wanted the shower was ruined with two spectators. René thought of how it could be a problem if their shower voyeurism became a habit, but he decided he'd worry about it another day. He turned off the water. Gooseflesh puckered across his shivering body. He wrapped a towel around his hair and dried himself with a second one. After he finished, he tied the second towel around his waist and sat back on his bed with the Ouija board.

René sighed and said, "I know you were there the whole time. I bet I can even tell you apart."

You think so? One of the ghosts asked. Abrupt movement, it was Marcus.

"I know the difference," René assured them.

Can we test it? Bastion asked.

"I don't mind," René said. "Take turns touching my shoulder, and I'll call out who I think it is."

The first tap shoved René's shoulder back an inch. It reminded René of how a bee sometimes headbutted as a warning before stinging, and it made him laugh.

"Marcus," René said. The second touch was lighter but still abrupt and solid. "Marcus again."

The third touch was fast, but a quick dart of fingers glancing the tip of René's shoulder instead of an actual press. René's lips curved into a grin.

"That time it was Bastion."

As soon as René said Bastion's name, three more taps pushed against him, right, left, center.

"Marcus. So? What's my score?" René picked up his pen to write down their response.

You've had a few lucky guesses.

"That's also you, Marcus."

The planchette jerked back and forth as if both ghosts were pushing and pulling at once, but when it returned to spelling, they were clearly Bastion's movements.

How do you know the difference?

"Easily, Bastion." René's mouth dropped open as one of them slipped behind him and covered his eyes. The room blurred, almost as if a fog settled over everything. René shivered from the chill behind him. "Hmmm... Bastion?"

Bastion's hands dropped to René's neck. He tilted his head back. Meanwhile, a larger, broader touch rested against his thigh.

"And Marcus is touching my leg."

They both grabbed his arms. Bastion spider walked his fingers upward while Marcus dragged his nails down. René held his breath, savoring both touches before describing who did what. The springs in the mattress creaked as Marcus stood.

"Where are you going, Marcus?"

Why would you think that was Marcus?

"You're more graceful when you move," René told Bastion.

Bastion stood up as well. René reached out his hand, his fingers searching for the chill of either ghost. Before he opened his mouth to ask them where they went, a burst of frigid air shoved him against the bed and pinned his hands over his head. Dressed only in a towel, René's nipples hardened into small knots and gooseflesh puckered across his skin. He bit the inside of his lip, refusing to arch up, but that was precisely what instinct insisted he do. Something tickled his chest. Hair? Hair much longer than René's.

"I told you this sort of thing doesn't scare me."

The notebook floated in the air, and the pen scribbled *who* on the paper.

René opened his mouth to guess Marcus, who seemed the more forceful of the two, but a gut instinct made him change his mind at the last second. René continued to look at the paper and pen floating in the air.

"It's Bastion trying to trick me into thinking it's you."

Bastion released René, and René rubbed his chilled skin. Bastion distracted him by unwrapping René's hair from its towel and letting the damp strands tumble to his shoulders. Bastion traced along René's shoulder blades while Marcus held his hand out in front of René's chest, hovering but not touching his skin. The cold lingered where they almost connected. Although he still couldn't see them, René held out his hand and pressed it against Marcus's palm, mirroring him. Marcus's hand was there, but not quite solid, similar to the surface of a waterbed.

René reached out, tracing the shape and form of Marcus, imagining how tall he stood, and how he might look based on the feel of his body. After a few minutes, René turned and did the same to Bastion. Bastion's frame was thin, and Marcus was taller and more muscular. René massaged Marcus's bicep. Marcus flexed the muscle, and René chuckled and grabbed it with both of his hands. Bastion drew a spiral on René's back, and blew an icy breath against the nape of René's neck. René muttered who was who and looked at the notebook to see whether he was correct or not. Bastion wrote *you're right* on the paper. His handwriting was as curvy as his planchette strokes. They crowded around him, and he trembled from more than cold.

"Maybe I should get dressed," he said. Bastion wrote on the paper again. René squinted at the letters, but they weren't legible. "Your handwriting is worse than a doctor writing a prescription."

He noticed the planchette sliding along the Ouija board and leaned forward to read what Bastion spelled.

We're not done yet.

René raised an eyebrow. "Are you being sore losers? I've proven I can tell you two apart."

Well, what about this?

They sandwiched him between them. Marcus faced René and Bastion lingered behind. Both spirits rubbed their hands against René's bare skin harder than before. René closed his eyes for a moment, fighting the urge to grab one of each of their hands and thrust them under his towel. He hadn't thought of the touches as erotic at first. In the beginning, he'd simply been excited to come in contact with real ghosts. He enjoyed the sensations but didn't think of them as sexual until Bastion touched his lips. Now René had to consider they might not find the game so funny if they knew he loved men and their touches aroused him.

"Uh, uh guys," he squeaked, trying to clear his throat. They should know the truth, but René was never comfortable telling anyone about his sexuality. Bastion picked that inopportune moment to tickle René, but he was too aroused to giggle much. Marcus joined in and René couldn't take it.

"Stop." He laughed, a nervous reflex, not a physical reaction to their fingers. He grabbed Marcus's wrists and pinned him against the mattress. He held Marcus in place, but Marcus disappeared, and René plopped onto the mattress. Marcus rematerialized behind René and Bastion, shoving them on top of each other.

"Even if you are a ghost, disappearing and rematerializing is still cheating." The pillows muffled René's voice.

The pressure of the two ghosts on top of him almost had René moaning their names. Face buried in his pillow, René breathed deeply, trying to calm himself. René sensed them laughing above him. He opened his mouth to tell them why they should stop but found it hard to force the words out.

"I-I need to unpack. I've wasted the whole morning." He muttered the excuse even as delicious shivers snaked through his body. "And I'm hungry. I can't go all day without eating."

Marcus released him, spelling on the board. *You're no fun. Things were finally getting interesting.*

René held the towel in place, changing in his closet while talking to his *roommates.* "We'll have plenty of time to research the physics of natural and supernatural interactions, but right now, you're not the ones who are cold and naked."

Finished, he glanced at the board.

Marcus continued to spell. *How do you know we're not?*

"Naked?" The thought was too much for René's already-addled brain.

Cold.

"Of course." René rubbed his shoulder, an embarrassed grin on his face. "Are you cold?"

You're cold, Marcus answered.

"What do you feel like to each other?" René asked.

Warm, Bastion replied.

"That's fascinating," René muttered, his mind back on the topic of paranormal mechanics and out of the gutter.

We'll have to do more tests. Marcus wrote again.

"After breakfast," René said, then walked out the room and descended the stairs. A chill followed René around the kitchen and lingered beside him as he ate and while he unpacked. He spoke to them, but kept to random information about himself, wishing he could have a conversation without the Ouija board. Three times, he tried to explain to them why they couldn't watch him shower, or why they shouldn't wake him in the mornings by caressing him, but each time, he stuttered and babbled something ridiculous. During his lunch break, he used the board to learn about them. In life, they'd been musicians, local, but popular enough to avoid regular jobs. As ghosts, they couldn't go very far beyond the house, but aside from boredom, they enjoyed being dead. Like René, they didn't care for large crowds, so they didn't miss dealing with people, and death had no bills, no social rules, and no responsibilities, so it suited them.

At the end of the night, René read on the sofa, facing the fireplace. Even when his eyelids slid shut between sentences, he shook his head and turned to the next page, avoiding his bed, or rather, avoiding the temptation he'd find there.

Both Marcus and Bastion rubbed his shoulders. A quiet sigh slipped out of René's mouth. "That's nice," he whispered, half asleep.

When he woke the next morning, the novel lay on the rug with a bookmark tagging his place. René's favorite blanket was wrapped over his body as well. He smoothed his hand over the comforter and thought of how every ghost movie ever shot got all the important details wrong.

Chapter Two

"WELL? DOESN'T THIS look better than an empty house?" A week later, the house looked like René had always lived there. He sat on his bed with his legs folded beneath him and the board in front of him.

Are you trying to make it look like a haunted house?

René shrugged. "That's just my style. If I wasn't this way, I wouldn't get along with you jerks so much."

You're so mouthy.

René rested his chin in his hand as he transcribed their responses. He leaned against Bastion's shoulder. When he draped over their bodies, he was a bird catching an invisible wind current and gliding through the air, and it thrilled him. However, part of him always feared falling through them.

"There's something I should tell you." René swallowed, licking his lips twice. He was still working up the nerve to confess his secret to his roommates.

Instead of listening, Bastion tickled him. One of their favorite games, their petting and tickling always ended in wrestling, and René couldn't remember his last warm shower. Bastion pushed him into Marcus's lap and leaned on top of him, slipping his fingers under René's shirt to tickle his bare ribs.

René wiggled in between them. It aggravated his frazzled, aroused nerves, but he couldn't help squirming when their fingers dug in his sides, and their cool, stormy presence pressed against him from both directions. He slapped at their hands, but his protests were playful, and he didn't try hard to get out of the entanglement.

Although they were ghosts, their breaths tickled René's neck and face. He shivered from the chill and wondered if the act of breathing was a mental reflex one couldn't quit, even after death. He imagined how it felt blowing from their mouths—warm by their perception, his breath cold instead. They both breathed hard, and René thought it was unfair. His every expression and repressed moan was exposed to them, but theirs veiled to him. They could be enjoying the moment as much as he was, and he wouldn't know. They could be moaning in anticipation with hooded eyelids as they surrounded his body, and he wouldn't know.

René's eyes rounded at the thought. The bastards *were* seducing him, and he was so preoccupied with staying respectful that he'd passed himself off as a tease. The entire time he'd let them pet and paw at him, but always retreated before they could push further. René looked down at himself. With his legs spread wide and his shirt bunched half up his chest, he couldn't fathom how he'd been naive enough not to understand what had progressed since that first morning of delicate touches.

But now it was a different game entirely. A smile raised his lips as René resisted the urge to laugh. He tossed his head back, letting his hair tickle his shoulders and Marcus's face. He pretended to fight harder, pushing back and bucking forward. Marcus restrained one of René's arms to keep him still, so René kicked out with his legs— not enough to hit Bastion in front of him, but enough to position their groins closer together.

René continued to restrain the moans threatening to push through his lips but permitted a few grunts to sneak past his clenched teeth. His added resistance was met with more aggressive pursuit from his companions. Their mouths drew closer to him. Their forms seemed more solid than usual, and both of them were stiff as he pressed himself back and forth between them, feigning a need for escape.

He wanted to beg, to plead for their cold mouths to meet his and their icy fingers to travel lower than his ribs, but there was too much fun to be had with the game they'd been playing to ruin it for a quick orgasm. He wanted them to break first. He wanted to drive them so crazy that they took him in a fit of need. René rolled off of the bed to untangle himself from his soon-to-be lovers. He laughed as if the entire experience had been another afternoon roughhousing with the guys.

"Okay." René pushed himself on his hands and knees, chest heaving from hard breaths. "I'm cold." It was his go-to excuse when he became too turned on and didn't want to embarrass himself. He peeked up at them, this time knowing they were as frustrated as him, and he reveled in the knowledge.

The Ouija board lifted off of the bed and slammed on the tiled floor, planchette moving to the *No*.

"Sorry." René stood up. "I have to get ready soon. My friend May is taking me to the Dive." He paused on his way out the door. "She doesn't have as much love for the occult as I do, so please, *please*, behave tonight. Don't touch her. She'll scream and I don't want to deal with the headache of explaining a haunted house to her."

The board slid closer to him again. *Why should we behave?*

René sighed, then said, "Oh, Bastion, play nice. Look, I know you guys get bored stuck in this house all the time, so if you don't scare my friend, I'll think of something entertaining for us to do after she leaves."

FOR LUNCH, RENÉ assembled a plate of chopped vegetables, lunch meat, cheese, and crackers, food he could pick up with his fingers and put straight in his mouth. They always watched him, so René decided to tease them in every *accidental* way imaginable.

"Can't go out looking like this." René strolled up the stairs, his movement languid.

He pulled his shirt up over his head as he entered the bathroom. The rest of his clothing dropped to the floor as René stripped. He hummed as the water heated up in the shower. He stepped beneath the spray and exhaled as the water flowed over his body. When the chilling air perked his nipples, René smiled. He didn't mind them watching anymore. In fact, he'd counted on it. René dragged his fingers over his stomach, up his chest, and to his hair. He bent forward, giving them a nice view of his ass as he combed through the strands of hair, wetting them. René forgot to use the washcloth and lathered the glycerine soap between his palms. He smoothed the bubbles across his body and caressed each inch of himself before rinsing the suds away. The temperature dropped lower as the spirits drew close to him. He rinsed the soap from his body and slipped his hands down his stomach and thighs. After the water grew tepid and he had to end his shower, René turned and slid the shower door to the side.

"If you're both going to stand there, might as well be useful and help me dry off." He snatched his towels from their drying bar and smiled.

A pause hung in the air as the ghosts held a conversation his living ears couldn't hear. Disappointed they didn't take the bait, René dried himself, but Marcus snatched the towel from his hands and wrapped it around his shoulders. Bastion grabbed the second towel and dabbed it across René's chest. René braced his right hand against the damp, tiled shower wall while Marcus and Bastion rubbed the soft towels along his skin and hair. Eyes closed, René waited for something other than cloth to touch his skin. Lips, fingers, a tongue, he stood naked between them, obviously not minding their attention to his body, but they hung the towels back on their racks and retreated to a different room. René couldn't tell if they were playing coy or if he'd somehow upset them; however, as he dressed in his bedroom, the futon in the spare room next to his creaked. René buried his face in his pillow shams to suppress the hysterical laughter bubbling from his chest once he realized what the noise meant. He exhaled and leaned against his mattress, listening to the soft shuffling sound of bodies moving furniture.

This was a chance to release some of this own tension. René snatched the lotion from his drawer and tissues from a box and relaxed on his bed. He pressed the pillow over his mouth, not trusting himself to keep quiet. He could ask to join them, but he wasn't going to. He'd wait, driving them further and further, until they begged *him* instead, because those were the unspoken rules to the game *they* had initiated.

He massaged his cock in his hand, drawing out the full length of his shaft. A shiver ran through him. It'd been too long since he'd had a chance to touch himself. René sighed into his pillow as his hand moved in time with the creaking futon in the other room. It excited him, thinking about what they were doing with only a wall between them and René, knowing that his display in the shower was the reason they'd gotten so hot and bothered. He arched his back and bucked into his own closed fist. René fantasied about being inside a ghost. They'd be colder internally, but he was getting used to their cold touches and thought he might like the chill. He enjoyed using ice cubes in bed.

René didn't need long. Between the last week's caresses, the quick strokes of his hand, and the quiet noises sifting through the wall, he climaxed after three minutes. René caught his breath afterward and dressed for the evening, parting his hair to the left and tying it away from his face. He examined himself in the mirror, while the noises in the other room reached a crescendo. René thought he even heard a ghostly moan. *That* was a hilarious explanation to all the rattling, moaning, creaking stereotypes that appeared in dozens of ghost stories. René clenched his hands into fists, licking his lips. He wanted them to hurry before he ran in there and jumped in between them after all. The thought of them banging in the next room was enough to turn on René all over again. But before he lost his resolve, the sounds stopped and René exhaled in relief. He jogged downstairs to wait for May. René read on the couch when the spirits joined him fifteen minutes later.

"Oh there you are," he said, licking his fingers and turning the page to his book. "I wondered where you'd gone off to. I was thinking of the promise I made earlier, and..." He looked above the pages. "If you leave May alone tonight, I'll give you both a massage." He set the book to the side so he could put his hands on both of his roommates' shoulders near their necks. "Nod yes or no. I think I can tell the difference without using the stupid board."

Both men nodded yes and René smiled. "Okay, it's a deal. No haunting, and you'll get a back rub." The smile dropped. "Is that okay? You don't have muscles to get sore."

Bastion took René's hand and placed it on his cheek, nodding yes again. René exhaled, glad they were able to communicate, even in a small way, without the Ouija board.

"Then that's what I'll do," he whispered, hypnotized by his roommates. With his hand on Bastion's face, René wanted to lean over and kiss him, then do the same for Marcus.

The doorbell rang and broke the trance. René forced himself up from the sofa and walked to the door.

"May, it's been a long time." René let her in, shut the door, and hugged her.

"I know." She returned the embrace. "And if I go one more night without getting drunk, I'm going to scream. Show me around your new place so we can find some Gregs to buy our drinks."

May and René had met in junior high when they were fourteen, both crushing on a boy named Greg Thompson. At first, they treated each other as competition, but when Greg started dating a too-skinny cheerleader, they banded together with sleepovers, ice cream, and scary movies to get over the boy who had broken both their hearts. Since then, all boys they'd known were no good for them, but were still pretty enough to chase, were Gregs.

René held May's hand. He led her upstairs to show her the guest room, his bedroom, his office, and then he showed her the kitchen, dining room, and living room. They ended outside in the garden.

"Shit, there's even a pool out here. It's small but better than nothing."

"Yeah, I was thinking about adding a hot tub over there in the corner." He pointed to the spot.

"Hell yeah, you should." May rested a hand on her wide hip and grinned. "We can drink champagne in it. Fucking classy."

"Speaking of drinking, let's go. Those shots won't drink themselves."

The city was quiet as they strolled to the nearest bar three blocks from René's house. A few cars passed, but traffic was sparse. It was a struggle to keep their hair tamed in the cold wind, and René chuckled at May's heels striking the cement.

"I don't see why you wear stilettos when you know we're walking and we'll be too drunk to even crawl by the end of the night."

"They make my legs look sleek in this dress," May said. "Don't judge me. I noticed you look extra gorgeous this evening as well. This is the first time I've seen you do something with your hair since you dated what's his face."

"What's his face's name was Vincent."

"Why'd you dump him again?"

"He's the one I hit with a shoe, remember? The guy who had a thing with mirrors. Where we couldn't fuck without him staring at his own damn ass in the mirror—didn't exactly make me feel attractive, and it was annoying."

"Oh my god, how did I forget? Yeah, I remember Vincent now, and he was the one who basically demanded you moisturize your skin daily and dust the mantel with a pair of tweezers, right?"

"Pretty much. I used to fix my hair around him because he'd bitch that I looked sloppy if I didn't." René rolled his eyes.

May's expression turned sly. "Then why'd you do your hair tonight?"

"So I looked pretty for you." Before she could call him out on the flattery, René added, "Really, I was just bored waiting for you. It was something to do."

"Yeah, I put three coats of polish on my toes, trying to kill time this afternoon. Why don't more people drink at three p.m.? When you're as old as us, you need to get drunk by dinnertime so you can be in bed by ten thirty."

"Damn straight," René agreed, thinking. "We've been friends for twenty years. When the hell did that happen? It doesn't seem that long."

"Oh god, I feel so old!" May slapped her forehead. "Don't ever mention how long we've known each other again. I'm trying to pass myself off as a twenty-seven-year-old."

"You can. Easily," René said.

May smiled. "For now. It'll get more difficult when I'm sixty-five and still trying to do it."

They reached the Dive, an old, square building. The bar loved featuring live music—albeit usually not great live music—but there was always an open pool table for them. René ordered a pitcher of beer and a tray of shots while May claimed a pool table, brandishing a roll of quarters from her purse. They took their time playing pool, chatting and drinking a shot between games. May always won the first few rounds, when they were sober, but as the night progressed, she missed more while René picked them up.

"I don't get how you become magically good at this game when you're drunk." May pouted as René hit his third consecutive solid into the corner hole.

"I always thought you just got worse when you're drunk." René laughed.

"Whichever." May shrugged and looked around the bar. "There is nothing worth our time here tonight.

René glanced around for the first time. Most of the people sat in couples or clusters, listening to the music. The few actively prowling for companionship were obvious creeps.

"If anyone comes up to flirt with either of us, I'm your boyfriend, okay?" René whispered in May's ear.

"No kidding. Some of these guys look like the type to throw you in the back of a van and drive you out to the woods."

"I might appreciate that as long as they didn't tie the ropes too tight." René winked at May.

"You would say that." May choked on her beer. She covered her mouth and laughed.

"We better go, before some of these losers become acceptable options." René tapped a finger against one of the empty shot glasses. When the quarters ran out, they finished the last of their shots.

"I don't think I've ever been *that* drunk." May blew air between her lips. She dug through her purse for her cell phone and searched her phone book for the cab company. They waited outside to be picked up. Their breath furled from their mouths in thick, white streamers.

"Fucking hate the cold," May mumbled with a bit of a slur. She tugged at the hem of her skirt. "Why did I wear such a short dress?"

"So your legs would look sleek," René said.

"For all the good it did. Usually there's at least one or two potentials."

"Guess tonight was just our night to get trashed." René found he enjoyed the cold night air. It reminded him of his secret roommates. He felt sorry for May but didn't mind the lack of potential one-night companions for himself. René closed his eyes.

May stepped closer to him, shivering. He took off his jacket, wrapped it around her shoulders, and hugged her close, rubbing her arms to warm her while savoring the gooseflesh pricking his own skin.

"You're such a sweetie." May snuggled herself into his jacket.

Their cab arrived five minutes later, and they crowded in the back seat, cuddling to keep warm. When they got home, May paid the cabbie—it was how they always split the evening. May paid for pool and the cab, René bought the drinks—and then they raced to René's front door.

"Honey, I'm home!" René shouted into the visibly empty house.

"I don't believe you found such a nice place so cheap." May gave it a second look-over.

"It's haunted." René winked at her as he locked the front door.

"Oh?" May kicked off her heels so she didn't fall. "Do the ghosts fuck with your lights and move your furniture around?"

"Sure, all the time." René waved his hand. "They make the books float in the air and slam all the doors. You know, the usual bullshit."

"Maybe you should hire a psychic."

"I'm better at sensing ghosts than those wannabes. I just whip out my crystal ball and Ouija board and it's an instant party at our house." René snorted laughter, unintentionally calling it *our house* instead of *my house*.

"Ouija board, huh? In this day and age, you'd think a computer would suffice." May crashed onto the couch.

They had tried, but the spirits talked late into the night and René's computer was in his office. He'd also tried paper and pen, but their handwriting was a headache. In the end, it was more comfortable for René to curl up in his bed and read the letters off the board. René didn't say anything out loud. He was drunk, but his brain still worked.

"What's the fun in that? Crystal balls all the way," René muttered instead of his actual thoughts.

"Oh, so they play with your crystal balls, do they?" May snorted laughter.

"You want a T-shirt and some boxers?" He changed the subject.

"Yes, fuck this stupid dress." May tugged at the tight hem of her dress, but the fabric didn't move any farther.

René jogged up the stairs to his room, stumbling on the third step. He braced himself on the wall and continued. Upstairs, he unbuttoned his shirt and rummaged through his drawers for comfortable clothes for him and May to wear. The spirits stole the opportunity to surround him. They rubbed their hands through his hair and over his chest. René opened his mouth wide in a voiceless moan. He slung his arms over their shoulders so they could support his weight as they kneaded his body like pastry dough. He permitted them to play with him until Bastion undid his pants. Chuckling, René wagged his finger at them.

"We can't play our flirty game when May's here." René gave them a wolfish, drunken stare. He shimmied out of his slacks and replaced them with pajama bottoms, leaving his chest bare.

Grabbing a shirt and boxers for May, he brushed past his roommates and sang Chris Isaak's "Wicked Game" under his breath as he walked down the stairs. He dropped the clothes on May's face.

"Thanks, René." She went to the downstairs bathroom to change. René sat on the couch and waited. Marcus grabbed his ponytail and pulled his head back. He couldn't see anything except the ceiling but knew he was staring at Marcus. Bastion straddled his lap, and René swallowed. He couldn't hear them, but he was positive they growled dirty fantasies against his lips as he looked up at faces he couldn't see. René licked his lips. He wished they'd kiss him, but they didn't.

"Would you turn on the stereo?" he asked. "I want to listen to some music."

They retreated and hit the radio to a random rock station as they stormed up the stairs. René had a suspicion of how they'd spend the night. He was envious, but this was a bro's night out. They'd have to wait. There was no way he'd risk getting caught by May.

May returned, singing with the radio, and dropped hard onto the couch. René leaned against her chest. They lay pressed together as they so often did when they were tipsy after a night of pool and drinks.

"The only time I don't mind breasts is when I'm drunk and I need pillows."

"I know. Any other guy trying to pull this shit would piss me off, but you're okay. Too bad you don't have a hot tub, yet. It would come in handy right now."

"Are you still cold?" he asked.

"No, I'm good. Hey, isn't this how we used to spend every Christmas break?"

"Yes." René smiled at the memories.

May's parents sucked and both René's were dead, so they celebrated Christmas each year sprawled on René's couch and singing Christmas carols. They ate ramen and corn nuts for dinner the first few years, before René began collecting cookbooks and taught himself how to cook. Talking about past holiday adventures, they ended up staying awake until three in the morning, laughing until they couldn't breathe.

RENÉ JOLTED AWAKE with a gasp. He didn't remember falling asleep. He sat up and looked around.

"May?"

None of the furniture was his. He wrinkled his nose at the zebra-print couch. René jumped in his seat as a guitar chord rang through the air and looked behind the sofa—it faced the fireplace—to discover Marcus and Bastion standing in the middle of the living room. They were familiar without needing an explanation. Bastion's disheveled, black hair hung past his waist, and his skin was pale like René's. Marcus's skin was the color of worn leather, his ash-blond hair fanned around his head. They both wore jeans but no shirts or shoes. Both wore thick eyeliner, and René bit his bottom lip at how attractive it was on them.

Marcus strummed the guitar again, tuning the instrument. He practiced a few chords while Bastion warmed up his voice.

"Can you see me?" René asked.

They didn't answer. Instead, they started playing. They were better than any of the bands at the Dive where he and May drank, and René enjoyed the music, but they stopped often and fussed at each other. Bastion accused Marcus of trying to speed the tempo, and Marcus complained about Bastion singing sharp.

René laughed. He'd never heard their voices, so he sat on the couch and listened to their banter as much as their music. Two Jim Beam bottles sat on the floor and they reached down from time to time and drank directly from their own bottles. After a while, their arguments accelerated until Marcus set his guitar on its stand and smacked Bastion's shoulder. Bastion countered by punching Marcus in the mouth. René curled on the couch while the two wrestled on the rug. They both smirked as they fought, as if they enjoyed it. Some time in the middle of the fight, René couldn't tell when it transitioned, the biting and scratching grew needful. Bastion clawed at Marcus's back until it bled, already furrowed with old scars from previous encounters between them.

Marcus yanked Bastion's hair and bit his shoulder. They ripped each other's pants down and kicked them off to the side. Marcus shoved Bastion's face into the rug, grinding him from behind. Bastion pushed him off long enough to crawl across the floor to reach a bottle of lube. René laughed when he noticed there were three scattered around the first floor of the house. René put his hand over his mouth and groaned as Marcus slid inside Bastion's ass. Their toned bodies moved hard and fast. Marcus thrusted and Bastion pushed back to meet him. René wanted to be on the floor with them.

He woke up as dawn broke into his living room. René blinked, looked around again, and shook the odd dream from his head. The quiet of the room jarred him; the radio no longer played. René lay half on top of May. A blanket curled around both of them. He smiled at the thought of his roommates covering him and May with a blanket while they slept. He pushed himself half up, head swimming.

"Oh," he groaned, "forget hungover. I'm still fucked up."

"Go back to sleep." May dug herself deeper into the sofa.

"I'm going to my bed." René struggled to his feet, then rearranged the blanket on May.

May grunted but otherwise ignored him

"Shit, how much did we drink?" René stumbled up the stairs to his room. He held his forehead in his hand and crashed onto the mattress.

Marcus and Bastion nestled beside him. The dream rushed back to René's thoughts. He swallowed as he imagined them writhing on his bed—in between his legs. His cock throbbed, and René took a deep breath to push aside his lurid fantasies.

"I'm still drunk," he muttered to them. René rolled over Marcus and burrowed in between them.

The two spirits stirred awake. Their fingertips rubbed his temples and their hands massaged his shoulders. Every touch was gentle, nothing like the vision he'd seen, but exactly what he needed with his head pounding from too much vodka. René arched his back as they caressed him.

"That's so nice," he breathed. He wanted them, and he couldn't be bothered with the game, not when his bed was comfortable and warm, not when their touches were soft and cool, not when the gray morning light made everything beautiful, and not when he was drunk enough not to care who won anymore as long as they took him hard and quick. Just as they'd done to each other in his dream.

As always, the initial light touches turned into heavier petting, but this time, René didn't resist. He gripped the sheets with both hands and stifled his whimpers, wanting to stay quiet since May slept downstairs. They teased him, and pinched his nipples, and traced the lines of his abs. Bastion dipped his fingers below the drawstring of his pajama bottoms but stayed away from his erection. René bit his lip to keep from begging.

He raised his hips, digging his heels into the mattress. He sighed and squirmed, moving his hips to guide the ghosts' touches where he wanted them, but both Bastion and Marcus shifted and dodged their hands around his body. Revenge for the shower tease, René guessed. It didn't daunt him. He parted his lips, inviting them to kiss him.

He couldn't see them, see their reactions. He couldn't hear them, hear their satisfied purrs as they drove him closer to madness. He imagined them swearing at each other...

Don't fucking touch his dick, Bastion. The little brat needs to learn not to be a tease.

Me? Fucking him was your bright idea in the first place. Don't tell me what to do. I've gotten you to beg for it plenty of times, haven't I?

It was his imagination, surely it was. Nevertheless, René would bet their house they said something along those lines. His whimpers changed to grunts. They were driving him crazy, and he couldn't take it anymore. He ran his fingers down his stomach, about to grab his own damn cock to get things started. The thought excited him, made him nervous, tied his stomach in knots.

René jerked to a sitting position. Instead of grabbing himself, he covered his mouth with his hand as his stomach lurched and turned upside down. The nausea was enough to break sweat across his brow, and René scrambled over Marcus to reach the bathroom across the hall from his bedroom.

René's knees struck the floor as he doubled over the toilet bowl in time for the rush of liquid to spew from his mouth. He choked and sputtered as he vomited in quick bursts. Bastion smoothed the bangs out of his face as Marcus stuffed a wad of toilet paper in his hand.

"Thanks," René whispered as he wiped the rim of the toilet seat. "Damn, haven't gotten sick from drinking since college."

René hobbled to the sink to wash his mouth and drink some water since further dehydration would make his oncoming hangover even worse. He stumbled back to his bed. His stomach hurt. His head hurt. His balls hurt.

René rested his hand on his feverish cheeks. Marcus's and Bastion's chilled bodies pressed against him. They laid him on the mattress and pulled up the covers while holding him from both ends. René shook, not because their bodies felt cold, but because he wasn't used to being held by his lovers—all the more odd since he hadn't slept with his roommates yet. He couldn't hear them, but their breath tickled like snowflakes against his ears as they whispered to him.

"I saw you in a dream," René whispered back, "I heard you play. Then you fought and made up on the bearskin rug behind your couch. That's the ugliest fucking couch I've ever seen, by the way."

Marcus shifted and René knew he was complaining, defending the couch.

"If it was still here, I'd burn it," René said. "You both are very attractive. Very. Attractive."

He fell asleep. The next time he opened his eyes, May stood in the doorway, leaning against the frame. Her hair was a wrecked nest, and her complexion was waxy.

"May? Are you okay?"

"I've gotten well acquainted with your downstairs toilet this morning." She gave him a queasy smile.

"Yeah." René nodded from the bed. All she saw was him, but Bastion and Marcus also slept in the bed with him, making the situation awkward. "I spent some quality time with the upstairs one earlier."

May walked to the bed and flopped down. René winced, but Marcus disappeared and reformed on the other side of Bastion before May hit the mattress. May nuzzled her head into René's shoulder.

"Hey, Rem, let's eat pancakes."

"Are you fucking serious?" He kissed her forehead.

"We always go out for pancakes the next day."

"I feel shitty, May. I probably look shitty too. I'm not leaving the house today."

"I've never seen you not look gorgeous. Stop fussing. I'll drive." May poked his chest.

"No," René said. "Let's stay here. I'll make you pancakes instead."

May pursed her lips together, considering it.

"I have chocolate chips."

"Okay." She grinned and hopped out of the bed.

"Still think you're crazy, and tomorrow, you're going to bitch at me for letting you eat so much."

"That's why I go to the gym." May waved her hand to dismiss his complaints.

"Do you need me to wash your dress?" René shook his head at her.

"It's dry clean only. I have a change of clothes in my car. I'll go get them now."

"I'll put a clean towel for you in the shower," René said as he went to the bathroom to fetch a towel.

While May showered and changed, René went to his kitchen and gathered flour, salt, oil, milk, baking soda, and various flavored extracts. He warmed a cast-iron skillet on the stove and found the chocolate chips and pecans. He mixed the batter and divided it into two bowls. One was for chocolate chip while the other batch became butter pecan. Whether drinking or eating pancakes, he and May did nothing in half measures. He poured batter on the hot skillet and searched the cupboards for plates. René checked his skillet to find small bubbles building and popping on the raw batter surface. Marcus and Bastion rubbed his shoulders.

"Thanks, that feels great, but I promise I'm okay. I don't even have a hangover. How's that for a miracle? Still, I'm sorry I got sick earlier."

He bit his lower lip, thinking and deciding he wanted omelets to go with the rest of his breakfast. René rummaged in his fridge and removed eggs, swiss cheese, mushrooms, spinach, and cherry tomatoes. He set everything down on the counter. He flipped the pancakes and found another large bowl to mix the eggs. Bastion grabbed his wrist and pulled René against his chest. Marcus stood to René's right.

"Guys, I know you don't like being ignored, but May will be back any second."

Bastion touched along René's face and lips to show he didn't care if May walked in on them. Marcus slid his hand across René's bare ribs. René turned to the skillet, removing the first set of pancakes and ladling a second batch into the pan. This time, Marcus clenched René by the hips and pulled him close. Bastion grabbed René's chin and tilted his face. René's heart raced in his chest, his breath erratic, and he wished he didn't enjoy their rough handling quite so much. He glared in Bastion's direction, daring him to do something.

Bastion glided a finger along René's lips, and René wanted them. Badly. Marcus slid his hands beneath René's pants, but only held René's hips. The front door opened and shut, and May shouted something from the other room.

They released him. René sensed their tantrum in the air. He wanted to get the board and talk to them, but he had to flip his pancakes again. They stormed out of the kitchen, and René sighed in frustration. Once he finished cooking, he arranged everything on top of the table.

"Why don't we do this every weekend?" May sat in her chair and grabbed her first plate of food.

"Because I hate dishes," René said.

"I'll help before I leave," May promised.

They ate the omelets first. René poured orange juice in champagne glasses and they clinked the crystal together—a toast to debauchery. They saved the pancakes for dessert.

"Lucky bastard," May complained, "with your godlike metabolism."

"I can't get away with as much as I could in my twenties," René confessed.

After breakfast, René started a load of laundry and May helped him restore his kitchen to order. They watched a movie, *Ravenous*, one of their old favorites, and then May hugged and kissed him goodbye and went home. As soon as she left, René searched the house until he found them in the guest room playing gin rummy.

"Hey, she's gone," René said and turned to leave. He paused inside the doorframe and looked over his shoulder. "I feel grungy, so I need a shower, but you guys are welcome to watch...if you want to."

Chapter Three

RENÉ TURNED ON the shower, leaned against the back wall, and relaxed as the water poured down his chest. The prickle of the spray teasing his skin made him hard before he touched himself. He washed his body and hair. His nerves registered every fiber of the washcloth as the rough fabric brushed over his skin. After the last suds slipped off of his body, René took his dick in both hands and stroked himself. Each action felt rushed as if he kicked underwater, desperate to reach the surface and breathe. He clenched a hand into a fist and hit the tiles behind him as he loudly moaned.

The water warmed his body, but a chill in the air announced the other two watched him. René slid the fogged glass door aside, allowing steam and a fine mist to drift out of the cubicle and onto the bathmat. He stared in their direction while lidding his eyes and arching.

"I know you enjoy watching me in the shower." He turned away from them. "Go ahead, then, watch." He squeezed himself harder, gasping at the friction of his palm around his shaft.

René started when two foggy shapes materialized, entered the shower cubicle, and shut the door. Their outlines were fuzzy, but he could make out the difference between Marcus's broader and Bastion's lithe body shapes.

"Why didn't you do this before?" René shook his head to dismiss the question. "Never mind, we'll talk later."

René continued to pleasure himself, cupping his balls with his left hand and hissing quick breaths through his mouth. Bastion and Marcus stood on each side of him, leaning close. Their presence made René self-conscious, but it also thrilled him. The misty outline of their fingers reached out and caressed René's skin. René tilted his head up, moaning. An orgasm welled from deep beneath his stomach. The spirits leaned closer, almost warm because of the hot shower water and curtain of steam. René moaned again, and when they traced the contours of his ears with their icy tongues, René cried out. His legs buckled and he dropped to his knees, shoulders hunched forward.

Marcus rounded his hand over the curves of René's ass while Bastion toyed with his inner thighs. They went for his neck at the same time, sucking hard. A loud cry poured from René, and come shot down the shower drain. René jerked as he climaxed and curled on his hands and knees afterward.

They pushed him back in a sitting position, shifted their fingers through his wet hair, traced along his jawbone, and drew over his lips. Hazy satisfaction intoxicated René, and he melted into their caresses. René leaned toward Marcus and hovered his lips near the ghost's cheek and mouth— then he switched to Bastion and repeated the action. They both groped his chest before nibbling against the sides of his neck. Traveling upward, their lips brushed along his jaw and across his cheeks. They each kissed one corner of his mouth. The second time they caught a bit more of his lower lip. They kissed him one last time, their mouths pulling on René's bottom lip. He sat on the shower floor with his eyes closed while gasping and raising his hands to their faces. René guided Marcus's and Bastion's mouths together.

"Let's go back to the bedroom," René said as he stood up and turned off the water. He snatched his towels, but the spirits took them from his hands and dried him as they did before. As Bastion fondled René's balls, Marcus bit his lip and then the juncture between his neck and shoulder. René was aroused again; he felt sixteen and insatiable.

"I owe you both a massage," he said as they kissed his shoulders. Each took one of his hands and led him to the bedroom. René found his notebook, and Bastion spelled on the board.

We were beginning to worry that you'd never take the hint.

"Sorry. The idea of ghosts being real was too good to be true. I didn't have any room in my imagination for hot, gay ghosts." He poked the foggy outline of Bastion's midsection. "You've been hiding from me this whole time."

We've never shown ourselves to anyone on purpose before.

René carded his fingers through Bastion's hair. The strands parted around his fingers like silvery white streams of liquid smoke. The planchette moved out of the corner of René's eye so he focused on it.

You mentioned backrubs. Marcus shoved the board to the side and lay on his stomach. Bastion copied him on the other side of the bed.

"I did." René maneuvered in between them and kneaded their necks with his hands, one hand for each. Moving to their shoulders, he used both hands on Marcus's back, and then switched to Bastion's. René continued to alternate between them and move down their bodies with deliberate, languid attention. He couldn't pull his gaze away from the mirage-like glimmer of their forms. At times, if René stared long enough, the mist would lift and he'd catch a hint of color from their skin or hair, but the moment he blinked the illusion disappeared, returning to fog. When he reached their lower backs, he circled his palms against their tailbones. René darted his fingers over their asses and sometimes the back of their legs. Each time he strayed from their backs he could feel them hitch their bodies into the movement of his fingers, and René knew if he grabbed their cocks, they'd be hard.

"Wait a moment, you're solid." René stopped and blinked at the mattress.

Marcus grabbed René's hand and placed it back on his tailbone, encouraging René to continue. René spread his fingers across the cold and stormy shape of Marcus's back. The skin was chilled but firm, no longer like the surface of a waterbed.

"You're solid," René repeated. He swung his leg over Marcus's ass, straddling him. Bastion shifted up to watch the scene. René leaned close and rested his cheek on Marcus's shoulder. He no longer felt like a bird caught in a wind current; he merely laid on top of a naked lover. "You're still cold, but you used to only be half there. Now I can feel your heart beating."

Bastion reached over them, handed René his notebook, and took the board. *We've always had heartbeats.*

"This is the first time I could feel your heartbeats, and you always felt like gel." René squeezed Bastion's shoulder and his arm, relishing the silky texture of Bastion's skin. "Can you make yourself invisible again?"

The wavy image of Bastion's form vanished. René patted down Bastion's sides. Holding Bastion in place, René's mouth searched out Bastion's nipples, and his tongue prodded them before circling around his chest. Even invisible, Bastion remained solid in René's hands and against his tongue. René forgot himself as he kissed up Bastion's chest until Marcus bucked upward and reminded René he was in the middle of a massage.

"You're still solid. I don't understand," René said.

You were always solid, Bastion answered.

Marcus snatched the board. The planchette jerked a bit because René still sat on him and he couldn't get a firm hold on the pointer. *If you can feel us better, it means more fun for all of us.*

"But what changed?"

The planchette swerved along the board in the shape of a question mark.

"You guys aren't very helpful. Isn't there a handbook like in *Beetlejuice*?"

The planchette swung to "No" and then the board lifted off of the bed and dropped to the carpet below. Bastion's shape filled in once again as Marcus rose and lay René against the mattress. The ghosts leaned over their pale, living companion, predators closing in on prey. Then they were on him in a flash of teeth and nails. René screamed in anticipation. The last of his questions shattered, window glass in a storm. The way they could materialize or disappear, the dream of their past, how they'd become more solid beneath his touch, each thought blew away in the gale of their fingers and lips. René thrust his hands between their thighs and massaged their balls. He fought to his knees as Marcus sucked on his nipples, and Bastion bit his shoulder. René took both their cocks and stroked them.

They groaned, quiet and far away as if from another room. He leaned against their bodies, his fingers firm and steady paced around them. Marcus bucked in René's hand while Bastion pushed his cold tongue into René's warm mouth.

Marcus spoke, a muffled, whispered sound René couldn't translate. Bastion pulled his mouth and body away and wrapped his arms around René's waist, guiding René on top of him. René groaned in delight as his belly and cock ground against Bastion's body. The spirit sucked on René's bottom lip and brought their mouths together in unhurried, leisurely kisses.

Meanwhile Marcus rummaged through René's dresser drawers. René lifted himself to ask what Marcus was doing, but Bastion captured his face and locked their mouths together for another kiss. Marcus found René's bottle of Gun Oil and a dong hiding in his sock drawer. René giggled as Marcus's translucent shape carried the opaque lube and purple dong to the bed. René's giggles melted to pleading whimpers the moment two wet fingers wiggled into his ass. Bastion broke their kiss to give René a moment to breathe. He bucked his hips against René's groin, and René groaned. Bastion grinned, tracing René's lips with long, slender, fingers. René snatched Bastion's mid and pointer fingers in his mouth and sucked while rocking his ass backward to make Marcus's fingers push deeper.

René sighed as Marcus's fingers pulled away from his ass, but an exciting rush filled him as Marcus replaced both the fingers with the silicon dong. René huffed, raising his ass higher and relaxing to the opening sensation of the toy. Bastion wiggled a pillow below his hips to press harder against René while giving Marcus better access to both of them. It was difficult for René to think of how he'd appear to an observer—floating above the bed in a cloud of fog and getting fucked in the ass by a self-moving dong—but if he kept his eyes closed, he felt their bodies in such specific detail that his brain ignored their wavy appearance.

More moans from them, catches of vocalization so faint it sounded like imagination. Marcus entered Bastion. His thrusts were quick, but he maintained his hold on the dong he used on René. The thought of he and Bastion pressed together, getting fucked at the same time, awoke a lust in

René he'd never known. Bastion's hand fumbled between them until he reached René's cock. He pulled at René's shaft and teased the tip with his thumb.

"Fuck. *Fuck,*" René hissed and reached for Bastion's cock in return.

Bastion's hold loosened as René pumped his wrist. The quiet, otherworldly sighs became discernible. "S*hit, shit, shit, shit, shit,*" Bastion swore as he clawed René's back with both hands. A shocked gasp slipped from René's mouth as Bastion came. Cold coated René's stomach and hand, and he shivered.

He didn't have long to process the sensation because after Bastion's hips relaxed, Marcus tossed the dong on the ground and snatched the bottle of lube in his hand instead. René sucked in a breath as Marcus's head rubbed against his asshole. The breath choked in René's throat as Marcus entered him. Lube dripped down René's thighs. He was saturated, but he still burned with the friction of Marcus moving inside him. René clenched his teeth and screwed his eyelids shut. Bastion caressed René's chest and face. René held onto Bastion, unable to do anything else as he adjusted to Marcus's width.

"Goddamn." He shuddered out a weak breath. There was potential behind the discomfort, but at the moment he was overwhelmed. Bastion stroked René's shaft and cooed in his ears. René let them work, too absorbed in the moment to care if he was their doll. As long as they continued to toy with him, and as long as they pushed him over the edge. After a few minutes, his muscles relaxed, and each time Marcus rammed into René, he called out in pleasure. René buried his face in Bastion's chest, muffling his moans and screams. He held Bastion's shoulders and clenched his ass in time to Marcus's thrusts until his body trembled with orgasm and his semen burned hot against his body.

Although, he knew to Bastion it felt burning cold.

Marcus sped his pace. He clawed at René's outer thighs. René heard Bastion's echoed and distant voice, and imagined he could hear what Bastion said to coerce Marcus.

"Marcus..." René whispered. "Bastion."

Bastion's voice grew louder and Marcus thrust four last times, then came. René gasped from the force and the cold shooting inside him. He collapsed and panted. Shivering, René pulled the blankets around him to help dispel the cold. The spirits lay beside him, Bastion to René's left and Marcus beside Bastion. They spoke to each other, but in soft tones René couldn't understand. Bastion looked around until he found the board on the floor. He slipped out of the covers to retrieve it, resting it on René's belly.

Still cold? he asked.

"No, I'm fine." René turned away.

Bastion tapped the planchette against the board to draw René's attention back to it. *If you're not cold, why are you shaking?*

"Maybe a little cold."

Marcus reached over Bastion and took the planchette. *Liar.*

"It's not the cold." René stared at the ceiling. "This is...scary."

He looked back at the board while Bastion spelled. *Fucking ghosts?*

René laughed. "No, that part's awesome. Staying in bed together afterward... I'm not used to it. Usually if I follow a guy home from the bar, I leave or make him leave when it's over."

What about boyfriends? Bastion asked.

René shrugged. "Only two ever got serious enough to be called boyfriends, but it took longer than a week to stay in bed afterward." René smirked. "What of it? You think you're my boyfriends now?"

You could do worse. Marcus spelled the statement.

René snorted. "Trust me, I've done much worse than a couple of punk musicians."

Marcus smacked the side of René's head with a playful tap of his hand.

"Ow." René pretended to rub the spot Marcus hit although he didn't hurt.

Do I get to hold your hand and call you Rembrandt, now? Bastion teased.

"Don't call me Rembrandt." René scowled at the message.

He turned away from them again, letting the board slip between him and Bastion. René held his pillow and closed eyes to fall asleep. Before he could get comfortable, Bastion rolled over him. Both ghosts mashed René in the center of a tight hug.

"What's this about?" René laughed as they crushed him in their arms.

They returned the board to where René could see it. *You're cute. We want to keep you.*

"I'm not a sex toy you can keep in a drawer." He thought a moment and then added. "How many times have you done this before? Both of you with another person?"

Before we died—or after?

"After?" René asked.

No one. You're the first.

"Okay, how about before?"

We didn't keep count, but it's not the same as this, René. Bastion argued.

"How sweet, was this special because it was your first time as ghosts?" René shifted to his back and raised his knees so he could lean back against his pillow shams but still read the board.

You're different because none of them ever lived with us. You're not the only one who's sent a guy home with cab fare, Marcus added.

And we gave up casual lovers years ago. It'd gotten old, but we care about you. Bastion scribbled in fast swipes of the planchette.

We do, Marcus wrote.

"I..." René felt his cheeks burn. "Well, I don't plan on moving out anytime soon, so we have plenty of time to see where things go."

Do you want us to go to the other room? Marcus asked.

"No." René heard himself say before he'd given it any thought. "Uh, no. I...this is actually nice. Please. Stay." He settled beneath the blanket and didn't complain when they held him again.

Chapter Four

IN THE MORNING, René awoke with his legs tangled around Bastion's calves and his right arm draped over Marcus's chest in a hug. He blinked as his mind came to in stages. They were invisible again, and their breath suggested they still slept. René traced his fingers along Marcus's chest and his toes down Bastion's calf muscle. The tickle from René's foot woke Bastion, and the spirit squeezed René hard with one arm and used his free hand to caress René's blond hair. René had grown accustomed to their soft touches in the morning, needed them. Marcus rolled over to face René and Bastion. René stumbled his fingertips across Marcus's face until he found his lips for a kiss.

Bastion fetched the board and leaned over so he could spell. *Do we get pancakes?*

"If you could eat them, I'd cook you pancakes and eggs Benedict and a triple-layered chocolate cake smothered in ganache if you wanted it."

Where the hell were you when we were alive? Marcus asked.

"Probably dating some jerk," René answered, slipping out of bed and heading toward the shower. He felt stiff from the night before in the pleasant way one felt sore after a good workout. A hand rested on his shoulder. He stopped and turned toward the touch. "Is something wrong?"

Marcus grabbed the soap.

"Oh, you want to shower with me. Sounds like fun." René watched the soap float in the air despite knowing Marcus held it. Bastion joined them. They edged René inside the shower cubicle and Marcus turned on the water for him. René shrieked when the cold jet of water hit his back.

"It's cold." René squirmed closer to Marcus. "You're cold too. I can't win."

René laughed again and clung to Marcus until the water heated and steam filled the shower cubicle. With a sigh, René eased beneath the warm flow and let the water wash the gooseflesh from his skin. Marcus rubbed the soap across René's body. He knelt to reach René's legs and even his feet. Then he turned around and did the same to Bastion. The bubbles gave a slight outline to Bastion's form, and René reached over Marcus's shoulder so he could smooth two fingers down Bastion's soapy chest.

Bastion stole the soap and worked lather over Marcus's arms. His hands rubbed Marcus's lat muscles and over his firm ass and thighs. They rinsed off, and both Marcus and Bastion vanished once the soapy water spiraled into the drain. René's fingers continued to slide along the arms and shoulders, Marcus's back and Bastion's chest.

"Never showered with a lover before," René muttered. "None of them ever *wanted* to."

Marcus's and Bastion's outlines filled in with swirling mist, almost as if the steam from the shower decided to take the shape of two men. Marcus's hand cupped his face, and he kissed René. Bastion guided René's face in his direction so he could do the same. René closed his eyes, and sighed, and enjoyed the moment for just a little longer before he turned off the water, dried off, and returned to his room to change. Breakfast was not pancakes, nor chocolate cake, but scrambled eggs and asparagus, and René only made enough for himself. The thought swept him with melancholy. He'd never be able to cook for them, but when Bastion touched his cheek, René turned and smiled and pushed his thoughts away.

He spent the morning in his office, working from his computer. It was the one time he asked them not to disturb him, but René daydreamed about them regardless. When he went downstairs for lunch, René found his roommates sitting on the couch reading a book together. He smiled and leaned against the cherry railing. The book hovered in the air; the occasional page mysteriously turned. A blanket stretched over their laps, and the fabric etched a vague outline of their lower bodies.

"You know," René teased as he finished descending the stairs. "You're bad examples of semi-abusive, alcoholic musician ghosts. Put some cocoa on the table and a Christmas tree behind you, and I'd have a Hallmark card." René disappeared into the kitchen to heat up some soup.

Marcus and Bastion entered the kitchen, two silhouettes holding the Ouija board and notebook. They set the items on the table and sat in chairs. Their smoky shapes both grabbed for the planchette, but Bastion reached it first.

"You keep switching back and forth. Is it easier to be invisible?" René asked before they had a chance to spell anything. The planchette swung over to the "Yes." After a pause, Bastion added.

We have to consci— The planchette scribbled around the board for a moment then continued, *consciousle—*

Marcus stole the planchette from Bastion's hands. *We have to do it on purpose.*

"No E," René said.

You need a laptop.

"What? You don't think the Ouija board is quaint? I could do séances for money. We'd freak people out."

Bastion stole the board again. *It's hard to talk this way.* Marcus added, *Takes too long.*

"I know." René stirred his soup without eating any. "I'll go to the store tomorrow." René wrinkled his nose in a grin. "Jeez, you guys are the second most high-maintenance lovers I've ever had."

Who was the first? Marcus asked.

"None of your business." René took a bite of lentil soup to avoid saying anything further.

Are you done for the day?

René nodded his head yes.

Good, because we're bored, Bastion said.

"Yes, having to entertain yourself for an entire morning. I don't see how you managed." René snorted as he washed his dishes in the sink. Bastion nuzzled into René's neck and nipped at the tender flesh near his collar.

They both grabbed his hips and pulled him away from the sink. René reached out to put his bowl in the dish rack before succumbing to them. He thrust back, grinding his ass against Bastion, who was closest to his backside. Then René marched away, but he stopped at the doorway and turned around with a smile on his lips. He left the kitchen and walked to the living room. Marcus shoved him onto the sofa. Bastion crashed beside René and licked the outer shell of René's ear. The cotton of Bastion's shirt bunched beneath René fingers as he grabbed for Bastion's chest. Without warning, the cloth disappeared, and René's fingers rubbed Bastion's soft skin.

"What do you do with your clothes? Do you just think yourselves naked?"

Bastion took René's hand and pointed to the kitchen.

René sighed. "Yeah, the board. Fuck it, it takes too long to spell everything out."

Marcus tapped René's shoulder as he kissed his neck.

"Yes, yes. Laptop. Tomorrow. I promise. Don't stop," René said.

Their hands clawed his clothes. They grabbed, and tugged, but never moved toward his zipper. René bucked into the air, but they continued to tease him until he finally grabbed Bastion's hand and held it against the tent in his jeans. Bastion grinned and kneaded René's dick through the pants material. René's breath hitched and so did his hips as he struggled for more friction against his cock.

Marcus growled, but it only reached René's ears as a haunting purr. Marcus yanked the shirt off René's shoulders and bit along René's collarbone. René tumbled to the floor to give the three of them more maneuvering room. He kissed their chests as they switched from his to each other's. Marcus tugged at René's zipper, but René pushed him to the rug, straddling him.

"You first." René bent low and sucked on Marcus's neck.

He swung to the side to give Bastion room to join them, and together they kissed Marcus's chest and abs. Bastion clasped his fingers beneath René's chin and pulled his face close to kiss him. His hunger for kissing was endless. Bastion half climbed over Marcus's chest in order to deepen his kiss with René. He slipped his tongue into René's mouth even as he slipped his hand down Marcus's pants.

Marcus's jeans disappeared, and both Bastion and René stroked his freed cock as they kissed above him. Marcus shouted. It wasn't so much a noise as a frequency in the air sending a shiver through René. Their fists continued to tug at Marcus's dick. René twisted Bastion's nipple between his fingers until Bastion was breaking their kisses with tiny, sharp intakes of breath. Marcus bucked up, and they held his cock more tightly to keep it in place as Marcus raised and lowered his hips. They stroked him in unison. The vibrations in the air grew stronger. They thrummed right into René's core. Marcus's cock pulsed and come fountained over René's and Bastion's joined hands as Marcus came.

René panted for air. He tackled Bastion onto the rug and ground his hips downward. Marcus helped pull René's pants down to his ankles and leaned over him to reach around and stroke René's cock. Below him, Bastion became naked, and René pumped at Bastion's cock while Marcus pumped his. The sensation of touching and being touched both at once overwhelmed René. His cock swelled until his cockhead was red violet and precome dribbled from his tip.

The air puffed from René's mouth in a white cloud although a fire roared beside him. Bastion's cock burned with cold René's hand, and when Bastion trembled and came, it felt like sleet pouring through René's fingers. That didn't stop René from bringing his hand up to his mouth and licking his fingers as if to clean them. Even without physical come, the sight of his tongue trailing up the side of his palm and his mouth sucking each finger would be seductive for them to watch, and the warmth of his mouth helped lessen the stinging cold.

Marcus flicked his wrist faster, and Bastion slipped his hand between René's legs so he could massage René's balls. The cold thrilled him; their touch thrilled him more, and René's muscles clenched, and he shivered, and he sputtered on top of Bastion's stomach.

"I'll get a towel." René gasped for breath after he finished.

His seed stuck to Bastion instead of sinking to the rug below. René stretched out his tongue and licked one of the gleaming pearls off Bastion's stomach before going to the kitchen to fetch a towel and returning to wipe up their mess. Bastion thanked him with a tender squeeze to the shoulder.

"We can play a game of cards to kill some time," René suggested as he shimmied into his jeans. The vaguely defined shapes of their heads nodded in agreement, so he found a deck of cards. He sat cross-legged and shuffled as Marcus brought the board to the rug and set it down between them.

Strip poker? Bastion asked.

"Little unfair for me, don't you think?"

But fun for us.

"You've done half the work already." René pointed to his discarded shirt on the floor. He rested the deck on top of Marcus's belly. "Cut."

Marcus held the cards in the air and cut them. He passed the deck to Bastion who dealt three hands for five-card stud. René looked at his hand and then raised his eyes to where the other cards floated in the air.

"I should warn you." René smirked. "I'm very good at this game. Lucky for you we aren't playing for money."

René filled the dead air with his own voice. Talking about this and that, anything to make the room less quiet. They responded with the Ouija board. They tried to talk back, but anything past a sentence or two became hard to read, and in the end, they gave up and played their last game in silence. René won seven games, Marcus won four, and Bastion won two. When they finished, René set the cards on the coffee table for later games.

"I'll be back in a little while." He put on his shirt and grabbed his jacket from the closet and walked toward the door.

Bastion grabbed his arm to stop him.

"I'm sorry you're stuck here, but I'm not. I have to interact with the rest of the world once in a while." René sighed, not needing the board to understand the question.

Marcus lightly smacked his shoulder. This. too, he could translate.

"What? You expect me to tell you where I go every time? I didn't before we slept together."

Bastion cupped René's face for a moment. René understood Bastion was looking at his face, but it was unsettling because René couldn't truly look back. Bastion and Marcus spoke to each other, and Marcus grabbed René's hand, kissed his knuckles, and let go. Half a minute later, Bastion let go as well.

"I'm just going to the grocery store," René muttered before opening the front door.

He left the house and forced himself to deal with the crowds at the supermarket and electronic store. When he returned, not only did he carry several bags of food, but a laptop as well. Marcus set the computer up on the kitchen table as René sliced onions and peppers in strips for the fajitas he'd chosen for dinner.

While browning the fajita meat, René put away the rest of his groceries and found Tupperware to store the leftover fajitas for tomorrow's lunch. As the vegetables sizzled in his cast-iron skillet, he swept the kitchen floor and watered his houseplants. The chores felt strange and mundane—cooking dinner, storing leftovers, and cleaning—everyday, ordinary actions. Even reading Bastion's and Marcus's texts on the computer had all the excitement of an online conversation instead of breaching the lines of life and death. René thought it should feel different. He should sense some great, mysterious rule broken, or a sacred taboo violated, or a tear in the veil, but it was another nice Sunday evening. They were dead, but they had breath and heartbeats. Nothing changed for them after dying except the size of their world. As René ate dinner, his left hand snuck across the table to trace along Bastion's palms and Marcus's wrists. He glanced in their direction, wanting to see their faces. He found it hard to swallow his food, his breath faint and his heart fast beating. The only thing that ever frightened René about the spirits was the way they made him feel.

Bastion shook his shoulder.

"Yes?" René asked.

Bastion tapped at the computer screen and René read the tail end of their conversation. They spoke of music, one of their favorite topics, but one they knew more about than René. He could only mutter a vague answer about his preferences.

After René washed the dishes and mopped the floor, it was late enough to go upstairs. The moment René crossed the threshold of the room, Marcus seized Bastion's long mane and René's ponytail and dragged them to the bed. He slammed them onto the mattress. René grunted, ecstatic. He had a thing for hair pulling, but none of his previous lovers ever pulled hard enough. They yanked and teased his fine, pale-blond strands, but only enough to make René want more, or they'd jerk his head one way or the other, trying to be forceful, but managing to only irritate René. Not Marcus; he pulled up, not back, going hard without hurting René's neck. This time there would be no erotic teasing, no mock resistance. He'd do whatever they wanted.

Marcus tore René's clothes from his body. Bastion tossed him the bottle of lube and Marcus eased two fingers into René without the coy drawn-out process of foreplay. As he fingered René, Marcus sucked Bastion's cock. René remembered his dream and how they'd looked. Bastion was gorgeous, so pretty it hurt to stare at him, and Marcus was a golem twisted together from hard muscle and leather-tanned flesh.

"I want to see you in detail," René moaned. "I want to see you so bad."

Marcus raised his head, and he and Bastion stared at René. He hated it. They could stare at him, but all he saw were white shadows. Marcus withdrew his fingers and pulled Bastion up. He situated René on his hands and knees and pushed Bastion against René's rear. Marcus gave Bastion instructions, his voice a shuddering, ghostly whisper that René heard, but couldn't translate. Bastion stayed behind René while Marcus went to the front of the bed. He grabbed the top of René's head, guiding René's mouth toward his thick cock. As René swallowed Marcus's length, Bastion entered René. A moan caught in René's throat, half strangled by Marcus's girth. Bastion shifted back and forth in graceful, tireless thrusts. René focused on performing fellatio, but occasionally paused with his lips sealed tightly around Marcus's shaft. He clawed at the blanket and screwed his eyes shut. The tremors of pleasure snaking through his body were too distracting for him to focus. René bucked back, facilitating each forward shove of Bastion's hips and using the movement to help him bob his head along Marcus's shaft.

After several minutes of fucking, Bastion reached for René's cock, Marcus snarled a command, and Bastion laughed and removed his fingers. René tried to smile, but Marcus's width stretched his mouth too wide. He sucked more fiercely, sliding his mouth up and down despite his sore jaw. René's teeth dug into the back of his lips, but he didn't stop because he enjoyed giving the blowjob as much as he enjoyed getting fucked. Marcus's head swelled. His shaft grew fatter as he approached orgasm. Behind, Bastion shuddered and pushed with the last of his endurance as cold shot through René.

With Bastion spent, Marcus pulled out of René's mouth and flipped René on his back like the 185-pound man was a doll. He hoisted René's legs up over his shoulders, reapplied the lube, and bore down. René screamed and clenched his eyes shut. His body waited for each new thrust, and when it struck, René's stomach looped as if he rode a rollercoaster. Marcus lifted René's legs higher and said something to Bastion. With René's legs in the air, and the weight of his lower body resting on Marcus's shoulders, Bastion had plenty of room to lean in and lick René's shaft.

"Ah!" René wailed when his cock entered Bastion's mouth. He didn't notice the cold anymore. His body was scalding enough to thaw the chill of his ghost-lovers' bodies. "Don't stop. Please don't!"

René never begged in bed before, nor did he care that he begged. His toes curled and bursts of color bloomed behind René's eyelids as he came in Bastion's mouth.

Marcus ejaculated last, his growls savage and violent. This time, when the three of them dropped into the haven of blankets and pillows surrounding them, René didn't complain when they shrouded him in their arms. He didn't have enough breath, or will, to argue or feel awkward from the proximity. He lay between them, gasping and shaking from sheer euphoria.

Chapter Five

WEEKS LATER, RENÉ sat straddled on top of Bastion's cock. He rocked back and forth, just so, squeezing his pale thighs and dropping hard enough for his ass to smack against Bastion's body. René held his breath as a spasm shook through him. From behind, Marcus reached around René, teasing René's left nipple with one hand and stroking him with the other. He trailed up the nape of René's neck with bites, and René gasped each time teeth pricked his skin. René arched his back against Marcus's chest as his semen arched across Bastion's stomach and the bedsheets.

René hunched forward. He rolled onto his back to catch his breath. Marcus grabbed a vibrator he'd set aside and angled it up Bastion's ass. Bastion hadn't come yet. Every time he neared release, they'd ease back and stop before he could finish. Now Bastion's rough moans echoed in the bedroom, loud enough for René to hear. René stroked Bastion as Marcus pleased him with the vibrator. Bastion shook his head side to side. His ass rocked against the toy. René lavished his chest with kisses, stroking and stroking and stroking until Bastion bowed upward as he climaxed.

Once it was over, René relaxed into his pillow, asleep before he registered the process. His cell phone woke him, Blue Oyster Cult's "(Don't Fear) The Reaper" playing in a loop. René grabbed for the source of the noise, half asleep and half blind in the darkened room. It was past 6:30 in the evening.

"Damn, I slept all day," he murmured, only answering the phone because May's name appeared on the screen. "Where the hell have you been? You haven't returned my texts in over a week."

"I know. I'm sorry," she said.

"Well?"

"Not over the phone, Rem. Want to go out tomorrow night?"

"Always," he answered, sitting up, "but are you okay?"

"Yeah."

"Come over tonight, May," René said, "I want to have a slumber party. We can make Rice Krispies Treats."

"Damnit, René." May laughed, but it was a sad noise. "Why aren't you straight so I could marry you?"

"We could still get married and cheat on each other with gorgeous men. We'd save money on taxes and health insurance."

"Okay, I'll be over in about an hour. I'll bring pizza and an engagement ring." May laughed again, more sincere.

"You better get down on one knee when you propose to me, May. I want this to be a romantic moment, and I want a black wedding dress."

Her laughter rolled through the phone. "Can I have a slutty red one?"

"Why the hell not?" René shrugged, though she couldn't see the gesture over the phone. "It's going to be a disgraceful marriage. Might as well be a disgraceful wedding."

"Great, see you soon." May ended the call.

"Damn her." René tossed his phone on the dresser. He clenched his jaw.

Bastion opened up a word document on the laptop sitting on René's nightstand, asking, *What's wrong?*

"When she shows up, she's going to have on sunglasses and extra makeup. The only time she ever ignores my calls is when some Greg hits her and she doesn't want me to see the bruises." René shook his head, standing up and rummaging in his closet for clothes to wear. René chucked his clothes on the bed. "I didn't even know she was dating someone. I'm going to fucking beat his face in."

Greg? Marcus asked.

"Y'know, a guy you fool around with." René gestured with his hand.

Bastion nudged René in the ribs and asked, *So, are we your Gregs?*

René turned away from the screen. "I thought so at first, but...no, I don't consider you Gregs. Gregs break your heart by dating cheerleaders, or hit you, or threaten to leave if you don't keep your nails manicured. Gregs don't ever hold you afterward, or take showers with you, or play card games on the living room floor. Gregs don't last very long."

The three of them sat in silence for a moment. Bastion broke the quiet by asking, *So you like living with us?*

"Well." René grinned. "It's my house too."

Too bad you're going to marry that broad and ruin it all. Marcus wrote on the screen.

"Sorry, guys." René took his clothes and went to take a shower. "You've been demoted to my mistresses."

After his shower, René dressed and took his laptop downstairs. He started a fire in the fireplace and sat on the sofa. Bastion sat beside him, and Marcus sat on the rug facing them.

Bastion wrote a message. *I refuse to be a mistress.*

"Well, if you don't approve of my wife, I guess you guys will have to sleep in the guest bedroom," René teased.

Marcus said something and Bastion typed. *He's right. You'd miss us at night.*

"I guess I would. Oh well, I'll just have to bring a Greg home to keep me company."

We'll make knives fly through the air, Bastion threatened.

Marcus jumped on the couch so he could type. *We'd have him scared to death before you reached second base.*

René thought about what they said. He'd been so caught up in the fact ghosts existed—and wanted to touch him—that René hadn't had time to think about another relationship, or how they may or may not work it out.

"What if I did meet a guy and want to bring him home one night? Would you really scare him away?"

They discussed it; Marcus typed. *He better be into ghosts and four ways.*

"That's fair." René leaned onto the sofa arm and smiled. "But I don't think I'd like sharing either of you."

He expected a sarcastic reply. When Bastion grabbed René's hair with both hands and kissed him, it caught him off guard. Marcus copied the action and René sat back, panting. His heart went wild, pounding in his chest, and René grew dizzy from the thrill.

"Wh-what was that for?"

Marcus wrote, *We're also selfish, jealous bastards who'd rather have you to ourselves.*

"Then let's make a deal, I won't bring any living boys home if you don't invite any other ghosts to live with us." René toyed with loose strands of hair.

Deal, Bastion agreed.

"Bastards," René swore, "I didn't want a relationship. I just wanted to fuck some ghosts and then have you both go haunt the attic or something."

Well, Bastion typed. *This house doesn't have an attic, so your plan was stupid.*

May knocked on the door, and René closed his computer. "*Deus ex Machina* to the rescue. No more conversations about how we're going steady for the entire weekend. What a relief."

The mist of their forms evaporated, leaving them invisible. René walked toward the door. Marcus slapped his ass as he passed, and René chuckled. He opened the door and stepped back to let May inside.

"I bought a frozen pizza and stuff for Rice Krispies Treats." May stormed in, heading for the kitchen. She tied her hair in a knot and preheated the oven.

"No sunglasses?" René leaned against the fridge with his arms crossed over his chest.

"It's eight p.m. and you're not stupid, so I didn't bother." She walked to him and kissed his cheek.

"You did a good job. I can barely see the bruise around your eye." He held her chin, examining her face.

"Primer. It's fucking awesome, lets the makeup stick better."

"When'd you meet him?"

"About a week after the last time we went to the Dive." She spoke rushed, stilted sentences, repeating a story to René she'd rehearsed a dozen times in her mind. "He was hot. I slept with him. He stuck around for a few days and left. He knocked on my door at two in the morning about a week ago, drunk and wanting some ass. I told him to fuck off. He hit me. I slammed the door in his face and ignored his calls ever since." May stopped to suck in a heavy breath. "I didn't want to talk to you because if I did, I would have gotten upset, and when I get upset over a Greg, you kick his ass, and then I have to bail you out of jail."

"You only bailed me out of jail the one time," René said.

"Well, it was the last time, so I'm still expecting it." May knelt to the kitchen floor.

"May, what are you doing?"

"Give me your hand, René," she said.

"If you give me a cigar band and call me Molly Brown, I'm not making you Rice Krispies Treats."

"There was a quarter machine at the grocery store." May stuffed her hand in her pocket. "Almost everything in there was plastic diamonds and flaked gold paint, but this is the one that randomly popped out." She slipped the small, black ring decorated with a white-painted skull on René's pinkie finger. "I think it was destined for you. It's creepy, just your thing."

"I'm wearing this tomorrow night at the Dive. If anybody hits on me, I'm telling them I'm engaged." René smiled at the little, black ring.

"You better." May stood up, dusting the knees of her jeans. "No looking for Gregs tomorrow. It's bro's night out."

"That suits me just fine." René grinned, glad to have an excuse.

THE NEXT EVENING, while May showered and René tossed on a pair of old jeans and a red hoodie, Bastion brandished a tube of liquid eyeliner.

René frowned at the floating makeup. "Don't steal May's stuff. Put it back before she notices it's gone."

Bastion leaned over to the laptop sitting on René's vanity. *Let me make up your eyes.*

"Hell no." René wrinkled his nose.

But it was fun to do our eyes for shows—stage makeup.

"Do your own eyes."

Why? So black lines can float in the air? That'd be weird. C'mon, I'll make you sexy.

"I'm not even brushing my hair. The last thing I want is to look sexy."

Bastion sat in René's lap, wrapping his arms around René's neck and leaning close. René moved his head back as far as he could while in Bastion's grip, looking over to his bed.

"Marcus, help me out here?"

Marcus waved from the bed, and René rolled his eyes because he knew Marcus wouldn't do shit to save him. Meanwhile, Bastion nuzzled his nose against René's forehead and cheeks, begging with subtle body language instead of on the computer.

"This is coercion." René laughed.

Bastion leaned back and typed. *If you let me, I'll vacuum, dust, and wipe down all the stupid moldings while you're out tonight.*

"Oh no." René frowned. "Last time you helped me clean you broke two glasses. I'm surprised you haven't broken the laptop yet."

Hey, do you have any fucking idea how much willpower it takes to move shit when you don't have a physical body? Kiss my ass.

"That's why you don't clean." René grabbed his ass instead.

*I'll manage it without breaking anything. Let me do something fun...because if I get bored...*He kissed René's neck.

René looked over to Marcus. "I'm going to remember this, remember how you sat there and did nothing. Next time he pulls this shit on you, don't ask for my help."

Marcus shrugged.

"Fine, Bastion, just hurry up before May finishes her shower. I don't want her seeing makeup floating in the air. It's going to be hard enough to explain why I borrowed it."

Bastion grinned and applied a thick line of the liner. René tried to blink the offensive liquid away from his eyes, but Bastion held his cheeks and forced him to stay still. Finished, Bastion disappeared to return the makeup to May's bag, leaving René to sit in front of his vanity, staring at his face. René looked away, embarrassed at how much he admired the look, but his eyes kept darting back to catch quick glimpses.

Marcus walked to the laptop so he could type. *He does a good job.*

"I'm so pale. I look dead." René glanced back at the mirror.

Marcus grabbed René's chin and forced his face close. The temperature dropped until René could see his breath. His eyes watered. He blinked to avoid ruining his eyeliner. Marcus spoke to his face, but all René could do was shake his head *no* because he couldn't hear anything past a faint murmur.

"I can tell you're upset, but I don't know why," René said.

Marcus growled and turned to the computer. *"Not dead. Never say that."*

"Oh, damn. I'm sorry." René touched the back of Marcus's hand with two fingertips. "I won't ever say it again. I'm sorry."

In the bathroom, the sounds of water stopped, so René closed his laptop and set it on his nightstand. He flipped the hood up on his sweatshirt, hoping it'd distract from his eyes, and waited for May to return.

She entered the room wearing a tight-fitting black T-shirt and boot-cut jeans. May carried her makeup case with her, and René sighed at the thought of it.

"Your water pressure is the best ever. I should come over every day to shower—and eat brunch." May applied multiple layers of sprays and creams to her own face as she spoke.

"Then you're paying the water bill and washing the dishes," René said.

"I'm okay with that. Well, maybe not the dishes. I have enough trouble keeping my own washed." She fanned her face to let the cream dry, looking up at René. "Holy shit, Rem, when did you start using guyliner?"

"I, uh... I saw a video on YouTube and thought it'd make me look like a vampire or something. You know, for shits and giggles." He averted his eyes.

"You look like a supermodel."

"Whatever." He blushed, cursing Bastion. "I wore the baggiest clothes I could find in my closet."

"René, you should know by now you're one of those people who could walk around in a sack and make others jealous."

"Then I'm washing this crap off. I don't want guys messing with me all night."

"Oh, don't wash it off. I know I said no Gregs tonight, but seriously, if you see a cutie don't turn him away just for me." May caught his hoodie and pulled him back toward the bed when he tried to walk away.

"I'm done with Gregs," René said.

"That'll last about as long as a New Year's resolution." May laughed.

"I really don't have time for them anymore."

"Yes, because moping around this old house all day with the ghosts takes up so much of your time."

He started at her words, prepared to explain, but then he realized she was teasing him. He grinned, as wide as he could.

"At least the ghosts can carry on a good conversation, which is more than I can say for all the Gregs I've ever slept with."

"Yeah?" May asked, "What do you talk about with your Ouija boards and your crystal balls?"

"Music and literature, mostly. The bastards have me reading *Carmilla* right now, but you know I'm more of a Poppy Z. Brite fan." René chuckled, amused by the situational irony.

"You should write a freaking screenplay about your pretend ghost adventures, but maybe change *Carmilla* to the *Necronomicon* or something." May shook her head.

"With my sordid imagination? Anything I wrote wouldn't be appropriate for cinema."

"I'd watch it." May did her own eyeliner and eye shadow, giving her eyes a smoky look. When she finished, she touched up her hair in René's vanity mirror.

"We look awfully pretty for a Greg-free night." René frowned.

"Isn't that how it works? When you try, you look okay, and no one talks to you, but if you don't give a fuck, you look fantastic. Watch, everyone at the Dive will be a babe. We'll both end up at hotels tonight."

"Are you ready?" René dodged the question.

"Yes, let me get my boots and we can go."

Chapter Six

"DID WE EVEN buy a single drink?" May stumbled across the threshold, slung over René's shoulder and shaking from the cold night air. It was past 2:00 a.m.

"We bought our first round." René closed the door and wobbled over to the fireplace.

"Most of them were after you, but that's okay as long as they're buying both of us drinks. I'm so surprised you didn't like the one with dark hair. He was hot. Oh baby, so hot."

"I've seen hotter." René stacked logs into the hearth.

"No you haven't," May said.

"Once or twice I have." Catching a shadow out of the corner of his eye, René turned to the stairs and winked. The room chilled as they walked closer. The cushions on the sofa shifted, but fortunately May was too drunk to notice.

"Hurry up with the fire. It's freezing in here. Are there any Rice Krispies Treats left?" May flopped on the rug and wiggled the boots off her feet.

"In the kitchen." After he got the fire roaring, René concentrated on returning the grate to its proper place.

"Mmmmm, drunken munchies," May slurred as she fumbled her way to the kitchen.

With May gone, Bastion and Marcus crowded against René and teased their fingers through his hair.

"I love that," he whispered as softly as he could, afraid he'd scream without noticing. He closed his eyes, "I love you. I love you both."

They stopped and laughed.

"Yes, I'm drunk," René hissed into their faces. He wondered if they could smell the alcohol on his breath, or just feel the cold air he blew on them. "Yes, I'm saying it because I'm drunk. Don't care. It's true. I love you."

Marcus pinched René's nipple.

"Yeah, I love boobs when I'm drunk too. Well, you're a pair of boobs, 's all the same." René crawled away from them and climbed onto the sofa.

May brought a plate of Rice Krispies Treats with her. One hung from her mouth. Her other hand held a tall glass of water.

"Shouldn't it be milk, or something? And cookies?" René squinted at the glass.

She set the plate on the floor, taking the Rice Krispies Treat from her mouth to answer, "I don't want a hangover. We should drink water."

They split two treats and drank some of the water. Sitting on the rug with their backs to the couch, both rambled about their past few days, complained about annoyances in their jobs, and laughed again at how many free drinks they'd scored at the bar.

"We should do something," May insisted.

"Like what?"

"We need a game."

"Like a drinking game?" René laughed.

"Like a board game." May gestured with her hand.

"Like the Ouija board?" René fell back on the rug laughing.

May jumped to her feet and searched the closet where René stored his cards and board games. She frowned at his selection, then cheered, "Jenga. Is this the same damn one we played with in college?"

"No, that was Jumbling Block Tower, remember? Didn't have the money to buy the official one when I was in college. I had the dollar store version." René stared at the ceiling.

"Let's play this." She cradled the block-filled tube in her arms and danced back to the rug near the sofa. "Okay, I know we're smashed, but that's no excuse for us to suck at this. René, we are going to become the motherfucking Jumbling Block Tower champions of the world."

"But this is Jenga."

"Don't bother me with details. I'm setting up this tower."

They took turns stealing wooden blocks and stacking them on top. Neither rushed. Instead, they tapped the blocks to check for loose ones before removing them and setting them back on top. Once they reached thirty-five levels high, May held her hands out in a stop gesture.

"René we're done."

"You're suppose play until it topples over."

"I know, exactly. I can't stand to see it fall, and that's why—we're done. We're going to quit while we're ahead and leave the damn thing standing. This tower isn't going to fall."

"It'll probably fall while we're asleep," René spoke matter-of-factly, drunk, but not as drunk as when they came home an hour before.

"No negative thoughts, René. You'll jinx our poor tower."

"Okay. Let's leave it up. I want you to prove me wrong when it's standing in the morning." René rested his chin in his hands and stared at the tower.

"The woman is always right, René. Of *course* it's still going to stand in the morning."

"That was pretty sexist, May."

"I won't tell HR if you don't." She winked at him. "It's time for pj's."

May went to the downstairs bathroom to change, and René staggered to his feet. He was careful to avoid their wooden tower as he stumbled to his room to put on his pajama bottoms. As he changed, Marcus grabbed him from behind as Bastion crammed his hand down the front of René's pants.

"Oh, oh yes," René whispered as he swayed beneath their touches. "Guys, I want to, but I can't. May will see."

Marcus bit the nape of René's neck, and Bastion kissed his lips before they both let go. They disappeared, and René buried himself under his blankets. He sucked in steady breaths, releasing them slowly to calm himself and stop his cock from swelling. He was back to normal before May jumped next to him on the mattress.

"I'm cold, let's cuddle." She nuzzled beside him under the covers, an old habit from when they were teenagers.

"Do you want me to turn on the heat?"

"Nah, it'll be okay. Although, this house is drafty."

"I've never noticed." René grinned.

"If our tower falls, I'm going to cry," May muttered, drunk and falling asleep.

"It won't fall," René promised.

"Everything we do falls, René. We both know it. It's probably leaning right now. I just wanted to win a game for once."

"It won't fall. Not until we knock it down," René said.

"Do we have to knock it down? I want to take it down one level at a time."

"Okay."

"You're the best friend ever." May squeezed René's shoulders.

"We'll take a picture first, to prove it stayed up all night."

"RENÉ, HEY RENÉ? Rembrandt."

"What?" He awoke with May shaking his shoulder hard and repeating his name.

"You were joking when you said your house was haunted, right?"

"What?" Her question made him jolt up to sitting.

"The lights keep flickering on and off." May gave him a guilty, sheepish grin. It was somehow apologetic, as if she knew the question was stupid but she couldn't help asking.

"What the fuck?" René yelled at whichever one of them was at the light switch flicking it up and down, but May thought he was shouting because of the lights.

"I mean, we're drunk, right?" May asked him.

Bastion walked in with a sheet over his head. He raised his arms out in front of him like a zombie, which made him look like an idiot, not a ghost. René stormed to Bastion and ripped the sheet away. He dropped it to the ground while punching him in the shoulder.

"What the hell do you two think you're doing? It was two nights. Two fucking nights for you to entertain yourselves but you had to act out? What are you? A couple of teenagers? Marcus, touch that light socket one more time and I'll find a way to break your hand. Bastion, a sheet? A sheet? You couldn't do better?" René smacked his shoulder again, though not as hard as the first time. "You couldn't make the knickknacks float around the room or something? You had to put a sheet over your head? You're the worst ghosts ever."

René stopped his rant when he realized he was yelling at them more for their shoddy haunting than for scaring May. He glanced over at her. She curled under the blanket, eyes wide, face pale.

"I-I'm sorry, May," René stuttered.

"René, your house is haunted," she said, trying to grasp the idea.

"Yeah." He sighed.

"You know their names?"

"Yeah."

"Why didn't you tell me?" she yelled.

"I didn't want to frighten you." René shrugged. "Or be sent to a mental hospital."

"Yeah, you're right. I wouldn't have believed you." She glared at him. "So all those jokes you've been making? You don't actually talk to them with a Ouija board, do you?"

"The Ouija board was annoying, so they made me buy a laptop." René scratched the back of his head as he walked toward his nightstand. He opened the computer and a word document, glancing over his shoulder. "You're taking this well, May. I thought you'd be screaming."

"It's a quarter past four in the morning and I'm still kinda drunk. I reserve the right to freak out about this later, but right now I'm just confused." She blinked, her bottle-blonde bangs a mess around her face and her blue eyes wide and bleary from sleep.

"Good enough." René scooted over so Marcus and Bastion could reach the keypad. "Well, assholes? You wanted attention. Mind explaining to me why you thought this would be a cute idea?"

Don't be pissed, René. We were just trying to say hi.

It seemed funny at the time, and you were both so piss-faced drunk we didn't think you'd wake up.

René examined May, her face frozen with shock as she watched the keyboard type by itself. She covered her mouth with her hands.

"This, this is really happening, right René? I'm not dreaming, right? I don't think I am...but this is crazy."

"I'm sorry, May. I'm so sorry. I thought they had more sense than to out themselves." René gave her hand a comforting squeeze.

"How long?"

"How long?" he asked.

"How long have you known about them?"

"I figured it out on the second day I was here," he answered.

"They don't scare you?" May laughed at her own question. "Of course they don't! You probably talked to them first. You probably squealed like a child on Christmas morning when you found out you lived in a haunted house."

"Yeah, kinda," René said.

May grew thoughtful, tilting her head to one side, and asked, "So which one of you was dumb enough to put a sheet over his head?"

Me.

May looked at René for clarification.

"Bastion." René pursed his lips.

"Doesn't it freak you out? I mean, people you can't see always walking around your house?"

"I can kind of see them, sometimes, and I always know when they're near because the room will get colder."

It's our house, Marcus wrote, *we're just letting him stay here to amuse us.*

We scared everyone else away, Bastion added. They wrote *m* or *b* before their dialogue so May knew who said what.

"Yeah, I bet whatever you did to scare the others away excited René." May snorted when she read the last part.

Yes, Bastion agreed.

René bit his lip to keep from screaming at them, hoping May didn't catch the subtle insinuation. He watched May's face, no longer pale or shocked. She edged closer to the monitor, forgetting to be afraid as the conversation progressed. René smiled.

"So, what was that all about?" May gestured to the sheet on the floor.

Seemed funny at the time, Bastion answered.

We were just trying to say hi, Marcus responded. *You spend a lot of time with René and so do we. Better to be friends, yes?*

"No," René interrupted, "better to hide so she didn't know you existed."

Now, now, Rembrandt, you sound ashamed of us, Bastion wrote.

"Poor René, they already know how to push your buttons, don't they?" May laughed when she read René's full name on the screen.

"You have no idea." He pondered the rows of text on the screen. "What made you want to be her friend? You don't like people."

You only drink with her, and you're cute when you drink. And we don't want to sit in the guest room every time you two hang out together. It's awkward, Bastion answered.

"Awwww, you're cute when you drink. Maybe I should come over next weekend too." May ruffled René's hair into his eyes.

"Our livers couldn't handle more than every other week." René swatted her hand away and fixed his hair.

"Every other weekend it is, but don't stay up for us, ghosts. If we find some hot Gregs to waste our time with, we'll be at the hotel till morning."

"May," René held both her hands in his.

"Holy shit, René, you're boning them!" May's eyes sobered, and she shouted out the words before he had time to finish his sentence.

His expression crumpled. Being gay was awkward enough without having to admit he was sleeping with ghosts too.

"I don't care—but how does it even work? I mean *physically,* because they're ghosts." May caught his look, squeezing his hands to comfort him.

Bastion and Marcus phased into their mirage-like images. May squinted her eyes as if she saw the air shift, but couldn't make out how. Bastion rested his hand on her shoulder. May jumped off the bed and stumbled three feet backward, almost tripping on her pink pajama leg. She stopped and rubbed her shoulder. After a minute, however, she walked back to the bed and reached out her hand. Bastion held it. She took his palm and ran her fingers over his invisible skin.

"Well," May admitted, "I guess it could work. It'd be creepy as hell, though." She shook her head, her yellow ponytail swinging back and forth. "Then again, this is *you* we're talking about, so it makes all too much sense." She narrowed her eyes at René. "Actually, this explains a lot. You've had this crazy glow the last couple of times I've seen you, and you smile more now."

"Whatever, you're just imagining things."

"Hey, René, does this make you a necrosexual?" She lay on the bed and giggled.

"Please shut the fuck up, May. I'm not digging up corpses from their graves."

"No, no," she agreed, "that would be weird, wouldn't it?"

"They breathe, and they have heartbeats," René said.

"No you don't," May accused them directly.

Marcus placed her hand on his chest.

She paused a moment and said, "You do. That doesn't make any sense." May laughed off her confusion. "So, now my best friend has two Gregs and I have none. Looks like I have some catching up to do."

Oh, we're not Gregs, Bastion corrected her.

"Hah, all guys are Gregs," May said.

Marcus reinforced Bastion's statement, *"René said we weren't."*

"You did?" May stared at René, raising an eyebrow.

"It's five in the morning. Can we please go to sleep?" René tucked the blankets up to his chin.

May turned back to the computer. "He's never said that before, about anybody."

Marcus asked, *What about his ex-boyfriends?*

"There are Gregs we fuck, and Gregs we date, and Gregs we move in with until we realize we made a mistake and then move right back out." She smiled. "He must think you're special if he said you weren't Gregs."

"May, go to sleep. In the morning I will convince you this was all a drunken hallucination."

"Yeah, but I'm not drunk anymore. Hell, I'm not even afraid anymore. Your new boyfriends are fracking adorable. Tomorrow, while you make us pancakes for breakfast, I'm going to tell them about your awkward teenage years. The red will never leave your cheeks by the time I'm done."

See, René. Bastion tilted the computer so René could read his words. *This is why we like her so much.*

"May? You're honestly okay?"

"I know they're like ghosts and stuff, and I should be freaked out." May snuggled back under the covers. "But you're such a creepy nerd. This somehow makes more sense than any other guy you've ever dated."

René sighed. "Okay."

"Hey, Marcus, since you're so good at turning lights on and off, why don't you turn them off now?" May closed her eyes and grinned.

"Yeah, Marcus, that's a good idea," René said.

Marcus grumbled, but he turned off the lights before crawling beside them once the room was dark.

"René, there are four people in this bed. You're a whore." May snickered.

"This is the most platonic four way I've ever been part of," René confessed.

"We're still engaged, right?"

René kissed her forehead. "Yes."

Chapter Seven

RENÉ WOKE TO the clacking sound of long-nailed fingers striking computer keys. He blinked his eyes open. The room glowed with afternoon sunlight. May sat in the bed and giggled as she read something on the computer.

"Uh-oh." René cleared his throat as he remembered the night before. "How long have you guys been talking?"

"Over two hours." May stretched her lips in a wide grin.

He peered over her shoulder at their conversation. May closed the document. "Sorry René, girl talk is sacred."

"What did you tell them?"

"Your favorite color. Your favorite season. Your favorite baseball team. Seems you've been very closemouthed to your poor roommates about certain details. That's not very nice, René."

"May, stay out of my love life." René hid his face beneath his pillow.

"You should go make pancakes and give me some more time to gossip." May rested the laptop on top of René's black comforter.

"Nothing about what you just said sounds appealing."

"So you're going to stay in bed for the rest of your life instead?" May pushed his hair into his eyes.

"No pancakes. Too much sugar. I'll make bacon, egg, and cheese biscuits. I don't want to puke again."

"We puked before we ate the pancakes," May reminded him, "but biscuits sound great. I'll take it."

"You have to go downstairs with me," René said.

"Really?" She batted her eyelashes at him, faint traces of her eye shadow haunting the outlines of her eyes from the night before.

"Yes," René insisted. "I don't trust you and Bastion together. You two could cause a lot of trouble."

"We're angels. I promise." May waved René's concern away with her hand.

"If you're angels, then you won't mind flying downstairs while I cook breakfast." René stood and stretched. He raised his arms high in the air and let them drop to his sides.

Marcus slapped René's shoulder at his last statement. A chill spiked through the air and puckered the skin on René's arms.

"What?" René asked, wondering what Marcus found offensive. René didn't wait for an answer. He went to the kitchen and preheated the oven.

"René, you never let me have any fun." May followed him, pouting.

"But I do cook you breakfast," he said with his arms full of ingredients.

"True, you do spoil me when it comes to breakfast." She blew him a kiss, the red paint on her nails flashing with sunlight from the window.

"Did you notice? The tower didn't fall." René set flour and salt on the counter.

"Yeah, but now we have to try to disassemble it without it falling."

"Can't we just kick it and watch the pieces scatter?" René asked to rile her up, payback for whatever secrets she told Bastion and Marcus.

"No. It deserves better."

"May, you're getting sentimental in your old age."

May held a hand up to her ear. "What, René? Did you say I should let your sweethearts know you love bondage and rim jobs—especially together—but you're always too bashful to ask for them? Okay. Hey, guys—" May inhaled a deep breath, preparing to shout. René threw a dry dish towel at her face to silence her.

"Keep it up, and you can go to McDonald's for breakfast."

Marcus and Bastion were sitting at the kitchen table, so they had already heard, but it saved René the embarrassment of listening to May scream it a second time.

"Sorry, I couldn't help myself." May laughed.

AFTER BREAKFAST, THE four of them worked together. René, May, and Bastion held the blocks steady at the base, while Marcus grabbed three sticks at a time and put them back in the cardboard cylinder. Row by row, they were disassembled by near-invisible hands. May's face barely contained her grin as their epic drunken tower of Jumbling Blocks—but really Jenga—pulled itself apart and reassembled in its box. Only once did René think it'd fall, because his elbow cramped and he bumped against it while changing his position. The remaining blocks shook on their foundation. May held her breath and crushed her eyes shut when he did it, but Marcus smacked the top with the flat of his palm and no one moved until the wooden structure stopped trembling and Marcus could continue his work. Three, two, one, and they were victorious. The lid was screwed on and the game was returned to the closet, sitting triumphant on top of Taboo and Risk.

"And that, bitches, is how we beat the game. You have to build it up to thirty-five levels, leave it up overnight, then take it back down without it falling, because we make our own rules to play by." May smothered them in a group hug when they were finished.

René stepped back and examined the scene. May in his living room with her arms slung around Bastion and Marcus was quite the sight. She looked silly, like a scarecrow on a pole surrounded by dense fog, but them standing together made René so happy his chest hurt.

May noticed the clock. "Shit, I need to get home. We stayed up all night and slept all day, and now it's almost five, and I have work tomorrow." She rummaged through her overnight bag until she found a pair of pants, stripping off her pink pj's and shimmying into the jeans. Slinging the bag over her shoulder and heading toward the door, May stopped and held out her arms so she could hug and kiss Bastion and Marcus. They each took turns squeezing her.

"Where the hell were you guys before?" May shook her head. "We should have been hanging out together when you were alive. It'd be even more of a blast, but that's all our fucking luck, isn't it? Anyway, I'll see y' guys in two weeks."

May grabbed René's hand and they walked out to her car. She tossed her bag in the passenger's seat and turned around, staring at René.

"Am I about to get a lecture? You have a look on your face." He raised an eyebrow.

"They're nice, René. I like them."

"I can't wrap my head around the fact that you're already fond of them. I have to bribe you with dessert to watch ghost movies with me."

"The ghosts in those movies are jerks. René, be nice to Marcus and Bastion."

"No, I don't think I will be." He shoved his hands in his pockets, staring at the driveway with a small grin toying with his lips.

"René."

"May, they're ghosts."

"They're people, stuck in a different plane of existence, but still people."

"That's the closest to spiritual I've ever heard from your mouth."

"Talking to the dead can do that, I guess." She squeezed both his hands. "Rem, we both know you're good at hiding behind a shield. This one time... go ahead and drop it."

He looked up at her. "What the hell did you guys talk about?"

"Sorry, girl talk is sacred." She smiled.

"Then, just between us girls, tell me what they said."

"Nothing," she said, "they just wanted to know more about you."

René dropped his head again. "May, I can never cook them dinner. Never go out on a date with them. Never look at them and see more than a blur, and their voices are just whispers I can't understand."

"They told me when you first interacted you could barely feel them, but now they're solid, right? And you didn't notice they had a heartbeat for a long time?" May opened her car door and sat in the driver's seat, looking up at René.

René nodded his head.

"Well, they were solid to me right away, and I felt Marcus's heartbeat just fine. How could I do all that when I can't sense them at all? They have to let me know who's who on the computer, but they said you're good at guessing and you even know if they're laughing or yelling at you."

"So what?"

"So, apparently spirits and shit are real and you're sensitive to it. If you're having trouble hearing them, maybe it's not because you can't, but because René's force field of 'if I don't care, they can't hurt me' is activated."

René blinked at her. "You think I'm blocking some weird sixth sense?"

"If anyone had some stupid sixth sense, it'd be you, sweetie."

"That's...dumb."

"So is Jenga, but it's my new favorite game." She blew René a kiss. "I'm leaving for real this time. Think about what I said."

"Sure." René waved goodbye as she drove down the street.

He turned around and walked back to the house. René crossed the threshold and shut the door. Both his roommates stood in front of him, already waiting.

"Please don't tie me up and give me a rim job." René giggled.

René heard their soft laughter, or thought he did, May's words swirling in his mind. They stepped closer and pressed René against the door. Marcus reached out and traced his fingers along René's lips while Bastion caressed his cheek. René exhaled, his breath shaking and his eyes closing.

"Stop," he whispered, but even he didn't believe the words and they kept going, hardly touching him. René started panting. "Stop it. It makes me feel like gelatin."

They removed their fingers and touched each other instead. Their hazy bodies drew close, caressing as their lips met. René's mouth dropped. His fingers twitched, wanting to touched them, but he stood in place. The smoky outlines of their hands intertwined and they walked across the living room and up the stairs. They left René to stay or follow at his whim. When he trusted his legs enough to walk, he followed them. They lay on his bed, kissing and holding each other and in no hurry to progress. Their shapes twisted together. At moments, wisps would clear, and René could almost see a glimpse of how they *should* look, but those moments were brief. René held the door frame for support as want and need clenched the muscles below his abdomen. He staggered to the bed and dipped onto the right side of the mattress. He pressed his mouth against Bastion's lower spine and kisses his way up to Bastion's shoulders. Bastion sighed and arched into René's kisses. His toes rubbed René's calf.

Marcus slid his arm across Bastion's body and reached for René. He pulled René tight against Bastion's back. Marcus and Bastion continued to kiss while René worked his lips along the nape of Bastion's neck. His mouth wandered to Bastion's ear and back to his shoulder as he explored Bastion's skin with his tongue.

Impatient, Marcus pulled away from Bastion's mouth. He rose to his knees and grabbed the bottle of lube on the nightstand. René stole it from Marcus's hand, coating himself until his cock gleamed in the lamplight. René grabbed Bastion and pulled him onto his own lap. Bastion faced away from René, eased down René's erect cock, and sighed in pleasure. Bastion planted his feet on the edge of the mattress for purchase and gripped his knees. Marcus knelt on the floor in front of the bed and opened his mouth wide to swallow Bastion's entire length. René gripped Bastion's waist and held him, so Bastion couldn't move.

"René," Bastion whined, struggling to bounce up and down.

Marcus lifted up his head to smirk. "Yeah, hold him."

René shook his head. He told himself he couldn't have actually heard the words and must have imagined them. He held Bastion more tightly, and Marcus dropped back down. He sucked from base to tip and made Bastion grunt in wanton aggravation.

"Hmmm, you don't want to stay still, do you, Bastion?" René squeezed Bastion's hips, keeping Bastion's weight pressed down on his cock and whispering in Bastion's ear. "A fucking bedsheet? I don't see how you ever scared anyone away from this house." He bucked his hips up. Bastion's body squirmed in his grasp, encouraging René to buck upward a second time

Bastion called out and doubled his efforts to move. He settled for rocking his ass front to back against René's lap as Marcus sucked him into a frenzy. The longer Marcus sucked, the more desperate Bastion's moans sounded. René held him and listened, listened to the velvety, chaotic whispers he couldn't transform into coherent words, but he wanted to. He wanted to. He'd thought, for a moment, he had.

Still, he didn't need to hear the words to know Bastion was pleading with both René and Marcus. Trapped on the edge, the thin line between exhaustion and bliss, Bastion begged them to let him move how he wanted. René bucked one last time, and the scream from Bastion's mouth broke through the veil separating their worlds—loud like a bell. It reminded René of the dream of Bastion singing. He used his hands to guide Bastion's hips. It was exactly what Bastion wanted and he slammed his ass onto René's cock over and over. René grunted each time Bastion's ass struck his thighs. His own ecstasy climbed as Bastion rode his cock.

Marcus had to stop sucking, but he worked his fingers around Bastion's shaft. For several luxurious minutes, Bastion called out with pleasure, ass still bouncing. His nails dug lovely crescents into René's legs. Then he held his breath, trembled, and crashed onto René's thighs. Bastion doubled over and gasped, his body spent. René lowered him to the mattress and leaned forward, kissing him. Bastion held the side of René's face, his hand shook from his orgasm.

René turned to Marcus. "And you."

Marcus's voice echoed in the air. It sounded like the faint rumbling of distant thunder. René went to his toy drawer and pulled a medium-sized plug from the collection of treasures. He ignored the indiscernible grumble of Marcus's tough talk, and pressed him down beside Bastion. René attacked Marcus with his mouth. Kissing his hips, nibbling the meat of his thighs, and lapping Marcus's balls with his tongue. René slid the plug inside Marcus as his mouth covered Marcus's cock.

Bastion rolled onto his stomach so he could lean over Marcus and suck at his lips. René had fucked Bastion, but never Marcus. They used plugs and anal beads on him from time to time but predominantly allowed him to be the alpha of their lovemaking. René patted the back of Bastion's thigh. Bastion turned onto his side, watching René prepare Marcus.

René grinned and discarded the plug. He hooked his arms around Marcus, lifted him in the air, carried him for three feet, and slammed him against the wall. Marcus was almost too heavy for René to keep upright, but the chair rail provided enough support for René to maintain their position. René leaned close, Marcus's breath shallow and cold as sleet against René's cheek.

"Your light stunt woke May, but it wasn't scary at all. You're both terrible ghosts." René brushed his lips over Marcus's cheek and to his ear. "Tonight, I'm going to fuck you," he breathed, as low and sultry as he could while keeping the words clear and audible.

René slipped partially inside, holding still a moment when a strange choking gasp escaped from Marcus's lips. René didn't expect to get away with his plan. He waited for Marcus to throw him back on the bed, to regain dominance;

however, Marcus simply kept his arms wrapped around René's neck for balance. He turned his face so he could stare at Bastion, who spoke quickly and excitedly from the bed before shifting onto his stomach for a better view.

René embedded himself fully. He paused again to give Marcus time to adjust. René wondered how there was ever a time he couldn't feel their hearts, because Marcus's heartbeat pounded against René's rib cage too strongly to ignore. René withdrew and slid back inside. He stopped another moment and then repeated. René's mouth opened wide as Marcus's body squeezed around him. Each push was hot and tight, and jolts stabbed their way up René's stomach as he set a moderate pace. Bastion crept up behind René and rounded his hands along René's hips. René swayed back and forth. Bastion shoved his hand between their bellies, giving René enough space to move while he toyed with Marcus's cock.

Marcus and Bastion spoke back and forth. Jealousy crept into René's mind. They could speak to one another, but René couldn't. Marcus contracted his pelvic floor muscle and René's thoughts lost themselves to the tightness of being inside his lover for the first time. He filled Marcus with his length, his breath puffed from his mouth in time with each thrust. Marcus's thighs were thick, and they hugged around René's body. Bastion stopped teasing Marcus's dick and worked his shaft in earnest. He purred in Marcus's ear as he jerked his cock. Marcus grunted. The muscles along his biceps and deltoids flexed tautly across his body. René's cheeks burned and his lips grew tight and cold as he neared his climax. Marcus groaned, and the noises he made while coming sent René over the edge.

"Fuck!" René screamed as his body tensed up. Every single muscle tightened and quivered and then relaxed in a quick rush.

He almost dropped Marcus but readjusted and kept them pressed together for a moment while he recovered. Bastion helped René ease Marcus to his feet. René and Marcus collapsed onto the bed, but Bastion wandered out of the room.

René giggled without reason, his head light and giddy. Marcus sat beside him and combed his fingers down René's back as if to ask if René was okay. The tickle of Marcus's hand against René's sensitive nerves stopped his laughing, replacing it with a gasp, and René threw back his head and arched from reflex. He rolled to his side and stared at Marcus.

"I enjoyed that."

Bastion returned with the laptop in his arms. He plugged the machine in and turned it on, opening a word document and typing. *That was hot. No one's ever taken Marcus before. That was fucking hot, René, you bastard.*

Marcus snorted, stealing the computer. *Maybe I should make you do all the work more often.*

René tilted his head up and smiled. "Anytime you'd want."

You should have seen his O face. It was adorable. Bastion wrote for René's benefit.

"Bastion?" René asked.

Yes, René?

René grinned as he saw his name on the screen, but it wasn't good enough; he wanted to hear it. "Will you sing for me? I don't care what. I won't be able to understand the words. I just want to hear your voice."

Bastion paused. Marcus chided him, and he snapped a reply. Bastion passed the laptop to Marcus, and he started singing. René blushed, Bastion sang, *I'm Burning for You.* Apparently, May also told them his favorite band. As he sang, Bastion swayed from side to side, leaning close to René or Marcus and pulling away, his motions lithe and fluid. René lifted himself on his elbows but kept his eyes closed. He imagined Bastion's dancing form, hair spilling around his face and back in a mess of black flames, blue eyes intent on his audience, abdominal muscles trailing to his midline and forming a V in his pelvis—a shape which forced May and René to both agree perhaps God did exist. After all, something that sexy was strong evidence for at least perverted, if not intelligent, design. His mind was so focused on the fantasy, René wasn't sure when he began to hear the lyrics.

I'm not the one to tell you what's wrong and what's right. I've seen suns that were freezing and lives that were through.

René opened his eyes in surprise, but when he saw only Bastion's smoky shape, he lost the meaning of the words and the lyrics unraveled back to the whispers of a ghost. René cursed his mind and demanded his brain give him back the language he'd lost, but his frustration rendered his goal unattainable.

After the first song, Bastion sang a second one, something René didn't recognize.

"You wrote this?" René asked Bastion and Marcus. Marcus confirmed it on the computer. René settled into his pillows, listened to the melody of the song, and fell asleep just after it ended.

Chapter Eight

RENÉ TURNED IN a circle. The furniture was gone, replaced with a thin layer of dust. He was in another dream of the past. The door clicked open and René saw his realtor and himself walk into the living room. He remembered their awkward conversation. René wanted the house, but the realtor was too desperate to sell it to notice.

Marcus walked down the stairs in jeans and a black tank top. There was no question in René's mind he was a ghost, but René saw him as if he lived. He was older than in the first vision. Marcus died at forty and Bastion at thirty-nine, but in the last vision, they'd been in their early thirties. The extra years improved Marcus's features. He still wore his hair spiked, but shorter, and his shoulders were broader and more cut, the shape René was familiar with when he stared at his outline.

"Hey, Bastion, get down here. We have company." Marcus raised his eyebrows when he saw them.

"Damn, he's pretty." Bastion appeared a minute after. He wrapped his arms around Marcus's waist. As with Marcus, Bastion was noticeably older but also healthier. His hair gleamed, and his eyes were clear instead of bloodshot.

"Sure is," Marcus agreed, "Too bad he's not going to stay long."

"I don't know, maybe this one could stay for a little while." Bastion elbowed Marcus's side playfully.

"He would be something to look at. The street gets boring." Marcus smirked.

"You think he has any books? We could keep him long enough to read one or two before we scare him away," Bastion said.

"If his tastes are any good." Marcus snorted.

"Assholes, you love my book collection." René scowled.

Time jerked forward. René spread out his hands for balance. He saw his past self move the first boxes inside his new home. When time slowed again, René stumbled, despite the room around him not physically moving beneath his feet. René held his stomach. The fact that he was dreaming didn't stop the car sick feeling.

Bastion and Marcus sat near the double glass doors and watched his past self, having nothing better to do. Bastion sighed and turned his head toward Marcus.

"You know what I miss? Our bed, or any bed, really. Sleeping on this floor sucks."

"Maybe he'll share," Marcus teased, staring at the garden outside. "You know what I miss? My guitar. It's the only thing I can't stand not to have anymore."

"Yeah, even singing isn't as fun without you backing me." Bastion wrapped his arms around Marcus's shoulders, comforting with action instead of words. René crouched beside them, unable to comfort them because they couldn't sense him. They sat together as the day moved on. They were invisible to past René because they were ghosts, and current René was invisible to them because he was in a dream. The entire mess hurt René's brain. Night arrived and they slept on the floor, near the fire and near René's sleeping bag. In the morning they woke, and Bastion stared at René's past self.

"You know what's funny? I forgot he was even here. He's not annoying like the others."

Marcus leaned over and touched the first strand of hair. After a moment, Bastion threaded his fingers through the rest.

"He's cold," Marcus said.

"Were the others?" Bastion asked.

"I never really touched any of the others. Just threw things at them when they pissed me off."

"Yeah, me too." Bastion dragged his thumb along René's cheek.

René's past self sighed at the caress, a slight smile gracing his sleeping lips. He rolled on his side and muttered, "It's too cold to get up."

"He does not give a fuck that we're touching him." Bastion snorted.

"I think he's right. Let's not get up quite yet." Marcus pressed Bastion down on the floor and sucked on his lips.

Bastion laughed and turned to René's sleeping form. "Hey, do you know some crazy ghosts are making out beside you on the floor? You don't mind, do you? No? Okay."

"Quit talking to the living, Bastion. He can't hear or see you anyway."

"Then shut me up."

They kissed for almost twenty minutes. Bastion's hair flowed out behind him like a black river against the tiled floor. He wrapped his legs around Marcus. They twined their fingers in knots and dragged their lips together in languid, unhurried kisses. René chewed on his bottom lip.

"Bastards. You sexy, fucking bastards. I don't believe I missed this the first time—I don't believe I can't see you all the time!"

Another skip in time. René closed his eyes to avoid getting sick again. When he opened them, it was the second morning in his new house. René watched as they caressed him, and René's past self cooed at the touches without waking up.

"This isn't going to scare him. Let's wait until tonight when he's awake." Marcus shook his head.

"Yeah," Bastion agreed. "Still kinda fun though."

"It'll be more fun when he's awake and he starts screaming."

"Aw, but he's so cute when he's sleeping," Bastion teased.

They followed René around the entire morning. As René set up his bed, Bastion moved the bag of screws to the other side of the room. René scowled at Bastion, remembering having to look for them, but even as René frowned, he admitted it was a funny prank. His scowl became a laugh when his former self dropped onto the bed, daydreaming of a mystery lover and oblivious of the two already watching him.

"Look at him. Jesus. I want to pull up his shirt and kiss my way down until he's *begging*." Bastion gestured with his hands instead of actually touching.

"He does look like he wants to be kissed." Marcus sat on the bed, studying René's dreamy expression.

The René on the bed jerked up because of Marcus's weight and shook his head. The René standing next to the bed covered his face with his hands and laughed at himself.

"Come on. I saw a box of books. Let's go steal one," Bastion said.

"Good idea." Marcus stood up.

They snuck to René's office and completed *Frankenstein* before René finished unpacking the living room and kitchen. He remembered that evening, standing in the living room and looking at his progress when Bastion brushed the hair away from his face and Marcus rested a hand on René's shoulder.

"Hello." He heard himself say out loud.

"Did he just say 'hello'?" Marcus asked as they stepped away from René and gazed at each other.

"Yeah, I don't get it. This is usually the part where they scream and run." Bastion waved his hand in front of René, but not close enough for René to register it—not back then.

"Wait, don't leave."

Bastion and Marcus laughed. "Is he...?" Bastion twirled his finger around the side of his head, suggesting René was crazy.

Marcus shrugged.

Meanwhile, his alternate self said, "Follow me. Please?" He climbed the stairs.

"Well," Marcus said, "we have nothing better to do."

They followed him upstairs. René's current self shook his head. The book box lid was tossed on the floor and *Frankenstein* sat three feet behind his past self, but René hadn't noticed because he'd been so excited.

"Hell no. I'm not playing ghost with this brat." Marcus held out his hands and shook his head when he saw the Ouija board.

"Let's do it," Bastion said.

"Bastion, really?"

"Yeah, why not? Aren't you bored? This might be worth a few shits and giggles. No one's ever tried *talking* to us before."

"Fine, whatever, we'll see if he has anything interesting to say." Marcus crossed his arms over his chest.

René's past self addressed the air, "I know this is dumb, I know this is a stupid toy, but why not use it? Crap, I hope I'm not talking to myself. I just want to—"

Bastion pressed his fingers against the planchette and skidded it across the board, and their first conversation began. After he introduced himself, Bastion leaned forward and brushed his fingers along René's jaw.

"René, huh? Bet the kids at school teased him."

Marcus smiled and tangled his fingers in René's hair.

"Why do you keep petting me? It's not scary in the slightest." René's past self asked.

"Good question," Bastion said even as he played with René's hair. "Why do we keep petting him?"

"Because he's beautiful and letting us get away with it," Marcus answered.

"You have a point." Bastion smiled as his fingers danced through René's hair.

"Fuck, not again," René swore when time spun forward for the third time.

He skipped to the next morning when they crowded around him on his bed and slid their fingers across René's face, shoulders, and chest. René watched himself sigh and squirm from each touch. They'd done much worse to him since, but seeing the wanting expression on his own sleeping face was embarrassing.

"Hey, Bastion?" Marcus tilted his head to the side, his expression thoughtful and intent.

"Yeah?" he asked, not paying much attention to Marcus or René, just watching his own fingers glide across the fair surface of skin with the indifference of someone pulling blades of grass up from their roots while lying in a field.

"I think our new *roommate* is enjoying this...a lot."

"Did you see his DVD collection? Nothing but horror, I'm sure he's thrilled to have us here," Bastion said.

"No, no, Bastion." Marcus snapped his fingers to get Bastion's full attention. "Not because we're dead, because we're men."

"You think?" Bastion removed his hand, as if the idea of him doing something inappropriate just occurred to him.

"Look at him." Marcus leaned forward, closer to Bastion.

René turned toward Marcus's caresses and exhaled with content at the sensation. He wore a smile, and a quiet hum escaped him.

"Let's test this theory," Bastion said.

He ran his fingertip along René's bottom lip. The moan was equally embarrassing the second time he made it, and René blushed as he watched his previous self wake up and run for a sanctuary he'd never find in the shower.

"Okay...okay, hey, Bastion?" Marcus asked as René showered. "Remember our no-more-threesomes rule we started when we sobered up?"

"Are you thinking about making an exception to the rule?" Bastion smirked.

"Just saying—he's nice to look at, gay as hell, less annoying than anyone else who's ever moved in since we've died, and he treats us like we're regular people. Which you have to admit is nice. I was afraid he'd try to get us to do circus tricks or some bullshit like that when I realized he was a horror freak."

"Yeah," Bastion agreed. "He's not afraid of us, and maybe we could actually get along with this one—at least for a little while. He'll get sick of us after the novelty wears off."

"Eventually, I'm sure. We're not exactly likable people. Too bad, though... I think I could get used to this one hanging around, if he wanted to.

"I know what you mean."

"Notice how he keeps nudging the water to the cold side? I think he'd be more than a little interested." Marcus walked into the shower. His clothes evaporated at his whim.

"I thought *your clothes just disappeared. I wonder what else you can do?"* René snapped his fingers, speaking to himself. He ended his monologue and winced when his past self's body jerked in response to Marcus's finger slipping up his spine.

René's old self kicked Marcus out of the shower. The spirit's clothes returned, body dry without needing a towel. He and Bastion leaned together shoulder to shoulder.

"Hey, Marcus?" Bastion scowled.

"What?"

"Remember when we were on the road at that one scuzzy hotel? And I was freaking out because I was sure I was being watched in the shower? And you kept telling me I was drunk?"

"Well, you were pretty wasted."

"Yeah, but you don't think?"

Marcus grinned. "Probably."

"Shit." Bastion crossed his arms over his chest.

René's previous self left the shower and the current René watched them play their ridiculous game of *Marcus or Bastion*. At first, they genuinely tried to get him to guess wrong, but not long into their game, Marcus turned to Bastion and smirked.

"It's not like the movies where you go through people. We can interact with him."

"Should we see just how much we can interact?" Bastion mirrored Marcus's grin.

Marcus nodded. They groped his body as they spoke.

"You don't think there's some kind of rule against it, do you?" Bastion asked.

"I don't know, Bastion, let me just whip out my *Guide to the Afterlife* handbook and look up the chapter on interactions with the living."

"Prick." Bastion snorted.

"So how do we want to do this?"

"Let's make it fun. He has to ask for it. If he tells us to, we'll do it."

Marcus stared at René. The present René threw a hand over his face. He had worried about telling them he was attracted to men, but it was written blatantly on every line of his continence and every excited breath he exhaled.

Marcus chuckled. "Ask for it? He'll be begging in five minutes! This is going to be easy."

René stepped closer to Marcus. He smirked and, although they couldn't hear him, whispered, *"I wasn't quite as easy as you thought, huh, Marcus?"*

They tickled him, and he stopped them. They pinned him to the bed, and he squirmed away, armed with a list of excuses. By evening Bastion laughed each time another advance failed.

"Easy?" he asked Marcus. "I think he's cock-blocking."

"We haven't lost our touch. It's just more challenging to seduce someone when they can't see or hear you." Marcus crammed his hands into his jeans pockets.

"We could do that one trick. Remember how the first person who moved in accidentally saw us when we were concentrating and trying to figure out how to lift stuff up?"

"Should we do that now? It might be more fun to wait until we want him to see us enough to know where to touch."

"I think you've got a point." Bastion walked behind the couch and massaged René's shoulders. "Too bad he can't see us. If he could, I don't think he'd be able to resist." Bastion eyed Marcus's body up and down to prove his point.

"Don't sell yourself short. You're some sort of fucking siren." Marcus joined him in kneading René's shoulders. He brushed his nose across Bastion's cheek. They looked at René who'd fallen asleep on the couch. Marcus rolled his eyes. "No use letting a good bed go to waste. If he doesn't want to sleep in it, I think we should."

"His loss," Bastion agreed. "He could have slept cuddled between us instead of squished on the sofa, but no, he wanted to read."

Bastion stole the book from René's hand, saved his page with a scrap of paper, and placed it on the floor while Marcus found a blanket to wrap over René. Hand in hand, they walked toward the stairs. Bastion stopped right before them, frowning.

"Stop it, Bastion." Marcus held Bastion's shoulders.

Bastion glanced at René for a distraction. "I know. I'm sorry."

"I don't want you thinking about it," Marcus said.

"I'm not. Let's go."

"You're a bad liar." Marcus swooped Bastion into his arms and carried him up the stairs. René followed them. Bastion laughed the entire way to the bedroom, and Marcus laid Bastion down on the comforter and hovered above him.

"Hurry up and kiss me," Bastion whispered.

"Since you asked so nicely." A grin overtook Marcus's face and he teased his lips against Bastion's.

René lay beside them on the bed. He regretted how his physical body slept on the couch. He glided his fingers across their skin. To René, in that moment, they were real and he was the pale, watching ghost. Marcus spread Bastion's legs with his knees and slipped inside Bastion without resistance. Bastion dug his fingers into Marcus's ass and squeezed. They started slowly, barely shifting against each other. Their intensity built up as they ground their bodies together on René's bed. René licked his lips. The image ignited all the nerves in his mind and spread warmth across his entire body. Bastion's full lips stretched wide as he gasped for air, and Marcus's lateral muscles rippled as he thrust inside their soon-to-be shared lover. The box spring creaked beneath their weight, and the headboard rattled as they both drew close. They finished within moments of each other and then Bastion shimmied under the covers.

"Why are you under the blankets when we don't get cold anymore?" Marcus chuckled.

"The comfort of it," Bastion answered.

"Huh, guess it is nice." Marcus snuggled beside Bastion. He squeezed Bastion to his chest, and they slept.

RENÉ JERKED TO a sitting position. He'd expected another dream—vision—the night before when he and May drank, since that was when he had the first one. He did not, however, expect another dream the night after. René crawled out of bed and wandered to the shower. As the hot water drenched his skin, he thought about the memories he'd seen.

Nightmare? Marcus asked on the computer screen after René returned to the bedroom and dressed.

"No." René shook his head, thoughtful. "I dreamed of my first few nights here—from your and Bastion's point of view. You know, if you're going to have sex in someone's bed, then you should ask them if they want to join."

You were the one being difficult, Marcus typed without apology.

Bastion pecked on the keyboard. *"In retrospect, maybe we should have asked you to join us upfront, but, at the time, it was more fun to do things the hard way."*

"I've always been a fan of the hard way." René winked at them.

"I'm going out for a couple of hours." René walked to his bedroom door. He stopped, the dream still in his mind, before he added. "Just going shopping. I won't be gone too long."

He wanted to surprise them, so he jogged down the stairs and out the door before they could ask him anything else. It took him a while to find a pawn shop, and it took three different ones to find what he wanted. After the pawn shop, he did his regular weekly errands, and when he returned to his driveway, it was late afternoon. René sat in his car, staring at his steering wheel. He took a calming breath and wiped the palms of his hands against the fabric of his jeans.

"Quit being a coward," René whispered. He forced himself to step out of the car and grabbed his groceries.

As soon as he entered the living room, he sensed them both staring at him. "Sorry," René muttered, his eyes glued to the floor as he marched to the kitchen and put away the groceries. "The trip took considerably longer than I'd imagined." As he filled his fridge with milk and vegetables, the hair on the nape of his neck tingled from the drop in temperature. They stood at the edge of his vision. Their arms crossed over their chests, but they didn't ask him any questions.

René smiled. He tried to suppress the reflex, but the corners of his mouth refused to go anywhere but up. They must have sensed he was up to something, because when he walked to the front door, Marcus grabbed his arm to stop him from leaving the house again. The strength behind Marcus's hold made René's heart skip an excited beat. René leaned close to Marcus's face.

"I just have one more trip to make to the car."

Marcus dropped his hand, and René sauntered to the car. He opened the trunk and slung the guitar over his shoulder by its leather strap. He also grabbed an amp and crate full of wires. He stared at the ground to try to hide his grin as he walked back inside. His palms sweated and his heart raced from excitement.

"Um...surprise," René said and bit his lower lip. "I tried to find one similar to the one you had in my first dream. I really hope this doesn't suck, because I don't know shit about guitars—"

Marcus held René's face in both hands and kissed him hard. Bastion stood beside René. Both spirits trapped him in an entanglement of arms and passionate kisses and René permitted himself to sink into the embrace.

"Rembrandt..." Bastion said a complete sentence, but René only caught his name from it.

He opened his eyes. They hurt from trying to focus on something he couldn't see. "So you like it?"

They were talking, but he couldn't understand them. Marcus gave up and French-kissed René and then Bastion. Their excitement hummed in the air like static during a storm. René laughed, still breathless.

He handed Marcus the guitar. "Well? Play for me."

Chapter Nine

RENÉ LISTENED TO them play for the rest of the afternoon. He couldn't see the excitement on their faces, but it hummed in the air, tingling over his skin like a gentle exhale. After they exhausted themselves playing, they dropped on the sofa beside René. He felt the perspiration on their arms, droplets of stark cold glazing chilled flesh. René ran his hands down their skin.

"Are you hot when you sweat?"

Marcus groaned and stood. He climbed the stairs and went to the bedroom where they'd left the computer. While Marcus retrieved the laptop, René turned to Bastion.

"I'm trying to hear you. When you sing, I can catch snatches of lyrics, and when you talk, an occasional word or two."

Bastion spoke, a quiet, rapid whisper. René closed his eyes, catching *"and until then"* but no more of the monologue.

Marcus brought the laptop, turned it on, and opened their last conversation. He typed, *What were we talking about?*

Bastion typed on the keyboard so René could see what he was saying. *He asked if we sweat because we're hot.*

"I thought you didn't get hot or cold?"

The air never feels warm or cold, but if we jogged laps around the backyard we'd get warm, Marcus answered.

"I don't see the point in dying if everything's the same."
René shook his head.

We're technically not supposed to still be here, Bastion
said.

"But you never get hungry or thirsty?" René asked.

No, Marcus answered. *We vomit if we eat or drink
anything.*

"Did you choose to stay? Or did it just happen?" René
frowned after speaking the words out loud. He shook his
head. "You don't have to answer."

Bastion said a few words, but Marcus interrupted him
by typing, *We chose to stay.*

Bastion muttered something and Marcus told him to be
quiet—René heard the three syllables. He didn't ask them to
elaborate.

"Can we watch *Session 9*?" He asked instead, trying to
think of a distraction. "You'll like that one. The horror is
subtle." The movie finished after midnight. René, who'd
seen the film a dozen times, fell asleep. His eyes shuddered
open when Marcus lifted him up.

"Won't leave me on the couch this time?" he asked, as
Marcus carried him up the stairs.

Marcus grinned and said something. Bastion walked
ahead of them. In their bedroom, Bastion opened the
curtains, moonlight staining everything cold silver.
"...clouds...wouldn't be surprised if..."

And Marcus replied, *"Fuck winter."*

"You don't like the cold?" René asked as Marcus placed
him onto the bed. "Does touching me bother you since I'm
cold?"

They both turned and stared at René.

René stammered, "I-I caught the last bit. Nothing
much."

They spoke on top of each other in an attempt for René to hear more words, but René shook his head. Their ethereal whispers seemed louder, but René wondered if it was his imagination. He shook his head.

"No, no, talking at the same time makes it worse. You're overwhelming me with too many words."

Marcus crawled on top of René and peeled the clothes from his body. René raised his arms as his shirt yanked over his head. They didn't need words to kiss, to grab each other, and René moaned instead of spoke. Marcus's hands caressed over René's chest and stomach. Bastion joined them on the bed. Light spilled into the room from the window. Shadows from the blackjack branches outside lashed across the wall. In the streaked mix of shadow and light, the misty image of both ghosts slipped into focus as the moonlight reflected off them. René caught glimpses of their expressions as they kneaded their lips together. Marcus combed his fingers through Bastion's hair, breaking the contact of their lips so he could lick the hollow of Bastion's neck.

Bastion motioned for René to sit up. René propped his pillows against the headboard, and Bastion meandered his tongue up René's pale thighs, paying specific attention to the crevice where René's limbs joined his pelvis. René gasped and clawed at the bedsheets while their tongues criss-crossed along his body. Bastion licked and kissed his way higher until he reached René's shaft, rubbing his tongue along the underside of the head. René held his breath. His hands twitched. The skin of his cock was so sensitive he almost shoved Bastion away, but then Bastion swallowed René's length. René released the sheets to clench Bastion's tousled black mane of hair.

Marcus held Bastion's hips from behind. Bastion whimpered in anticipation, but the sound was muffled by René's cock. Marcus pushed himself forward. Bastion jerked, eyes closing as the pleasure swept him away. Marcus repeated the hard, quick slams, forcing Bastion to pant through his nose as he continued to suck on René's cock.

The mattress rocked with their movements. Bastion's hand felt like sculpted ice as he held the base of René's shaft. Raising his hips, René smothered his face with one of the pillows and cried out. He wanted to blot the silver-lit room from existence and hide in the beautiful sensation of Bastion's mouth around his cock. René's thighs squeezed as his climax unfurled from deep within his groin. The world condensed to nothing but darkness, pleasure, and motion. It all exploded in his mind, giving way to a burst of ice-bright stars as powerful and brilliant as the quivering in his lower body. Bastion spat on the mattress beside them. René winced, but knew Bastion couldn't swallow without getting sick—the same with food and drink—so he didn't complain out loud.

René shifted a little lower on the bed and reached for Bastion's cock. He pumped his hand in time with Marcus's thrusts. René leaned close to kiss Bastion's sleet-cold mouth. Bastion lingered against René's mouth a moment, before pulling away and bearing down on René's neck with his teeth, biting hard. René tugged at Bastion's long hair with his left hand and stroked with his right. He cried out and whispered tender, endearing encouragements into Bastion's ear. Cold sprayed from Bastion's cock and over René's stomach.

Bastion continued to gasp and plea. He screamed Marcus's name, and René's cheeks flushed with the sound. On an erotic whim, René echoed Marcus's name. He sensed Bastion's blue eyes fixed on his face. René opened his eyes for Bastion, although he only saw Bastion's misty shape dappled with moonlight and cloud shadow. Bastion said Marcus's name again, and René repeated it, hypnotized by eyes he couldn't see. Bastion called Marcus's name a third time and so did René. Bastion shouted Marcus's name near René's mouth between kisses, and René blew the sound back into Bastion's mouth. Marcus cursed out their names as he came, leaning heavily against Bastion's back once finished.

René breathed hard, face flushed, cock half-erect though he'd already come once. Bastion asked him a question, but he didn't understand it. René's face fell as he shook his head no. Bastion said something else, and René responded with an exasperated sigh.

Marcus dropped beside René on the mattress, *"What about...Bastion?"*

"His name," René whispered, afraid if he acknowledged he could hear it, he wouldn't be able to hear it again.

"Bastion?" Marcus asked, René only catching the last word.

Bastion added, *"...Marcus, Rem, René, Rembrandt?"*

"Do you often call me Rembrandt when I can't hear you?" René scowled.

"Only in bed..." Marcus grinned.

"Hearing a word here and there is worse than not hearing anything at all," René groaned.

"René," Bastion whispered, dissolving the frown on René's face.

"Stop saying my name. It makes me want it like I'm nineteen again." He stared at the window and watched the clouds eat the moon from the sky. Bastion bit René's collarbone, and René bit his lip to muffle his shout. "I mean it. If you're worn out from Marcus, you better not start, because it'd take too long to come a second time."

"Maybe...help." Bastion shoved René's legs apart, dove between them, and licked his asshole.

A mumble of sound burst from René's mouth. Bastion flicked his tongue along René's sensitive skin and René couldn't say anything more complex than *oh*. Marcus chuckled and whispered René's name over and over between gentle, teasing nibbles against René's earlobe. René forgot he couldn't see them, forgot he could only hear every few words. He could hear his name, and it was more than enough. Cold from their bodies surrounded him, and he was lost to it, lost to their touches, lost to their mouths. René moaned.

TWO WEEKS LATER, they woke to the first dusting of snow covering the ground, with more falling. René sat in his office and pretended to work while actually watching the heavy flakes drop past the window. A timid knock on the door broke him away from daydreaming.

"You can come in," he said.

The door opened on its own and a cup of hot tea on a saucer floated over to René and arranged itself on his desk. René smiled at the sight, but shook his head and said, "That's sweet, but I wish you wouldn't mess with the dishes."

Bastion snatched a pen and sticky note and scribbled *fuck you* before turning to leave.

"Wait," René's grin widened and he gestured for Bastion to lean closer. He sipped the hot tea and held the burning liquid in his mouth. As Bastion approached, his hazy silhouette appeared and René held Bastion's cheek and drew their mouths together. René swallowed the tea and kissed him. Bastion tilted his head to question René.

"Sorry." René gave Bastion a sheepish shrug. "That was probably cold to you, but with the tea burning my mouth your kiss was warm."

Bastion stole the cup before sipping tea but spitting it into a pot of ivy growing on René's desk. Bastion returned the kiss. René flinched, the kiss was frigid, but he laughed when they parted. Bastion brought the cup to René's lips so he could warm his mouth again. The moment he swallowed, Bastion worked his tongue into René's mouth. René moaned, pretending the heat from the tea was Bastion's body heat. They kissed until the cold returned to René's tongue and then Bastion vanished so René could finish working. Later that afternoon, René bundled himself in a jacket, scarf, and gloves. He gestured at the double glass doors leading to the backyard.

"First snow, we have to play in it."

Marcus scowled, and René heard half his sentence. *"Sometimes...eight years old."*

"Wouldn't hurt...outside..." Bastion smacked his shoulder.

"Never did like fresh air." Marcus snorted in return.

"Liar...can't keep you inside most days."

René sat and listened intently so he could catch every word possible. Over the last two weeks, René managed to improve his strange clairaudience enough to catch fragments of their sentences, but their conversations still sounded as if they came through a radio with bad reception.

"If we go, I'll make hot cocoa afterward." René grimaced. "Dammit, I'm used to bribing May with food. I meant to say—"

Marcus held René's cheek in his hand, his palm colder than the chill sifting through the glass door.

"I meant hot shower. We can take a hot shower afterward." René swallowed.

"Sounds good," Bastion said.

Marcus sighed, defeated, and followed them outside. Clouds hung low in the sky, and snow painted the yard white. The plants and trees were lost under domes of powder. René jogged across the yard, scooped snow in his gloved hands, packed it into a ball, and chucked it at Bastion. An every-man-for-himself snowball fight ensued. René hurled a snowball at Marcus, but Marcus vanished and dodged.

"Hey, no going invisible. That is clearly cheating." René hid behind a shrub as he packed together more ammunition.

Marcus reappeared in time for René to catch him in the center of his chest at the same time Bastion hit his arm with a second snowball. The game continued until melted snow soaked through René's clothes and his teeth chattered.

"Okay, okay." René squinted his eyes shut and held out his hands in a stop gesture.

Bastion used the opportunity to toss one last snowball at René's face. He shouted as the cold burst around him, laughing.

"I think I'm developing a Pavlovian reaction to cold. Let's hurry to the shower. If I'm going to be this frozen, I'd rather be naked and between your legs."

Marcus reached the door first, Bastion a few feet behind him. René darted across the yard to catch up to them. As he passed the kidney-shaped four-by-six swimming pool, René's foot slipped on a patch of ice. His hands shot out for balance, but there was nothing to grab. His body crashed through the layer of ice capping the pool's surface, and his head cracked against the cement lip bordering the pool. After the sound of his forehead striking concrete, everything turned black.

RENÉ WONDERED WHY he wasn't wet, cold, or injured. He wasn't outside anymore. He was in his bedroom. No, that wasn't right. He was in Marcus and Bastion's room. This was another vision. Bastion groaned and reached out for an empty space on the mattress. He opened his eyes, saw Marcus wasn't in bed, and sat up. The musician scratched his head. His dark hair hung greasy and unbrushed from his scalp. Bastion turned to his left and noticed the two college-aged boys sleeping under the blanket. His face twisted in a disgusted expression. Ribs poked from his sides, and his bony knees looked like swollen knots in the middle of his legs. Examining him, René guessed this was a time period in between René's first and second visions. Bastion coughed and found a pair of boxers on the floor. He wiggled into the underwear and staggered out of the room with one hand holding his head. Not finding Marcus in the house, Bastion checked the garden, full of twigs and dirt and dead plant matter. Marcus sat on the ground against the outside wall, his knees tucked into his chest, and watched the sun rise over the fence surrounding the yard.

"Marcus, how'd we even get home last night?"

"I think one of those brats drove. There's a car in our driveway." Marcus also looked thin and pale, grime darkening his sandy hair. "They look like a couple of idiot jocks, don't they?"

"They probably are." The disgusted expression returned to Bastion's face. "New house rule, no more fucking idiots. I'm sick of waking up with weirdos."

"You look like shit." Marcus didn't laugh at the joke. His sage-gray eyes shifted to Bastion.

"Fuck you." Bastion turned his face away.

"I looked in the fridge this morning. Do you know what we have?"

"Don't fucking care." Bastion grumbled with his arms crossed over his chest.

"Half a bottle of Stolichnaya and a box of expired baking soda."

"Surprised neither of us has drunk the vodka yet." A single, humorless laugh snorted from Bastion's throat. He slid to the ground beside Marcus.

"I have no idea what we did last night, Bastion. I can't remember shit."

"Me neither." A pause between them, Bastion placed a deliberate kiss to the side of Marcus's neck. "Instead of drinking from the bottles, maybe we should buy shot glasses."

"And groceries," Marcus added.

"And razor blades. You look fifty years old, not thirty-seven." Bastion ran a finger across the stubble on Marcus's chin.

"Also, laundry soap." Marcus hooked his pointer finger in the band of Bastion's boxers, pulling them back and snapping them against Bastion's skinny waist.

"So let's take a shower, kick those assholes out of our bed, and go shopping." Bastion stood, holding a hand out for Marcus to take.

René watched them in the shower, happy to be the voyeur for once, but bothered by the mildew creeping up the sides of the stall. Damp towels piled in the corner, the mirror was spotted and streaked with a splattering of shaving cream, and when René looked in the sink's basin, he groaned and covered his eyes.

"Not looking forward to the next few days." Bastion pressed his face against Marcus's chest.

"That's what we get for acting like some goddamned twenty-year-old rock stars."

"I hate DTs." Bastion frowned.

"Then stop being a fucking drunk."

"Then you stop being a fucking drunk. I only drink when you do."

"And I only drink when you do." Marcus smiled.

"Then this is going to be some easy rehab, as long as one of us gets his shit together."

"Or both." Marcus held Bastion's jaw in one large hand and kissed him. One of the life-sized Ken dolls barged into the bathroom while they made out in the shower.

"I need to piss," he announced to the room.

"Use the downstairs toilet, asshole. We're busy." Bastion slammed the cubicle door open and glared at the kid.

René winced on Bastion's and Marcus's behalf. The probably college-student looked at them, dick in hand trickling dark-yellow urine, and shrugged. René clenched his fist. He wound his arm back to punch the guy, but remembered he couldn't interact with his visions. Marcus held Bastion and closed the shower door.

"Ignore him," he said, kissing Bastion again before Bastion could argue.

"Need some help?" The Greg standing over the toilet grinned as he watched them.

Bastion wrenched away from the kiss, opening his mouth to shout, but Marcus held him with both hands, biting down on Bastion's lip to keep him occupied. Marcus let go of Bastion with one hand and pressed it against the fogged glass, middle finger extended. René laughed, but the Greg snorted and left the bathroom without washing his hands. René yelled after him to flush the toilet, but the past image couldn't hear him. René tried to push down on the metal lever, but his hand went through the object.

"Dammit," René swore, angry at the dingy piss in the bowl, and the mold ringing around the porcelain, and the fact that the bastard hadn't washed his hands. René thought of how he'd scream at them when he woke up. The back of his mind reminded him there was a problem with his plan, but René found he couldn't quite remember what he'd been doing before falling into the vision.

Marcus and Bastion finished their shower. They couldn't find a clean towel and made do with an old bedsheet. They marched to their room, wet and naked, and flicked on the light. Greg number two grumbled when the light came on and hid his face beneath a pillow. Bastion jerked the pillow away while Marcus hunted for clean clothes for them to wear.

"What the hell?" Greg number two asked.

"I'd say it was fun, but it wasn't. Now get the fuck out," Bastion ordered.

"You need some more beer." Greg number two rolled over and shut his eyes. "You weren't a nagging bitch last night when you were drunk."

"Weren't you listening? He doesn't need a beer. He needs you to get the fuck out." Marcus yanked the kid up by his hair. He cried out, but Marcus ignored him.

Greg number two scurried around the room, dressing in a rush before disappearing. René thought them gone, but when Marcus and Bastion descended the stairs, both Gregs lounged on the couch and watched TV as if they lived there.

"What part of 'get the fuck out' did you guys have trouble comprehending?" Marcus gritted his teeth.

"Seriously? You're kicking us out?" They both stared at Marcus with blinking eyes, as if they truly didn't understand his words.

Bastion waved bye-bye as he dug through the random trash on the floor for a pen and scrap of paper. Once he found what he needed, he jotted down cleaning supplies and basic food items.

"Dicks." Greg number one frowned.

Marcus pointed at the door while Bastion waved goodbye a second time. Both Gregs sulked out the house. Bastion scowled after they left.

"I'm serious, Marcus. No more boys. Ever."

"Oh, so you like girls now?" Marcus asked.

"My preference is you, asshole," Bastion answered. "We're monogamous now."

"That...sounds good, actually." Marcus frowned. "Are we old? When quiet nights at home together sound more appealing than binge drinking and an orgy?"

"Well shit, guess we grew old together. Who would have guessed, back when we were two punk kids starting their own band, we'd make it this far?" Bastion waved the shopping list at Marcus, letting him know it was time to go to the store.

Chapter Ten

RENÉ SPENT THE next few weeks watching them detox. More and more as time went on, he had to remind himself he was in a vision. He wasn't a ghost; he wasn't actually spending weeks with them; it was just a dream. Although he couldn't remember what he'd been doing when he fell asleep, nor did René know how to wake himself, so he continued to watch Marcus and Bastion as they went through shakes, nausea, short-tempered fights, and bouts of exhaustion. Once they recovered, they scrubbed the house from top to bottom. After everything was clean, they repaired the holes in the drywall, repainted the walls, and fixed the leaking pipes under the bathroom sink. Marcus tore up the dead plants in the garden and planted hyacinths and tulips around the house.

Time jumped—lurched—into the future. They slept in their bed again, but the curtain was drawn back and the sunlight spilled inside the room. René smiled and exhaled in relief at the change. They'd reached their current age. Their skin, lit up by sunlight, glowed. Crow's feet etched along Marcus's closed eyes, but their faces were handsome, fleshed out and content opposed to the sallow, hungover masks René had seen (what felt like weeks) before.

Marcus woke first, rolling over on top of Bastion and smoothing his fingers down Bastion's face. Bastion opened his eyes and smiled.

"Hey, Bastion?" Marcus grinned.

"What?"

"Have I ever, after all these years, told you I loved you?"

"No." Bastion smirked.

"Huh." He snorted. "Maybe one day I will."

Marcus bent low and kissed Bastion. He backed away, and Bastion rose up to continue their kissing. By slow degrees, Marcus teased Bastion out of bed and into the hallway. They leaned against the cherry banister, white hands running across bronzed shoulders, tanned hands ghosting over a pale chest.

"What do you want for breakfast?" Marcus asked between kisses.

"You," Bastion purred.

"I mean to eat?"

"What are my options, cereal and frozen waffles?"

"I can cook bacon." Marcus laughed.

"You burn it every time."

Bastion stuck his tongue in Marcus's mouth, and the conversation died. Marcus stepped back, edging them closer to the stairs and toward the kitchen. Near the stairwell, his foot caught on the rug leader and his sage-gray eyes opened wide as he fell backward. On reflex, Bastion grabbed him to try to stop the fall. They tumbled down the stairs.

René choked and shut his eyes when Marcus's neck hit the stairs with a loud snap. Their bodies crashed down the steps and stopped on the checkered linoleum floor. René raced to where Bastion and Marcus twisted together in a knot of limbs turned wrong.

"God, god, god," René chanted, prayed, as he reached out to touch them. Unlike the toilet handle, they felt solid under his hands, but he couldn't help them. René remembered the day his fingers brushed the rust-colored stains on the linoleum in morbid fascination, but now the

blood was fresh and gleaming. The sight made his stomach turn. *"Oh god, I'm sorry guys. I'm so fucking sorry."*

Marcus stood, but at the same time didn't. His standing form was translucent, and his physical shell lay broken on the floor. He scratched the back of his head, squinting his eyes.

"That's a bright light." He muttered. His own body caught his eye. "Well shit. Guess that explains the light." His voice was oddly calm. "Should we go toward it, Bastion?"

Bastion's spirit sat on top of his body. Bastion panted for air, holding his ethereal chest as if wounded.

"Bastion?" Marcus knelt down and rested his hand on Bastion's shoulder.

Bastion didn't reply. He whimpered in pain and gasped for breath. Marcus checked Bastion's body. The outside appeared undamaged, but blood dribbled from his mouth, something inside torn beyond fixing, and his body gasped in sync with Bastion's spirit.

"Shit, you're still alive." Marcus closed his eyes and held Bastion's translucent form.

"Marcus? I thought you were gone?" Bastion clung to Marcus and buried his face against Marcus's chest.

"I'm staying right here. I'm staying with you until it doesn't hurt anymore, got it?"

"I don't, I don't understand. What happened?"

"We fell down the stairs, Bastion."

"I don't remember that." Bastion shook his head in shock.

"It doesn't matter. Don't worry, it'll be okay soon."

"I don't want to die."

"You don't any feel different after you die. Actually, I feel ten years younger."

"Marcus, I don't *want* to die. I wanted to see you get old—gray hair, wrinkles, Viagra, the whole fucking package of being old." Bastion sobbed. The tearless, choking sobs shook both his spirit and his body.

René wept with him, for the first time in years. He hid his face, snatches of breath made him tremble. Then, as if something knocked loose inside him, heat stung his eyes. Drops fell in his palms, but René ignored them as he gasped for breath between the half-choked wails forcing themselves from his throat.

"It pisses me off. What a stupid way to die. We should have stayed drunks and burned in a car crash." Bastion clenched his teeth.

"We had more fun reading on the couch then we ever did getting trashed." The corner of Marcus's lips twitched in a forced smile, but the expression sunk as Bastion choked on the blood leaking from his lips.

"Can you see the light?" He asked to distract Bastion from the pain of dying. "It's beautiful."

"I see it, but I don't want it. I want to stay here with you."

Marcus tilted Bastion's face so their gazes met. "Then let's stay."

"What?"

"Let's stay. We'll just ignore the light for a little while. We'll go in when we're ready."

"Yeah? How long?" A weak smile fought onto Bastion's face.

"Until your hundredth birthday. We'll stay here until you're one hundred and then we'll move on." Marcus pressed his lips against Bastion's forehead.

"That's the most stupid idea...I've ever heard." Bastion laughed. His sobs faded, but his breathing was more labored.

"So you want to do it?" Marcus asked, excitement brightening his face.

"Yes, I do."

"Then we're ghosts."

"Yeah..." Bastion exhaled, closing his eyes for a moment. When he opened them again, his breath and expression didn't show any signs of pain. "We're going to haunt the fuck out of this house."

"And we won't share it with anyone."

"No, it's our house. No living allowed."

"Did you still want breakfast?" Marcus lifted Bastion off of the floor, carrying him up the stairs.

"You're not going toward the kitchen." Bastion smirked.

"I thought you said you wanted me for breakfast." Marcus laid Bastion on their bed and settled on top.

RENÉ OPENED HIS eyes, but the light hurt and everything blurred. He'd spent so long internally in the vision that the waking world around him felt wrong. Tears washed down his face and he shivered under a rushing stream of hot water. René stared at his naked body sitting on his shower floor. His skin blushed dark coral, not from the shower, but from cold. René trembled and looked around, confused. Marcus and Bastion knelt in the shower beside him

"Don't panic. I'm okay," René whispered, but he couldn't stop shaking. "I'm sorry," René cried, holding onto them. "I'm sorry."

"René, stop it," Bastion begged.

"I saw you die." René choked on his tears. "I didn't mean to, but I saw you die."

Marcus wrapped one arm around René and one around Bastion, as if protecting them.

"*Who cares?*" Bastion yelled, "*...you.*"

"I'm okay," René said. He shook less, but his body felt frostbitten. His sniffling changed to tremulous laughter. "You pulled me out and dragged me up here? You guys saved my life."

"*...texted May,*" Marcus said.

"Oh please tell me you didn't say what I think you said, and you *did not* text May."

Marcus nodded.

"Why?" René groaned. Pain stabbed through his skull. Reaching up, René touched the welt on his forehead. "She's going to spazz when she sees me like this."

"*...hospital.*"

"I don't want to go to the hospital. I'm okay." René's eyes widened.

Bastion yelled in René's face, "*...hit your...underwater... frozen...not breathing!*"

"Bastion, calm down. I can't understand you when you scream."

"You scared the shit out of us," Marcus said, his voice calm and easier to decipher.

René forced himself to his knees, turning the shower handle deeper into the red. The more the scalding water ran over him, the better he felt.

"I'm sorry I scared you." René dropped to the tiled floor, allowing the hot water to bring his body temperature back to normal. "But because you both were here, I'm okay."

"You should still go to the hospital," Marcus said.

"He's too damned stubborn." Bastion stood. "I'm going to heat some tea. You deal with him."

"What good is a hospital? I'll be cold in the waiting room. I'll be cold in the doctor's office. They'll only check my vitals and prescribe me something I don't need. At the most, they'll slap a bandage over my head and charge me a couple grand for it." René rubbed his arms and legs. He eased to his feet, his legs wobbling. He probed the egg on his forehead, wincing. "I don't need stitches."

Pounding on the front door echoed up the stairs and to the bathroom. René turned off the water and stepped out of the stall. He stumbled, but Marcus caught him.

"Okay, so I have a concussion. I don't need a doctor to tell me what I already know." He managed to wrap a towel around his waist before May blazed into the bathroom on full mama-bear alert.

"Rem, are you okay?" She grabbed his face with both hands and examined his forehead. "Holy shit, that looks bad."

"May, I'm cold. Let me find some clothes." René winced at his reflection in the mirror. An ugly, purple welt with a gash in the center swelled on his forehead.

"I'll be downstairs with Bastion." Marcus squeezed René's shoulder before exiting the bathroom.

May led René to his bedroom. She turned away while he dressed in sweats and a sweater.

"Are you going to let me borrow some of that primer stuff to help hide the bruise?"

"I bet you've spent this whole time convincing them you don't need to go to the hospital?" May ignored his question. He tapped her shoulder, and she spun around.

"You've known me for a long time, May." René shrugged.

"Well, we're going, and I'm staying here for the rest of the week in case you need anything."

"Or we can skip the hospital, and I could call you if I need something."

"You *could* call, but you *wouldn't*." May snorted.

"I don't want you to miss work because I'm a clutz." René frowned.

"I'll go to work and come straight here after. I'm already packed." May kissed his forehead, careful to avoid the welt. She offered her arm to escort René downstairs.

"How about we don't go to the hospital, but I let you stay to keep an eye on me?" René grabbed his cell phone and thumbed through the screens. "Look, I'll google it."

"WebMD will tell you that you have cancer." May dropped her arm and pursed her lips at René.

"No, see, it says you don't necessarily have to go, only if you have certain symptoms—oh dammit." René closed the window on his phone. "This isn't fair."

"What?"

"Loss of consciousness at the time of injury." René kicked the tiles with a sock-clad foot. "I did pass out."

"Yeah, you did. I already knew. I had ghosts texting me and freaking out after they dragged your unconscious ass upstairs to get you to the shower because they didn't know how else to warm your body." This time May didn't offer her arm. She grabbed René and half dragged him toward the stairs.

René halted before reaching them and stared at the tiles below. Numbness spread through him and his stomach churned, but it wasn't because of head trauma. It was simply grief.

May tapped his shoulder. "Hey, Rem? Are you okay?"

"When I was unconscious, I...had a vision, of Bastion and Marcus. I watched them fall and die. I don't know why it's upsetting me so much. They're already dead, so I shouldn't be bothered, right? But when I think about what I saw..." He couldn't finish the sentence, didn't know how to.

May rubbed his shoulder. "Come on, let's go see them."

"I can hear them talk now."

"I knew you'd be able to." May patted his shoulder. "Come on. Don't look at the floor. Keep your eyes forward."

Marcus and Bastion waited in the living room. Their anxiety tickled against René's skin. He stood in front of both of them with his head bowed low.

"May's driving me to the ER."

"Good." Marcus nodded his head.

"*You...better!*" Bastion shouted. René still struggled to hear him, and he suspected it was because Bastion was upset. The air around him stabbed at René like icicles.

"I wish you guys could come with me," René muttered. He bit his bottom lip, realizing he shouldn't have said the words. "I know you don't have control over that. It's fine—"

Bastion cut René off by grabbing him and crushing him in a tight embrace. René sighed and buried his face into Bastion's icy presence. They kissed his face, stroked his hair, and promised to wait up for him. Before René felt ready to go, May nudged his jacket against his arm.

"C'mon, René, sooner we go, the sooner we get back, all right?"

René nodded and stepped away from his lovers. May helped him wrap up in layers before they left. The ride was quiet. René didn't mind because it gave him a chance to daydream. He stared at the city lights streaking past the dark streets and wished he'd had a chance to watch one of Bastion and Marcus's concerts.

The waiting room was filled. The snow had brought a number of people. May distracted René with a deck of cards. They played twenty-one, five-card stud, and a facetious game of go fish, but all René wanted was to snuggle on his couch with a blanket and forget he'd ever fallen. Even when a nurse finally showed him to a room, he and May waited over half an hour before a doctor arrived. She asked René a barrage of questions while checking his balance, reflexes, and motor skills. Using a flashlight, she made sure his eyes could follow the beam, and in the end she taped a single square of gauze to his forehead and offered to write him a prescription for painkillers. René declined the pills, content with ibuprofen, and rushed toward May's car hours later. René kept his arms crossed while May drove them home.

"I'm sorry, but we had to go," May said.

"It was a waste of time."

"It was a necessary waste of time." May sighed. "Will you forgive me if I make you hot chocolate?"

"Yeah, I suppose." René nudged her with his elbow.

The moment they stepped inside the house, heat washed over René's cold face. Marcus and Bastion had a fire popping, and the couch was covered in three quilts and several pillows to make an inviting nest. They rushed to him, grabbing him, kissing his cheeks, grazing their thumbs beneath his bandaged forehead.

"I'm fine. The doctor said I'm fine."

"He's supposed to take it easy for a few weeks, but the doctor said he should recover quickly."

René gasped as Marcus scooped him into the air and carried him to the sofa.

"I can walk, Marcus!"

"René, let him spoil you. Besides, watching you being carried by a mirage looks really cool." May laughed.

As soon as Marcus set him down, Bastion swaddled him in the quilts. They disappeared to the kitchen while May unloaded her things from her car. René closed his eyes and dozed until an icy touch lighted against his cheek. He opened his eyes. Bastion and Marcus stood above him holding the tea cozy and a bowl of soup.

"Thanks." René flashed a tired smile at them as they placed the items onto the coffee table.

"You better eat this soup. It's hard to use a can opener when you're a ghost." Bastion joked, but his voice shook.

René took the bowl of soup. "Don't worry. I'll eat it."

"You're talking to them, aren't you?" May cocked her head.

René nodded as he blew on a spoonful of soup. "Can't you hear them at all?"

"No." May shook her head. "I've never heard them, and I can only see a faint waviness when I look at them."

"René, how well can you hear us?" Marcus asked.

René paused in thought. His eyes grew wide. "Say a few more things."

"Yeah, I have a few things to say to you, stupid idiot."

"Uh, Bastion, I'd be careful what you say. I'm pretty sure he can completely hear us, now."

"Good, then he can hear me say this house is haunted, not cursed, and I already had to watch one person I care about die from tripping like an idiot, and I'm not doing it again."

"I'm sorry, Bastion." René balanced the soup in his lap and used his free hand to cup Bastion's cheek.

"Oh shit, you really can hear us now. When did that happen?" Bastion's mouth dropped when René touched him.

"When I woke up," René answered.

"René," May whined. "Don't have conversations without me."

"Sorry, May." René yawned. He shook his head to dispel the fatigue, but his eyelids felt like cement.

"Tired?" May combed her fingers through his hair.

"Yeah." René nodded, yawning again.

"The doctor said you might sleep a lot. Why don't you go upstairs? I can find a movie."

"Play the movie. I'll stay here for a little while." René moved most of his nest down to the rug, but he left a pillow and blanket for May to use.

René finished his soup and tea while listening to the occasional commentary Marcus or Bastion made on the movie. That's all he wanted to do—listen to them talk, talk to them himself, but he was too tired to act as a translator for May's sake. Fortunately, when René glanced to his left, he noticed May balled up on the couch, asleep with her hand curled under her chin and her hair fanned out over the armrest.

"Let's go upstairs," René whispered. He tucked May's blanket over her feet and shoulders before tiptoeing away.

They followed him with the extra blankets and bundled him in enough layers so they could hug him close without making him too cold. Bastion stroked his hair while Marcus gave him a quick shoulder rub.

"I wish you'd stop pampering me." René exhaled a breath.

"Yes, heaven forbid you ever get used to it." Marcus snorted, his fingers combing through Bastion's hair in the same way Bastion combed through René's.

"Thank you again." René laced his fingers through both of their hands. "You literally saved my life today."

"I'd say my heart stopped when you fell in the pool, but..." Bastion sighed. "We were in the water and pulling you out before either of us knew what we were doing."

"I know it wasn't easy fishing me out and dragging me upstairs to the shower."

"Your clothes gave us the most trouble. Touching you is easy, but with everything soaked and us both panicking—" Bastion dropped the sentence, shaking his head.

Marcus frowned. "We didn't think we'd be quick enough. Your lips were purple."

Bastion added, "And we learned the hard way ghosts can't administer CPR. The chest compressions worked, but our breath didn't transfer to you."

"Which you'd think would be common sense," Marcus said, "but sometimes we forget we're dead."

"Especially when you're around." Bastion sighed.

"Isn't this better? Talking without a Ouija board or laptop?" René changed the subject. He helped Marcus finger comb Bastion's hair. "I've wanted to talk, really talk, since the first night."

Bastion squirmed in his spot, obviously aroused by their soft caresses. René shifted his fingers from Bastion's hair and traced his jaw, his lips, his collarbone. Bastion trembled beneath René's fingertips.

"René, you stop that right now."

René inched closer. "Does it drive you crazy? Make your breath quicken? Make your palms sweat?"

Bastion nodded, his lips parted. Now that he could hear them, René wondered if he could work on seeing them more clearly. Occasionally, the fog lifted and he'd catch a translucent bit of them, so perhaps it wasn't impossible. René settled on an elbow, fingertips migrating from Bastion's collarbone to his chest. Bastion closed his eyes and sighed.

"As much as I'd love to join in on this, we really should play nice tonight," Marcus said.

"Yes, I plan on playing nice." René's fingers slithered down Bastion's abdomen and swirled near his right hip.

"Forget it, you almost died today." Bastion disappeared and reappeared behind Marcus.

"What better way," René crawled to Marcus and kissed his shoulder, "to remind myself I'm alive than to make my heart race by touching both of you?"

Marcus gripped René's shoulders and eased him against the mattress. He brought their lips close and whispered, "No."

"You...can't be serious?" René blinked. "Don't you want to?"

"Of course we want to," Bastion said. "You scared the hell out of us, and now you're back home. I want to kiss your face off."

"But you were in the *hospital*, René," Marcus said.

"Only because you guys called May."

"You hit your *head*, René."

"But I..." René drew against his pillowcase. "Want to hear you call out my name again."

"Rembrandt, we can say your name as many times as you'd like." Bastion's tone was playful.

"Okay, maybe not like that." René blushed at his full name. "Come on."

"No, René," Marcus insisted.

"No amount of smooth talking is going to change our minds." Bastion poked the tip of René's nose.

"You can't be serious?"

"We are." Bastion lifted their twined hands to his lips and kissed René's wrist.

A smile crept over his face. "Will you at least talk to me? Until I fall asleep?"

"Now that..." Marcus kissed the knuckles of René's other hand. "Is a desire we'd be happy to indulge."

Chapter Eleven

IN THE MORNING, before he opened his eyes, he felt them staring at him.

"I already told you," he spoke with his eyes still closed and a grin on his face. "I'm going to be okay. Stop worrying about me or I'm going to scream."

"I'll worry about you as much as I want." Bastion pinched his ribs.

René stumbled to the bathroom. After washing and drying his hands, he peeled the bandage away and scowled at the discolored welt. After rebandaging the cut, René investigated the living room and found it empty, May already at work. He stole the blanket from the sofa and wrapped it over his shoulders. René wandered near the glass doors leading to the garden, staring at the snow. Marcus and Bastion appeared beside him a minute later.

"Don't worry. I'm not going outside today."

Bastion drifted closer, lips hovering just out of reach. René held his breath, waiting, but Bastion stayed posed beside him without bridging the space between them. René couldn't take it.

"Please," he whispered.

"I like when you ask nice, but I'm afraid I can't," Bastion purred in René's ear.

René closed his eyes, asking again, "Please?"

"Well..." Bastion drew out the word, stalling.

"No." Marcus grabbed Bastion by the hair and pulled him away.

"Sorry, Rem," Bastion said, but his smile wasn't sorry in the slightest.

René opened his eyes and pursed his lips, fed up with their chastity act. He was alive, not fragile, and he refused to wait until his bruise healed before they'd touch him again. Dropping the blanket to the ground, René marched to the couch and lounged against the cushions. Marcus and Bastion wandered closer to see what René would do. He raked his nails over the sofa's textured surface and stared at Marcus.

"Are you not sharing anymore?"

"That's right." Marcus demonstrated his point by tugging Bastion in an embrace and kissing him, keeping too far away for René to reach.

René bit his lower lip as Marcus kneaded his lips against Bastion's. His heartbeat quickened, sending a light throb pulsing through his head, but it wasn't enough for concern. Meanwhile, the ghosts eased down to the rug and kissed again. Marcus lifted Bastion into his lap and they both stole knowing glances in René's direction. René rolled off the sofa and onto the rug below, crawling toward them slowly on his hands and knees.

"Marcus," René whispered in Marcus's ear. "Please, Marcus."

"Yeah, please, Marcus. He's so precious when he asks nicely." Bastion snickered through his kisses.

"I don't know..." Marcus considered their pleas with a smirk. "He'd have to promise to take it easy."

René crossed his fingers in front of them. "I promise."

Marcus ignored René and worked his lips against Bastion's neck. He grabbed Bastion's ass with his broad hands. Bastion threw his head back and moaned. Marcus fought his way into Bastion's pants and stroked Bastion with deliberate, taunting flourishes of his wrist. Bastion's groans simmered to tiny, breathless, needy whimpers. His hold around Marcus's neck tightened as the muscles in his ass cheeks clenched.

"M-Marc-us." Bastion gasped. "You know, I can't...last long...when you..." His broken sentence dissolved as he groaned.

"Take your pants off." Marcus bit his neck, growling against his skin.

Bastion stood and inched closer to René. His hips wove in languid figure eights as he peeled the pants away from his body. Through the white fog, René would catch a flash of skin, a nipple, Bastion's grin, and René's gaze locked onto Bastion as the striptease ended. Once he was bare, Bastion straddled Marcus's lap. Marcus maneuvered a finger inside him. Pumping in and out of Bastion's body, Marcus used his other hand to jerk Bastion's cock. Bastion gripped Marcus and hitched his hips, huffing shallow breaths as he rocked. René closed his eyes and listened, almost seeing the way Bastion's face crumpled as he neared his climax. René's own breath entered and left his lungs in quick bursts as his imagination spun out of control.

"Don't slow down." A strangled whine escaped Bastion.

"Hey, Bastion," Marcus said. His tone feigned boredom as he ignored Bastion's demand.

"I said don't slow down!" Bastion grunted.

"I'm busy torturing you. Could you reach over and kiss René for me?"

Caught off guard by the statement, René opened his eyes when Bastion's cold mouth sealed against his. Bastion's sudden embrace chilled René. He shivered and dove into the sensation. Marcus quickened his strokes again, and Bastion bit down on René's bottom lip. One of Bastion's hands remained slung around Marcus's shoulders. The other one held René's head. Bastion writhed and screamed *oh, oh, oh*. René pressed their mouths together until Bastion's kisses unraveled. He curled into the crook of René's neck and moaned and shuddered and came, bucking twice before relaxing in the grip of the other two men.

Bastion heaved for breath, petting René's hair. "René, are you cold? You're shaking."

"A little cold," René confessed. He knew a lie would make them stop. "Please don't let go of me."

"Stoke the fire," Marcus said.

"Should I bring the blanket?" Bastion slipped off of Marcus's lap to stoke the fire and add more wood to the flames.

"Yes." Marcus guided René to the ground. "René, if we do this, are you going to behave?" René raised an eyebrow at the word behave. Marcus rolled his eyes. Bastion knelt to the floor and tucked the blanket around René's chest. "If you don't take it easy—"

"I promise I'm fine," René interrupted Bastion, "but I'm also aroused out of my mind, so if playing docile gets me what I want, then I'm game."

"Bastion, hand me the lube," Marcus said.

Bastion rummaged under the couch cushions and withdrew a bottle. He handed it to Marcus, and Marcus prepared René.

"Oh god." René moaned at the gentle flicks of Marcus's fingers against his prostate.

"Hmmm," Bastion purred in René's ear. "I believe last night you wanted to hear us call out your name?"

René swallowed and nodded his head. Marcus circled the tip of his slick cockhead around René's asshole. René sucked in a sharp breath when Marcus filled him. Bastion licked the shell of René's ear. René's eyes fluttered closed and then opened halfway, his lips parted, and his chest rose and fell in time with each careful jolt of Marcus's body.

"Too bad for you Marcus is rather quiet." Bastion wound strands of pale hair around his fingers. He sank closer, whispering as if Marcus couldn't hear him. "Though, to be honest, you've dragged a shout from him on several occasions."

"Bastion, touch me," René breathed in his ear. Marcus's gentle tactics hypnotized René, made him feel like a flurry of snowflakes settling in their eyelashes and dissolving from their body heat. He couldn't feel it, their heat, only cold, but he *knew* they burned because he melted when they caressed him.

"I *am* touching you." Bastion chuckled, his hand twining through René's hair.

"Help Marcus make me come." René whispered against Bastion's mouth in rhythm with Marcus's thrusts. "Please, Bastion, please. Please touch me. Please."

"Damn, René," Bastion exhaled. "I didn't realize you could ask so nice."

He freed one of René's hands out from under the blanket wrapped around his shoulders. René's fingers fumbled until he held Bastion's re-hardened cock. After a few strokes, Bastion lowered René's fingers and molded them around his own erection. They moved together, Bastion's hand overlapping René's.

"You two...fuck," Marcus swore. The brunt of his sentence became lost in his mouth as he watched his lovers while circling his hips.

"Marcus." René's groin hitched up as a preorgasmic spasm seized him. A fat pearl of precome swelled at the crown of his erection. René gasped and panted. The miniature climax brought him to a higher plateau. He tried to speak, to call out, but only managed breathy, hopeless noises void of specific meaning. Every muscle tensed as another wave of pleasure seized him.

"Come for me, René," Marcus growled as he slammed his hips forward.

René whimpered and tensed again. He quivered, the pleasure expanding, spreading out each time Marcus pushed in. René curled his toes, arched his back, and came. Marcus pulled out and kissed René's thighs as René caught his breath. Bastion scratched his nails down Marcus's shoulder blades. Marcus bent Bastion over so he straddled René's body. René seized Bastion's cock and stroked while Marcus entered him. Marcus maintained his previous speed and rhythm, languorous and almost timid in his movements. They took their time, toying with Bastion until his nails dug into the rug below René.

"I can't take this." Bastion rounded his back. "You two drive me up a fucking wall. Go faster!"

"Relax. Enjoy this."

"I am, but I need to come right now, Marcus." Bastion growled. Marcus fucked him from behind while René lay beneath him and massaged his cock.

"Then come for me," Marcus instructed.

Bastion twitched in René's hand. He was close but needed something to help tip him over. Bastion moaned again, and then asked, "Why don't you ask nice? Like René did."

"In the decades we've been together, have I ever once said please?" Marcus spoke in a low, gravelled in a low tone.

"I don't think so," Bastion admitted.

"Bastion," he whispered. "Come. Come. Come because I want you to."

Bastion grunted, shoving his hips back to meet Marcus's thrusts.

"Come," Marcus repeated.

Bastion whined, his eyes screwed shut and his jaw clenched.

"Bastion...please."

Bastion called out, overcome in the heat of his orgasm. Even as Bastion climaxed, Marcus continued to speak.

"I'm begging." Marcus's own orgasm stilted his words. "I'm pleading, I'm—I'm coming inside you. Oh please, Bastion. Yes."

"Goddamn, Marcus," Bastion all but sang out after Marcus stopped trembling.

They lay on the rug. No one spoke afterward, curling together side by side side with Bastion sandwiched in between René and Marcus. After a length of time, Bastion broke the quiet by asking, "If you're already dead is it *la petite renaissance*?"

"That's ridiculous." Marcus snorted.

They bantered. René listened as they spoke, but his postorgasmic high and the soothing rhythm of their voices lulled him to sleep. When he woke again, it was to May's warm hand on the uninjured half of his forehead. René looked around. He lay in his own bed, covers piled high on top of him.

"Hey," she whispered.

"Hey," René repeated.

"Want something to eat?"

"Yeah, I'll get up."

She held him in place. Her voice quiet as she said, "Stay in bed and rest. I'll bring something. What do you want?"

"Soup's good." René scowled at the question. He wanted to sleep more than eat.

"Okay, be back in a few minutes."

René checked the clock. It was seven at night; he'd slept all day. René fingered the welt on his forehead. It had shrunk to a smaller bump instead of a fat goose egg.

"How do you feel?" May returned ten minutes later with a bowl of minestrone.

"Better," he answered, blowing on the hot broth. "Tired."

"Yeah, they said you slept all day."

"At least in the future, when I do something stupid, I can blame the brain damage." René yawned.

"That's not funny," May said, but she smiled despite herself. She looked out the window, snow framing the ledge. "I was going to tidy up after I got home to be nice, but they already had everything done. Hell, Bastion even watered the plants and had tea waiting for *me*."

"He only makes tea because I don't want him fooling with the dishes."

"Rembrandt, are you listening to me? Everything I wanted to do to take care of you is already done because they did it for me. I had to fight to heat up the soup so I could feel somewhat useful. You tell them thank you when you're better."

"Gee, May, you make me sound like an asshole."

"I know you hate being vulnerable, and if you admit they took care of you, you'd have to admit you were hurt"

"I'm not hurt," René argued.

"René."

"I'm not."

"Then why'd you sleep all day?"

René scowled at his bowl of minestrone.

"We all get hurt once in a while," May said.

René thought of how they taunted and coerced each other to say *please* (not as a mere, pretty word, but as a legitimate plea), and a smile twitched on his face as he thought of how *thank you* might be equally fun.

"You know, May, you're right. I promise I will thank them properly once I'm one hundred percent again."

"Good." She combed hair over his eyes to annoy him. "Your injury is ill-timed. Now we can't get drunk this weekend."

"What should we do instead?" René asked, placing the empty bowl next to his alarm clock.

"Let's put up a Christmas tree."

"Isn't it a little early? Thanksgiving isn't until next week."

"René, when do we ever follow rules, or traditions, or good advice, or common sense, for that matter? It's time to decorate for Christmas."

"I have all my decorations, but I threw away my old tree when I moved."

"That thing made Charlie Brown's little tree look splendid. Let's get a real one this year." May crinkled her nose at the memory of René's old tree.

"I don't know if I want to water a real one, and it's so early. What if it dies before Christmas? It'd be our luck to have a dead tree." René furrowed his forehead.

"If it dies, you can lecture me about how you told me so and send me to the store to fight the crowds for a fake one to replace it, but between the four of us, I'm sure someone will remember to water it."

"The four of us," he echoed. René stared at the quilt on top of him, blue roses embroidered on a pale ivory surface. "When you say it out loud, it sounds real."

"Well, isn't this real?" May elbowed his shoulder. "Or are you still unconscious from hitting your head?"

"The first two mornings, I thought they were a dream, and then they were a mystery, but then they became my friends, and now I think if we got separated my heart would stop beating so I could jump out of my body and go find them."

"That's...so fucking romantic. You should say it to them." May pressed her right hand over her heart.

"No." René flinched at the thought. "God no. I'd sound stupid—I—I was just thinking out loud. This freaking concussion has me all loopy."

"Or maybe," May whispered, "your near-death experience is making you be a little more honest with yourself."

"No, I'm definitely loopy from head trauma."

"Whatever." May snatched the empty bowl. "I'm going downstairs right now and telling them what you said."

"May, you will not. They don't talk to each other that way."

"Don't worry. I won't say anything if it'd upset you. Get some sleep, Rem."

René nodded and sank beneath the blankets. The tree branches danced outside his window as their shadows writhed across the wall. Snow covered the naked blackjack limbs. A soft-howling wind blew a flurry of white against the transparent glass pane. The moon glowed through the clouds, a haunting, yellow blur disrupting the velvety, dark sky. René fell asleep watching the snow and dreamed he stood naked in an open field. White stretched below his feet and sable coated the sky. The cold, gentle flakes kissed the surface of his skin. René spread his arms wide and fell to the snow—the soft powder caught him and embraced him with its chill. He moaned, aroused by the cold surrounding his body. He squirmed, yearning to be buried in white.

The sensation changed. Instead of snow surrounding him, ribbons of ice teased his temples and cheeks. René moaned and woke. Only then did he realize the dream changed because Marcus and Bastion lay in bed with him, their fingers dabbing at his face.

"René," Marcus said, "are you okay? You're too cold. It hurts to touch you."

René licked his lips. He rested his hand on his forehead. It was blazing hot. René groaned, afraid they'd drag him back to the hospital.

"René?" Marcus asked again.

"I have a fever." René pressed his forehead against Marcus's arm. "Please don't make me go to the hospital. I don't have any other symptoms—I probably caught this *at* the hospital. The waiting room was packed."

Bastion crawled out of bed. "I'll get some aspirin and a glass of water."

When Bastion returned, they helped René sit. He swallowed the two white pills and drank from the glass until it was empty. As soon as he finished the water, he sighed and muttered thanks to Bastion.

"Does this feel good?" Marcus rubbed René's face.

René nodded. The frost-cold hands soothed his burning temples, but he also shook with chills. René wrapped the blanket tighter around his body and leaned into Marcus's touch.

"Are you nauseous? Or dizzy? Does your head hurt?"

"No. I'm a touch achy, but I don't have a migraine."

Marcus and Bastion exchanged a look. René lay back against his pillow. He wanted to sleep. The thought of another three-hour hospital wait hurt more than the welt on his head or the aches in his muscles.

"Please..." René whispered, closing his eyes and hoping. "I'm too tired to drive and sit in a waiting room. I'm better off here."

"I have an idea," Bastion said.

"What is it?" René asked.

"Marcus, remember that time you had a fever, but I was drunk and didn't care?"

"Yeah, fucker, I felt awful, but you wouldn't keep your perverted hands off me." Marcus grinned at the memory.

"Right, but when I was done, didn't you feel great?" Bastion smirked.

"It's true. I did." Marcus nodded.

"Not, really following..." René blinked at both of them.

"Oh good, then this will be a surprise." Marcus kissed René's chest.

René gasped, the sparks of cold against his scalding skin reminding him of his dream. Marcus meandered lower, unlacing the tie string on René's sweatpants and tugging the boxers and pants away from René's legs. René breathed fast as Marcus continued down his abs.

"Um, I'm not complaining, but, why—*oh*."

He stopped when Marcus wrapped his lips around René's cock, hard from his dream, and sucked.

"Why, exactly, are you sucking my dick, Marcus?"

Bastion laughed. "No one's ever asked that question before."

"No, it's just..." René paused to moan and lick his lips, squirming. "I—fuck, it's amazing—but what does this have to do with my fever?"

"It tends to help the aspirin along." Bastion kissed his neck, smoothing a cool hand across his forehead and into his hair.

"How, exactly?"

"Magic," Bastion mumbled, his face buried at the nape of René's neck.

René's teeth chattered from the cold of their touches. The chilled, light caresses felt good but made him shake hard. Marcus pushed René's legs wider apart and lifted his hips an inch off the mattress. He moved lower, licking the rim of René's asshole. René called out, but Bastion muffled the noise with his tongue. Suddenly René remembered May was in the next room and sighed an appreciative exhale against Bastion's lips. The more Marcus flicked René's entrance, the harder it became for René to muffle his grunts. He broke Bastion's kiss and covered his face with a pillow, mewling beneath it. Bastion lunged to René's cock, blowing him as Marcus continued ringing the tip of his tongue around René's asshole.

René's toes dug into the bedsheets and his arms squeezed the pillow tighter. He raised and lowered his hips, thrusting in Bastion's mouth. The aches vanished, and the mixture of heat and chills spurred him closer to orgasm. René's stomach looped in excitement. Their mouths against him were too good, and René hitched as his heartbeat quickened. René arched his back, holding his breath as he climaxed. Coming down from the high of orgasm felt like sinking through a layer of clouds. René's entire body relaxed, and he cooed at the lingering kisses dotting his skin.

"Did the orgasm break your fever?" Bastion asked after René finished. "We figured it out by accident, but it always seemed to work with us."

"I want to make you come," René muttered, sleepy and satisfied.

"That wasn't the point. Do you feel better?" Marcus crawled next to René and thumbed his forehead.

René winced when Marcus's hand grazed his bruise. He wasn't sure if his fever necessarily broke, but his fever chills were gone, and he felt pleasant despite the heat in his face and limbs. "He doesn't feel freezing anymore, just really cold," Bastion answered.

"I feel good," René answered. "My chills are gone."

"Good." Marcus nodded. "Then let's go back to sleep."

"Sleep?" René frowned.

"You're sick, asshole. You need to rest."

"At least let me watch. I'll be resting in bed the whole time." René gripped Marcus's forearm. "I hate the thought of being the only one who came."

"We are performers, Marcus, and we've never rejected a request before." Bastion nudged Marcus with his elbow.

"You two are relentless." Marcus scratched the back of his head, sighing. Marcus stood and grabbed the chair next to René's vanity, dragging it across the rug and next to René's bed. "You." He pointed to René. "Will not participate. You will lay there and watch only. You." He pointed to Bastion as he plopped down into the chair. "Get over here."

Bastion strolled toward Marcus, straddling his lap. "You know, you're really cute when you give orders."

Marcus grunted in reply.

"I have an idea." Bastion turned on a small MP3 player on René's nightstand. Queens of the Stone Age played through the tiny speaker. Bastion sang along with the song, dancing just above Marcus's lap. Marcus and René's lips curled in simultaneous grins as Bastion rolled his abs and circled his hips in a teasing lap dance.

Bastion's hair swayed along his back. His ass hovered just over Marcus's erection, teasing but not quite touching. He spun around, taking Marcus's hands and placing them on his stomach as he swiveled above him. Marcus kissed up Bastion's spine, groping and pinching Bastion's nipples.

Bastion grabbed his cock in one hand and Marcus's in the other, teasing them with his fingers. René clutched the quilt with both of his fists. He regretted his promise to stay in bed. Even satisfied, body tingling from his own orgasm, he wanted to help please them. He wanted to kneel beside the chair and bite Bastion's inner thigh while massaging Marcus's balls.

Bastion flipped to his original position, and another song began. He aligned his ass with Marcus's cock and sank down. Marcus grunted and guided Bastion's hips. René chewed on his bottom lip and nudged himself closer to the edge of the bed.

Marcus pointed at him. "No, you stay there. You're resting, remember?"

"I needed a better view of you in the dark," René answered with a sheepish smile.

"Clever line, but it's bright enough in here. I know you can see us." Bastion braced a hand against Marcus's thigh and jerked his hips hard enough to make Marcus gasp. Bastion glanced over his shoulder to taunt René with a sultry gaze. "Which means you can see my dick rubbing against his stomach, and the way his nails are digging into my back."

"It's a little dark. I could see better if I were closer," René said.

"Dark or not, you don't need to get any closer." Marcus snorted.

René sighed in defeat and stayed where he lay. Bastion circled his hips and his hair swayed against his back. He leaned back farther, moaning as his thighs clenched and released. It was sweet torture, watching them move together, watching the ripples of their outlines and the way their hands grabbed each other. And it took a long time, as good torture ought to, before Bastion sped his pace. His breaths came out in choked moans, and he called out, his hand busy at his cock, stroking and kneading himself until he was spent.

Marcus lifted Bastion up, bending him over the vanity and thrusting hard into his ass. Marcus's fingers tangled in Bastion's hair. René pulled himself to the edge of the bed, leaning over the mattress slightly

"I don't think I'll ever grow tired of watching you two," René whispered.

Bastion glanced in René's direction, his hands pressed against the flat, wooden surface, and when he spoke, the words were breathy and broken by Marcus's thrusts.

"Oh? So you—like—to watch—too?"

He was teasing, but René didn't care. He watched them with an intense gaze so they could snatch glimpses of his face and feel the thrill of his voyeurism. Bastion grinned at the attention until he couldn't focus anymore, and then he pressed his forehead against the vanity and moaned.

"Fuck. Shit. Fuck. Fuck." The curses spat from Marcus's mouth without eloquence as he threw his head back and relished his climax. They held together for a few breaths. Marcus circled his fingertips against Bastion's hips, pulled out, and gave Bastion's ass a playful smack. "I love your ass."

He chuckled as he walked across the room and to the bed, shooing René over. Bastion followed him to the bed, straddling Marcus and leaning close to his face.

"I love your cock." He nibbled on Marcus's bottom lip and finished with a light kiss. He shifted to the center of the bed, legs wrapped around René. "What about you?" A sly grin brightened the corners of his mouth. "Do you love my ass?"

René caught his face and brought it close to his own. "Bastion, I—" René stopped the last two words, sliding his fingers away from Bastion's face and curving them down the length of his body. "I think it's a great ass."

"Next time I'll give you a lap dance and we'll make Marcus watch."

"I have a feeling he won't play by the rules as well as I did," René said.

"You're right. I won't," Marcus agreed.

Chapter Twelve

RENÉ AWOKE WITH two main thoughts. First, he felt incredible. Second, he was starving. He snuck out of bed, his lovers snoring on each side of him. Dressed in sweatpants, René crept to the kitchen. Nothing sounded more delicious than over-easy eggs broken and soaking into two golden slices of toasted wheat bread.

René hummed and heated the skillet. It was one of their songs, and he hoped he wasn't slaughtering it too terribly. He also hoped May would be in a shopping mood when she returned from work. Her insane notion of Christmas decorating sounded fun now that René felt better.

Bastion and Marcus entered the kitchen. Bastion was slung over Marcus's shoulder, half asleep and uninterested with the morning.

"Good morning," René greeted them. He yanked the toast from the toaster and used a spatula to top each slice with an egg. "I've only had soup, so I'm hungry. Well..." René winked at them. "And you two always work up my appetite."

"How do you feel?" Marcus grazed his pointer finger down René's cheek.

"Great." René smiled. "Who would have guessed you guys actually make good nurses?"

He sat at the table and ate his breakfast. Before he could stand, Bastion snatched the plate off the table and put it in the sink.

"I can do it," René said, on his feet.

"I won't break them."

"Why go through all the trouble?" René tilted his head.

"It's…just," Bastion stuttered, looking at the floor.

"It's because you told him not to after he broke those cups. You know how Bastion gets when you tell him he *can't*. It becomes all he thinks about." Marcus leaned back against his chair, arms crossed over his chest.

"Yeah," Bastion muttered, "and besides, even if you feel better, it won't hurt you to take it easy for another day or two."

"Well, Bastion, don't try to mop or dust either." René grinned at him.

"Ha-ha, jerk."

"Can't blame a man for trying to get what he wants." René shrugged, his body language flirtatious.

"No, I guess not," Bastion said.

"You know, maybe you shouldn't be on your feet. You're still recovering." Marcus snatched René, pulled him into his lap, and grinned.

René bit his lower lip, breathy and eager as always when manhandled by Marcus. René wasn't weak and had won his share of four-on-one fights in high school and bar-room brawls in college. So when Marcus tossed him around without effort, René's stomach fluttered with excitement.

"It's too early." René squirmed in Marcus's arms, enough to put up a fight, but not enough to escape. "I don't want to sleep all day like yesterday."

"Maybe you should." Marcus flexed his arms tighter to prevent René from squirming.

"Look, the swelling is gone." René wiggled an arm free to brush his bangs off his forehead.

"The bruise does look better." Bastion placed the plate and skillet in the dish rack and wiped his hands on a dishtowel, out of habit more than necessity.

"I know I'm not the best at admitting if I'm hurt, but I swear I feel awesome today. Please don't worry anymore."

"You're so cute." Bastion teased his finger over René's lips. He dropped the dishrag on René's head and walked to the living room.

"I want a shower. My hair feels greasy." René snatched the towel off his head.

"Who says I'm letting go?" Marcus squeezed tighter.

"If you don't, Bastion will get bored and who knows what he'll think to do to us for entertainment." René pried Marcus's fingers apart.

"Good point." Marcus relaxed his arms.

René showered and changed into fresh clothes. He brushed his hair, putting it in a ponytail, but making sure the bangs hid his bruise. Downstairs, René stared out the window at the pool. Sunlight reflected off the snow and made everything shimmer.

"I feel so stupid." René shook his head.

"At least you didn't trip down the stairs."

René jumped at Marcus's voice. "I know. I saw."

"I still can't believe I—"

"We need more board games." Bastion interrupted. He stood in front of the closet, staring at René's collection.

"We need to be able to go farther than a block past the house," Marcus muttered.

"Why can't you? I mean, what happens?" René asked.

"We end up back here." Bastion took Yahtzee from the closet and went to sit on the rug. René and Marcus joined him. They sat in a tight circle. René elbowed Marcus, pretending he wanted more space. While distracted, Bastion leaned close to René and whispered in his ear.

"Hey, René?"

"I know that tone. That's your give-me-what-I-want voice." René snorted.

"You should get Wi-Fi so I can use the laptop to go shopping."

"With my credit card, eh?" René grinned.

"Didn't know you wanted to be a trophy wife," Marcus teased. "First you start doing the dishes, and now you want to spend all his money?"

Bastion sputtered several curses under his breath. René found it endearing. Each curse sounded flustered, more embarrassed than angry. René held Bastion's cheeks. He wanted to feel the hot blood rushing across them, but instead, Bastion's skin was freezing. Bastion jerked his head away, refusing to look at either René or Marcus.

"I can't get a job, so it's not fair. We had money when we were alive."

A hungry smirk curved Marcus's lips. Apparently he didn't see Bastion flustered often either and wanted more of it.

"The first thing you can buy is an apron."

"Shut up, Marcus."

"Well, I suppose you could always repay him in blowjobs."

"I'm not a whore. Fuck, Marcus, you can be such a shit." Bastion's expression stretched taut and angry across his face.

"May wouldn't let me have two wives."

"Assholes." Bastion marched toward the kitchen.

"Wait," René called after him, "I was teasing, I'm sor—"

Marcus pressed a thick finger over René's lips to silence him. René narrowed his eyes at Marcus.

"I didn't want to hurt his feelings."

"You didn't." Marcus shook his head. "But let's see how far we can push him. It's fun to make up with Bastion."

"What did you have in mind?" René considered Marcus's proposal, a smile sneaking across his face the more he thought of it.

"Well, when he comes back, I'll—"

A crash and the sound of broken glass interrupted Marcus. He winced. "Crap, he just had to break something, didn't he? Now he'll be too mad to tease. Maybe you should go in there and smooth things over so I don't get punched in the nose."

"But I don't want to get punched in the nose, either." René stood up.

"Eh, you still have a bruise. He probably won't punch you."

"Thanks, Marcus." René pushed Marcus's head to the side. "Good to know you have enough confidence in me to make up with your old man for you."

In the kitchen, Bastion knelt on the linoleum with a dustpan and hand broom. He cursed at the broken shards of what was once a coffee cup and stabbed them with the broom's bristles. Bastion growled and swept the three pieces in the pan and chucked them in the garbage. Turning away from the trash bin, he noticed René.

"I know, I know, I was trying to make some coffee and—"

René opened the cupboard and pulled out a juice glass. He tossed it in the air, and it shattered against the black-and-white checkered linoleum.

"Why the hell'd you do that?" Bastion's lips twisted in confusion.

"Because it's just a glass." René grabbed Bastion's face with both hands and smashed their mouths together. He whispered between rough kisses. "You're fucking great. You're both so fucking great. I don't care about a broken cup."

Marcus peaked into the kitchen, drawn by the sound of more breaking glass. He raised an eyebrow. Bastion shrugged in reply as if to say, *don't ask me, René's fucking crazy.*

"You're never going to get him to stop dropping dishes by kissing him, Rem." Marcus walked closer.

"Fuck the dishes," René grabbed the back of Marcus's head and sucked his top lip.

"How hard did you hit your head?" Marcus asked after they broke apart.

"No, it's just..." René sighed, "I just, I mean, I want— look, it's hard to explain. Just...just shut up and kiss me so I can feel less stupid."

"You heard the man." Bastion laughed. "Kiss him. I'll go sweep the glass he broke."

"He broke?" Marcus asked, shaking his head, "Fuck it, I don't even care."

He tugged at René's hair, outlining René's cheek with the tip of his nose. He worked his way to René's lips, brushing them together until René squirmed in his hold.

"More," René begged.

Marcus licked the outline of René's lips. René pushed his tongue out to meet Marcus's outside their mouths.

"I will break a coffee mug every fucking morning," Bastion snickered, storing the dustpan in the cupboard under the sink. He stole Marcus's lips for himself. René yanked Bastion by the hair and shoved him onto the table, chest pressed against the wood, ass bent over the side.

"I want to thank you both for taking care of me while I was sick."

They chuckled, understanding the game. René ground against Bastion's ass. Bastion's hair covered his face and fanned across the round, pin oak table. René paused a moment and then swore.

"Shit, spontaneous is hard to pull off. I need lube."

"I'll get it." Marcus volunteered.

"Thanks," René muttered before painting figure eights on the small of Bastion's back with his tongue. He spread Bastion's ass cheeks apart, flicking his tongue up and down Bastion's crack.

Bastion choked out several, short, desperate breaths as René worked his tongue around the delicate pink skin of Bastion's asshole. He settled into a light, flickering pattern. He squeezed Bastion's cheeks with his hands as he continued to move his tongue.

Marcus re-entered, chuckling. He passed the lube to René and circled around the table until he faced Bastion. Marcus swept Bastion's long mane away from his face, twisted it in a rope, and tucked it to the side.

"Thought you preferred blowjobs?"

"Well," Bastion gasped, face flushed. "Who am I to tell a man how to say thank you?"

"Bastion, say something next time. Flip over." René raised his head so he could speak.

"No, don't stop."

René caught Marcus's eyes and used his pointer finger to draw a circle in the air. Marcus nodded and he held Bastion's wrists as René grabbed his legs above the ankles. They flipped Bastion over, his back now on the table and legs framing the sides of René's body. Bastion shouted when they spun him, laughing once he landed.

"That was hot, but never, *ever*, do it again without warning me."

"Where's your sense of adventure?" Marcus pinned Bastion's wrists against the table and plucked kisses from his lips.

René knelt in the seat of the nearest chair. He shoved Bastion's entire length in his mouth. Bastion dug his feet into René's shoulders for leverage. René measured his pace. Each sucking motion grew exaggerated and aggravating. Bastion hitched his hips to compensate for René slowing down. René withdrew his lips from Bastion's cock and shifted lower, drawing Bastion's testicles in his mouth and rolling them around with his tongue. He gave Bastion's perineum a few playful slaps with his tongue before traveling to his cock.

"Rem, um, y-you can go lower," Bastion stammered, his breath short.

Marcus's lips split open in a large grin. "See what I mean? Tell him he can't have something, or do something, and it's all he wants."

"Marcus," Bastion hissed his name like a dirty, erotic curse. "Stop using your mouth to talk and start using it to make me come."

"No, I think it's my turn. Let's switch places."

"Hell no, you fucking asshole," Bastion growled. "I'm already—*ahhhh!*"

As they argued, René plunged his tongue as deep inside Bastion's asshole as he could. Taken by surprise, Bastion kicked out and René grunted as Bastion's foot landed against his shoulder.

"At least it wasn't my head." René rubbed his shoulder.

"Geez, Bastion, don't kick our Rembrandt. It's not like we can go to the store and pick up a new one if we break him," Marcus chided as René made Bastion squirm.

"I'll survive." René ducked down to Bastion's ass and licked his entrance. René's hand searched for Bastion's cock, seizing it and stroking.

"Fuck yes! Touch me, René! Oh Marcus, please. Marcus, please, please, please." Bastion whimpered in response, too far gone to care if they teased him.

"Why are you begging me? René's the one doing all the work." Marcus pet the crown of Bastion's head, leering down at him with a sinister grin.

"I know, that's why I'm asking you to help."

Marcus pinched Bastion's nipples and spiralled his fingertip around Bastion's chest. Bastion bit his lower lip, moaning. Sunlight slanted into the kitchen through the window. The glow illuminated the dust motes floating in the air and transformed René's kitchen to a fairy's grotto. René imagined the light striking against Bastion's black hair as it poured onto the tabletop. He envisioned the way the yellow beams would make Marcus's eyes glitter and gild the sweat of both his lovers' bodies, turning them to treasure. René sighed at his thoughts and cursed his imagination.

René slid his tongue up Bastion's thigh, enjoying the way Bastion hitched up. René curved his tongue across Bastion's body and licked up Bastion's long shaft. The skin of Bastion's erection was as taut as possible, and René's mouth watered in anticipation as he stretched his lips wide and descended to the base of Bastion's cock. Marcus continued to tease Bastion. He twisted Bastion's nipples and grazed his nails down Bastion's chest. René's plans of spoiling them with attentive oral pleasure had spiralled back to their original game of 'how pissed can we get Bastion without him hitting us upside the head with a whiskey bottle'.

Marcus swerved close, as if to kiss Bastion, but held his lips above Bastion instead. "Beg some more. You're sexy when you're not getting what you want."

"Marcus," Bastion growled his name like a curse.

"Say 'Please, Marcus. Kiss me, Marcus.'"

"Kiss me...please...you bastard."

"Close enough." Marcus massaged Bastion's lips with his own, his fingers still tormenting Bastion's nipples.

René's fingers roamed up Bastion's hip bones, and Bastion clawed at Marcus's shoulders in response. Marcus pulled away again.

"Marcus, if you don't stop teasing me, my revenge is going to be nasty."

"I've heard that threat before."

"I'm serious. By the time I'm done, you'll be weeping."

As Bastion threatened Marcus, René undressed and used the lube to coat Bastion's swollen cock. Bastion's words broke as René squeezed his slick fist around Bastion's shaft. Bastion bucked, grunting and clenching his jaw.

"What do you think you're doing?" Marcus asked with the feigned bored tone he used for bedroom play.

René tilted his head to the left, giving Marcus a pleasant smile while answering in a coy, sultry voice. "Fucking your man. You don't seem to be in the mood to do it yourself."

Marcus smiled as well, all teeth and possession, the smile of a dragon or a god gone mad. "First, ask for permission."

"Of course, where are my manners?" René bowed. "Bastion, do I have permission to fuck you?"

Bastion nodded his head, crushing his eyes shut and squirming for attention as René and Marcus parleyed.

Marcus dashed around the table. He caught René by the hair and slammed him against the back wall of the kitchen. His breath huffed from his mouth and onto René's face in frigid bursts. René kept his eyes open. Their faces floated close enough to almost touch and adrenaline rushed through René's bloodstream, making his heart stampede in his rib cage. René licked his lips.

"Ask *me* for permission." Marcus nibbled the lobe of René's right ear.

"Asking didn't work well for Bastion."

"He'll get it when I'm ready to give it to him. Now, ask me nicely."

"I'm going to fuck him," René said with slow, enunciated words.

"That wasn't asking. Maybe I'll fuck you against the wall, instead. Make him finish himself."

"I'm about to, anyway," Bastion threatened.

"You won't let Bastion finish himself off, because then *you* didn't make him come. Now…" René rubbed his thumb against Marcus's cockhead. "Tell me how we're going to make your lover come."

"Ride him, but face me," Marcus brought René back to the table.

René winked at Bastion before climbing on top and facing Marcus. He balanced himself on the tip of Bastion's cock. Bastion groaned as René impaled himself.

"Don't start until I'm fully in." Marcus nudged his tip against Bastion's asshole. Bastion squirmed, hooking a leg around Marcus's waist. Marcus withdrew and inserted halfway, refusing to fully sheath himself.

"Dammit, Marcus!"

"It'll be worth the wait when you're coming."

"For fuck's sake!" Bastion bucked. René grabbed Bastion's thighs for balance.

"Marcus, please." René closed his eyes, clenching his ass around Bastion's cock.

"There." Marcus sank inside Bastion as far as he could push.

"Mmmm, Marcus." Bastion ranked his nails along the tabletop.

"Damn," René gasped as he rocked his body back and forth. "Damn."

"Good?" Marcus asked.

René sighed in response, and Bastion groaned. Marcus bit René's neck before slamming harder into Bastion's ass. René struggled to keep pace with Marcus. The table shook and creaked under his and Bastion's body weight, but they all ignored it, lost in their pleasure. Bastion smacked the table with his hand. Each exhale came with a curse, and Bastion's thighs tightened.

"Is this what you wanted, Bastion?"

"Fuck you, Marcus!" Bastion swore as he jerked into a semi-sitting position, but his head flung back and he shivered. "Oh, fuck yes!"

René gritted his teeth while the sharp, frozen sensation of Bastion's orgasm filled him.

Chapter Thirteen

MARCUS GRABBED RENÉ and shoved him on the table next to Bastion. Lying on his stomach, René held his breath as Marcus's cock angled inside him. Bastion kissed him while Marcus pounded into René's asshole. René moaned and moaned and moaned, forgetting everything that existed beyond the kitchen walls.

The table groaned under their weight and then—*snap*—they fell stacked on top of each other like cards in a deck. The rollercoaster feeling in René's gut, from being fucked, swooped and rose as he fell to the floor. Marcus scrambled to his feet, and René pushed himself off Bastion.

"Bastion, are you okay?" René asked.

"I'm dead," he reminded René, wincing.

"But did it hurt?" René rubbed Bastion's chest with his hands as if his touch could heal injuries.

"It didn't feel good, but it can't physically hurt me." Bastion sat up, grabbing René's shoulders. "What about you?"

"I landed on you." René smiled.

Marcus scanned the damage they caused and laughed. The sound echoed across the kitchen. Bastion and René looked at him for a moment before they broke into their own peals of laughter. René covered his mouth with the palm of his hand but it did nothing to mute his chuckles.

"Well, I was going to have to buy new cups anyway. I guess I'll get a table too."

For no logical reason, they burst into a fresh round of hysterics. After it fizzled out, Marcus wrenched his fingers in René's and Bastion's hair and led them to the living room.

"I never finished," he said.

"Neither did I." René licked his lips. "So let's finish."

"Have fun, assholes. I've been teased enough for one day." Bastion sat on the couch as if uninterested and picked up their half-read copy of *The Hellbound Heart*.

At the same time, Marcus and René charged and crashed onto the floor together. They rolled over the carpet, wrestling to see who would dominate. Bastion dropped the book and watched them struggle. René managed to pin Marcus against the couch. The moment he did, Bastion hooked his legs over Marcus's shoulders to hold him and knotted his fingers in Marcus's hair.

"Consider this step one of my vengeance. Hope you like getting teased for a change," Bastion purred in Marcus's ear, tugging his hair harder.

"You're cheating. It was supposed to be whoever was stronger between René and me goes on top. You wanted a break," Marcus argued.

"With physical strength, you'd always win. Sometimes you need luck to beat the game, and René got lucky that I decided to grab you when I did." Bastion dug his heels in the space between Marcus's arms and torso to keep him in place.

"Thanks, Bastion." René licked up Marcus's body. He grazed his lips across Marcus's cheeks, snatching kisses from Marcus's mouth. "How should I tease him?"

"Pinch his nipples until he squirms."

René sucked Marcus's chest and below his collarbone. He wound his way down until he reached Marcus's left nipple. René nibbled around Marcus's areola and licked against the hardening bud. Marcus strained, testing Bastion's grip, but Bastion had him pinned with both his arms and legs. René bit above Marcus's nipple. There should have been bruises, beautiful red-violet roses blooming on tanned flesh, but the silvery mist of Marcus's body refused to darken.

"Lick his cock, but only the tip."

René flicked the cleft of Marcus's cockhead. Marcus lurched forward but couldn't break free. Bastion laughed.

"Now suck his fingers one at a time."

René obeyed, slurping Marcus's pinky into his mouth and drawing on it before switching to his ring finger.

"Do you really want to wait before you take me?" Marcus's gaze consumed René and made René's heart race.

"No." René shoved his hand between Marcus's legs. He stroked Marcus's cock three times, but then winced. "Goddammit, the lube is in the kitchen, isn't it?"

Marcus licked his lips. "Better get it quick, because if I break out of this trap, I'm shoving you to the ground and fucking you raw."

"Then maybe I should help you escape." René stood and walked backward with slow footsteps to the kitchen.

He found the abandoned bottle half buried under fragments of wood. In the living room, Bastion wound his fingers in Marcus's hair and tugged at the strands. They both argued over who broke the table. René stood on the sideline and watched. Marcus could free himself from Bastion's grip if he wanted to, but he sat there and argued instead, waiting for René.

"I broke the table," René said.

"We all broke it. We were all on it," Bastion answered.

"I wasn't," Marcus said.

"If anything, it's your fault for fucking us so hard." Bastion snorted.

"I'm the one who threw Bastion on the table." René straddled over Marcus's lap, tracing imaginary designs in his stomach as he spoke so he didn't have to look at Bastion. "When I saw you sweeping up the glass earlier, it reminded me of the last time I was in a relationship and made me realize how different you both are from him—how much better you are than him. That's why I threw the glass on the floor. I know I'm not making any sense."

Bastion released Marcus's hair and shifted his legs to a more comfortable position. With their eyes trained on René's face, both sat in silence as they waited for René to continue talking.

"I thought I was happy, but every day he added another rule for me to follow. First it was small things, always shower before bed and never interrupt him. So I thought, okay, whatever makes him happy, but the list never stopped growing. I—I don't really want to talk about it, but it got ridiculous. Had he dropped a glass, I would have been the one expected to sweep up the mess, and had I dropped one, he would have berated me and sent me to the store to replace it immediately. Don't ask why the fuck I stayed as long as I did. I guess I was just young and stupid. I thought if you loved someone, then you stayed until things got better." René snorted bitter laughter. "But he only loved his reflection and didn't give two shits about me and one day it clicked in my head."

René snapped his fingers, demonstrating how instant his epiphany had been.

"What'd you do when you figured it out?" Bastion asked.

René smirked. "I bitch-slapped him with a high-heeled shoe. Shit, I hope it left a scar so every time he looks in the mirror he has to remember me."

"Going Cinderella upside his head is beautiful, René." Bastion grinned. "I mean that unironically."

"We'll try not to piss you off, if that's what you're getting at." Marcus toyed with René's hair.

René averted his eyes, staring at the fireplace to have an object to focus on. "With you guys...there's never a list, you know? I can't imagine what my life would be like if I'd never moved here, other than boring. I know when I first arrived, I was a cute face you wanted to use to kill some time, and you were some neat ghosts I wanted to use to kill some time, but..." René shifted his gaze to stare at their faces. "But, I think moving here was the best thing I've ever done. So, thank you for letting me stay."

"René, we want you here." Bastion slipped off of the couch. He caressed René's cheek. Bastion and Marcus looked at each other. Marcus reached out and touched Bastion's lips, and then they looked back at René.

"You're not even going to laugh at me for being dopey, are you? You're both just going to kiss me." René's cheeks burned.

Bastion nodded.

"That's right," Marcus whispered, cupping René's chin and kissing René's bottom lip.

Bastion joined them, forcing them in an awkward, three-way kiss. He shifted behind René and coiled his right hand around René's belly. His left hand intertwined with Marcus's. Bastion kissed down René's neck, and Marcus sucked René's collarbone. Their lips wandered to his shoulders. René swooned and leaned into their mouths. His cock hardened and his heartbeat danced.

Marcus reached for the lube. He drenched himself with the silicone liquid. Bastion coated his hand with a generous amount before wiggling one finger inside René's ass and working it around. A moment later, he added a second finger. René tilted his head and groaned as Bastion scissored his fingers inside René's ass. Bastion gradually added more fingers, shaping all five digits like the beak of a bird as he inserted them. René dug his nails into Marcus's shoulders as Bastion pumped his hand into René's asshole.

"Bastion," Marcus whispered, a pleading quality in his tone.

Bastion hummed. "No, he's not ready."

"I—" René's words melted to desperate, needful whines and Bastion pushed his fingers deeper.

"René, tell Bastion you're ready." Marcus skimmed his tongue across his teeth.

René wanted to. They'd gone the whole morning teasing Bastion without their own release and then the table broke. René's erection throbbed, but every time René opened his mouth to say anything, Bastion pushed a little deeper and René could only moan.

"Hey, Marcus?"

"What?" Marcus growled.

"Beg me for permission to fuck him."

"Isn't that his decision? Shouldn't I ask him?" Marcus copied René's strategy from earlier, but impatience tainted his attempt at a seductive tone.

"Oh, I don't think he's capable of answering right now. Are you René?"

René shook his head no, moaning as Bastion fisted him and digging his nails into Marcus's skin.

"Fine, you want me to ask? Bastion, let me fuck him."

"No,"

"Please."

"No, I'm fucking him right now."

"Then jack me off."

"I could, but you're sexy when you're not getting what you want."

"Bastion, just tell me what you want me to do so we can skip the foreplay, all right?"

"Beg."

Marcus grunted, but lust overwhelmed his pride. "I'm begging you, Bastion, please, fucking please, let me fuck Rembrandt."

René's breath caught in his chest when Marcus used his full name. His orgasm welled inside his abdomen, and he fumbled for his cock to stroke himself.

"Don't let him come, Marcus; you're not inside him yet." Bastion nodded toward René's hand.

Marcus squeezed René's wrists, keeping both hands away from his body. René made a whining, begging noise.

"Bastion," René pleaded.

"Sorry, Rem," Bastion purred in his ear, "but Marcus needs to learn not to tease me when I tell him to touch me."

"Bastion, I'm going to go out of my fucking mind if you don't let me fuck him. Stop with your power trip, and let me fuck him."

"I see the appeal in making me suffer earlier. This is rather fun." Bastion chuckled to himself.

"Bastion," René whimpered. "I'm about to come." The words choked in René's throat as Bastion moved inside him. "Either way."

"He's all yours, Marcus." Bastion kissed the nape of René's neck before removing his fingers.

Marcus grabbed René's hips, lifted him, and eased his weight down Marcus's cock. Bastion helped guide René's hips, and René was glad for it because his thighs felt weak and jellied. René slung his arms around Marcus's neck, barely able to hang on as he gasped for breath. He lowered his right hand and stroked himself. Each flick of his wrist encouraged his pelvis to jerk forward as he squeezed his muscles tight around Marcus's shaft. Marcus's head was a hard knot moving inside him and prodding René's prostate.

"*Oh god, oh god, oh god, oh god,*" René uttered in one quick breath as he shot out onto his stomach. His body dropped; he couldn't move.

Marcus didn't give him a chance to recover. He arranged René on his side. René's left leg slung around Marcus's shoulder as Marcus straddled over René's right leg. René's mouth remained open in a silent *O*. His eyes wrenched shut and his hand braced the floor for support. Bastion slapped Marcus's ass.

"Well? You wanted to fuck him. So fuck him harder."

Marcus growled as he sped his pace, jabbing into René's body. The breath squeaked from René's mouth in embarrassing, high-pitched bursts he couldn't control.

"Yes, just like that," Bastion cooed in Marcus's ear. "Would you like me to make you come?"

Marcus grunted, his breathing hard and quick. Bastion forced one, two, then three fingers inside Marcus's asshole, allowing Marcus's momentum to pull and push around them while he curled his fingers upward. Marcus slammed back and forth over and over until he gnashed his bottom lip between his teeth as he came.

"You're cold." René curled his legs closer to his body as Marcus finished.

"Sorry," Marcus whispered in a shaky voice as he dropped his hands to the floor.

"God, sexy as it was, you two made it unnecessarily long." Bastion huffed a long breath from his chest.

"*We* did?" Marcus pushed himself to a sitting position. "It was half your fault."

"You started it. I finished it."

"Will you two stop being adorable and fetch me a blanket?" René managed to roll on his back, shaking with cold.

"Never, never, call me adorable again." Marcus left to find a quilt.

SITTING ON THE couch, snuggled next to Bastion and Marcus, René looked up from his book as May opened the door and let herself inside.

"Honey, I'm home." She shut the door behind her and slung her purse onto the coat rack.

"Did work suck?" René asked.

"Eh, it's the weekend now. I've already repressed work. How are you feeling?"

"Perfect," René answered, then added, "but, I can't say the same thing for my kitchen table. Can we go to the store? I also need more glasses."

"What happened to your table?"

"It's not in there anymore," René said.

"Why not?" May peeked inside his kitchen.

"I was leaning against it and it broke."

"What the hell have you been eating?" May laughed. "Seriously, René, stop being such a klutz, what if you'd gotten hurt again? I'd be stuck here playing nurse forever."

"Only the table got hurt this time." René smiled. "So, store?"

"I need to change, but sure, let's go to the store." May rubbed her neck.

A few hours later, they returned with a small, round, breakfast nook–style table, glasses, a few Christmas decorations, and one large Douglas fir tree. René wrinkled his nose as he entered the living room.

"Is something burning?"

"Smells that way," May said.

René glanced around but didn't see Marcus or Bastion. He lowered the bags of cups and ornaments to the floor and walked to the kitchen. René waved smoke away from his face. Bastion sulked, and Marcus leaned against the fridge laughing. A skillet filled with water sat on the stove.

"Don't worry, we're cleaning up the mess." Marcus continued to laugh.

"You tried to make me dinner?" René smiled.

Bastion grumbled something inaudible, and Marcus laughed harder.

"We really do suck in the kitchen." Marcus shrugged.

"We get fucking bored, y'know? Especially when you're gone. So I thought we could do something useful." Bastion slammed the skillet in the sink and scrubbed it with a steel wool pad.

"It was a nice thought," René kissed Marcus.

René pushed Bastion hard against the counter. Bastion tried to look away, pissed, but René held his chin and forced his face to straighten. "Bastion, I can teach you."

Bastion jerked his face away again, but René pulled it back for a kiss. Bastion sighed, his anger fading with each brush of René's lips.

"Yeah, teach me. Learning will give me something to do."

"While we were out shopping, I bought a router for Wi-Fi."

"René, you give in to him too easily. We could have drawn that out for at least two weeks and had all kinds of fun with him." Marcus snorted.

"I'm curious to see what kinds of games he buys." René chuckled as he peeked out of the kitchen to find May. "Don't worry. They didn't burn the house down."

"Just the kitchen?" May asked as she propped the tree against the wall.

"They seasoned one of my favorite skillets."

"Well tell them to get in here and do all the heavy, awkward parts of putting up the tree."

"That's probably a better idea than having them stay in the kitchen, or they really might burn the place down."

René batted his eyelashes at Marcus. "Hey Marcus, you're a big lug. Go help May set up the Christmas tree."

"Isn't it early to buy a—"

"Yeah, I know, but that's how May and I do things."

"Sounds about right." Marcus sighed in response and went to help May.

"Lesson one will be salad." René washed his hands and selected vegetables from the fridge.

"Fuck you, René. I'm not going to do this if you're going to make fun of me. I seriously want to learn how to cook."

"And I seriously spent over seven hundred dollars on my knives. If you fuck them up because you don't know the difference between chopping, dicing, and smacking the blades against the counter, I'll banish you to the realms of Cthulhu. I can't teach you how to saute or flambe until you know some basics, like slicing a tomato." René wedged his hands against his hips.

"Goddamn, seven hundred dollars?"

"You'd do it for an instrument, wouldn't you?"

"No, I'm a vocalist." Bastion found a cutting board and placed it on the counter.

"Whatever, you know what I meant."

He washed the produce and dried the vegetables on a paper towel. He placed a cucumber on the cutting board and his chef's knife in Bastion's hand. Standing behind him and keeping his hands over Bastion's, René demonstrated how to properly slice the cucumber. Bastion chuckled.

"No, it's not phallic, and no, this isn't sexy." René laughed.

Marcus entered the kitchen as René spoke. "Actually, watching you stand behind Bastion is kinda sexy."

"And these cucumbers are definitely phallic," Bastion added.

"You burnt the chicken I'd taken out of the freezer last night, didn't you?" René kept them both on topic. "I think I have lunch meat left. We'll boil some eggs and make a chef salad."

"You make it look easy." Bastion frowned.

"Let me guess." René sighed. "You dumped oil in the pan, turned it to high heat, slapped the chicken straight in, and couldn't get it to flip over, right?"

"Um." Bastion grinned. "Kinda."

"Medium heat, pan first, then oil, let them each get hot, and leave the chicken in the pan until a crust forms. Then you can flip it without fucking up my skillet—which didn't cost as much as the knives, but wasn't cheap either."

"Hey Marcus, do you believe this asshole spent seven hundred dollars on his kitchen knives?" Bastion pointed the knife in René's direction.

"Bastion, I'm alive, please don't point a knife at me."

"Damn. Sorry, Rem."

"Bastion, don't kill our lover." Marcus kissed the side of Bastion's neck.

"Does *la petite mort* count?" Bastion asked.

"I don't know, let's 'break in' the new table tomorrow when May's at work and find out." Marcus grinned.

Chapter Fourteen

BASTION LEARNED HOW to cook. René learned how to play *Dust in the Wind* on Marcus's guitar. All of them tried painting, but none of them had the talent for it, so René returned the art supplies he'd borrowed from May. René gave Bastion his credit card and let him buy the occasional new toy, usually a board game. René thought about giving him an entertainment budget but decided he'd see how much Bastion spent before trying to establish any sort of rules. They tried playing D&D, but their campaigns devolved into erotic meetings at random pubs. Each attempt ended in lurid faux LARPing with cheesy dialogue they couldn't say without laughing so hard that it made actual copulation difficult, sometimes impossible.

They decided to forgo a traditional Thanksgiving, May and René being the only two people who could eat the dinner. Bastion baked lasagne. René roasted kale and acorn squash. Together they prepared crème brûlée. He, Marcus, and May spent most of the day watching football while Bastion used the laptop to read. After May left, they went upstairs.

"I really hate winter." Marcus sat by the window. "The days are too short."

"Come to bed and I'll make you forget how short the days are and beg for longer nights." Bastion kissed the nape of Marcus's neck.

"He's right, Marcus; come to bed," René whispered as he settled into the sheets. Bastion followed him down, draping himself on René's body.

"Why?" Marcus smirked. "Is Bastion's poetic talk getting you excited?"

"Yes, actually," René confessed, smoothing his hand up and down Bastion's ribs.

"He's always had a way with words. He can make 'fuck you' sound like a love song, but 'I love you' sound dirty."

"As if I'd ever say 'I love you' to jerks like you two." Bastion snorted.

"Oh?" Marcus asked, "You don't think we could make you say it?"

René chimed in, adding, "Over and over again."

"It does not count if I say it under duress." Bastion wagged a long finger at both of them.

"But it'd be fun, to hear you say it while we teased you." Marcus crawled on top of Bastion. "With your hips jerking up and your hair in your face, because that's when you're most beautiful."

"I could make you say it too." Bastion raked his nails down Marcus's chest as they kissed.

"Probably," Marcus admitted.

"It'd be useless." René shook his head. "To hear him say it. It's always on his face when he looks at you. I remember that clearly from my dreams of when you guys were alive."

"And what about you?" Bastion tugged René closer by his hair. René brushed his lips near Bastion's but not close enough to touch.

"There was a time when I could push away and act indifferent, but it's gone." René bridged the gap between his and Bastion's mouths. His hand intertwined with Marcus's fingers. "I had never let my lovers hold me until I moved here. Now, when I think about it, I try to remember why. Why did I hate getting close? And the only answer I can find is—because I wasn't with the two of you."

"You're cute when you're coy, but I prefer you sweet." Bastion purred in René's ear.

"What about when I'm rough?" René gripped Bastion's wrists. Their faces hovered close together. René held Bastion's gaze though he could only see fog.

"Also fun."

"What about you, Marcus?" René shoved Bastion to the side. He pounced on Marcus, pressed him against the mattress, and pinned Marcus's arms over his head.

"Oh hell yes." Bastion clenched the sheets with his fists. "You only ever did it one time, but I want to see you take Marcus again."

Marcus stared at René. Even as a vaporous ghost, it was obvious he was daring René to make good on his threat. René kissed Marcus's jaw and traced his tongue around the shell of Marcus's ear. He rose to his knees, stole Bastion's hand, and kissed it before guiding it down between Marcus's legs.

"Get him ready for me."

Bastion laughed, biting Marcus's nipples and rolling Marcus's balls in his palm. René found the lube and covered himself in the thick liquid as Bastion worked his fingers in and out of Marcus's ass. René spiralled his fingertips along Marcus's chest. Marcus groaned as Bastion prepped him.

"Well, Marcus? Are you ready?" Bastion asked as he shifted to the side.

"Fuck me." Marcus growled, low and predatory.

"How do you want me to fuck him? Fast or slow?" René smothered Bastion's chest with kisses as he asked the question.

"Fast," Marcus answered for himself.

"Start slow." Bastion grinned capturing René's lips and sucking on them.

"Bastion," Marcus cursed.

René bit Bastion's lower lip, soothed the bite with several deep, lingering kisses, and arranged himself between Marcus's legs. He lined his tip against Marcus's asshole, waiting until Marcus's thighs twitched before easing himself forward. Marcus's breath caught in his throat as René entered. A shiver wracked through René. Instead of heat, frigid muscles gripped around René's cock. He gasped and closed his eyes as he moved, hitching as lazily as he could manage despite the pressure around René's cock begging him to speed up.

"Marcus."

"Goddamn." Bastion exhaled as his fingers danced along Marcus's body. "I could watch this all day."

René groaned. He couldn't take it anymore and slammed forward. Marcus called out and the sound of it sent René's thoughts spinning. He rammed deeper into Marcus's asshole, craving another cry of pleasure from him.

"Slow down." Bastion dragged his fingers down René's spine.

René grunted, thrusting with deliberate pushes of his hips. Bastion kissed his way up Marcus's abdominal muscles and traced his tongue around Marcus's nipples. He sucked and bit Marcus's nipples until they poked out from his chest, and then Bastion kissed back down to Marcus's navel. René quickened his movements again, unable to resist. Marcus gasped, squeezing his thighs and digging his heals into the mattress. Bastion positioned himself behind René, holding René's waist and forcing him to stop.

"Bastion," René pleaded. "Not now. No games tonight."

"I said go slower. Let's make this last." Bastion guided René's movements with his hands. René allowed Bastion to control the pace for a few minutes, but the pressure in his groin swelled and ached.

"Bastion, let me go." René tilted his head back so he could plead in Bastion's ear.

"In a minute."

"No. Now."

Bastion bit René's collarbone and crawled up the bed. He stared at Marcus before tracing his fingers across Marcus's lips. They quivered under Bastion's touch. Marcus panted from René's thrusts. Bastion drew his pointer finger across the tip of Marcus's cock until it was slick with precome. He brought the finger to his mouth and sucked.

"I love seeing you this worked up." Bastion grabbed Marcus's hand and brought it to Bastion's dick. Marcus rubbed his thumb against the head, making Bastion sigh and roll his hips. "Yes. Touch me, and beg René for more."

"René," Marcus called out, not so much to say his name, but to beg for him to hurry. Marcus's legs twitched on either side of René as one hand continued to fondle Bastion while the other hand pulled the sheets off the bed.

"I..." René exhaled, speech eluding him. He dug his nails into Marcus's outer thighs. Instinct drove René, He bucked, crying to the ceiling. Even as their chill surrounded him and made him shiver, the heat from his own belly melted the ice around him and made him burn. Bastion whispered a string of curses and dirty imagery, but René couldn't hear the words as his orgasm scrambled the thoughts in his mind. He was only aware of the sweat tickling his temples and the breath pushing his chest up and down as he sunk to the mattress, heart pounding.

Marcus grabbed Bastion, slamming him belly down against the mattress and biting his neck and shoulders. Bastion grunted, shoving his ass into Marcus's groin and teasing Marcus to enter. With his fingers digging into Bastion's ribs, Marcus ground against Bastion's rear, teasing him in return. René watched, face half buried behind his arms as he caught his breath. A contented sigh sifted out his mouth. His brain hazy with endorphins.

"Remember, Marcus, he wants it slow," René said.

"He's getting it fast and hard." Marcus directed his cockhead against Bastion's asshole. He rolled it along Bastion's opening, pushing the head inside and then withdrawing it.

Bastion clawed at the wrinkled sheets but didn't beg or call out. He held his eyes shut tight, and his lips pressed together in a thin line. Muffled noises pushed from his throat, increasing in volume as Marcus readjusted his hold on himself to allow two inches of his dick to sink in and out of Bastion's body. He toyed with Bastion until Bastion was gasping before halting and gripping Bastion's hips with both hands.

Bastion raised up to his forearms and knees. Marcus shoved his body against Bastion's ass, inserting himself as deeply as he could. Bastion sucked in a loud breath. The bed creaked, the springs groaned, and the headboard smacked the wall. Bastion choked short, quick, breathy ohs from his mouth as Marcus crashed against him.

"You're so hard," Bastion moaned, "I feel like I'll tear open."

Recovered from his climax and wanting to get reinvolved, René inched closer to his two lovers, sliding his hand along Bastion's stomach and wrapping his fingers around Bastion's cock.

"Lightly, René." Bastion winced.

René released his hold on Bastion, using his thumb, pointer, and middle finger to caress Bastion's shaft, avoiding his swollen head. Bastion hissed at René's delicate strokes but didn't tell him to stop. Without warning, Marcus slowed his thrusts.

"You're so fucking hard," Bastion repeated.

"Yeah, you two have that effect on me," he said in between slow, purposeful glides of his body.

René stretched up to kiss Marcus, overcome by the sudden need to taste him. The cold of his mouth shocked René's warm tongue. René released Bastion so he could crawl to the floor. He lifted Bastion's face and kissed him. Bastion's cold saliva tasted sweet. Marcus tangled his fingers in Bastion's long hair to gain momentum.

"Bastion," Marcus said.

"Yes?"

"What do you want?"

Bastion licked his lips as he thought about his answer. "I want you to come inside me."

"You don't want to come first?" Marcus asked.

"Fuck me harder, Marcus."

Marcus smirked. "If that's what you want."

Bastion exhaled random curses as Marcus moved with quick, jabbing thrusts. René traced his fingers across Bastion's cheeks and chin. Bastion tilted his face toward the touches as *shits* and *fucks* poured from his mouth.

"Marcus is right. This is when you're most beautiful," René whispered to Bastion.

Bastion stared at René, his mouth dropping slightly. He tried to speak but only managed a soft whine.

"Fuck, you're both beautiful." Marcus spoke the words between pants. His hands shook and he pumped his body five times, muttering *shit* for the first four and holding his breath for the last one. He dropped his head against Bastion's back and rubbed his hands along Bastion's sides. As soon as his chest stopped heaving, Marcus nudged Bastion to the edge of the bed. "Your turn."

"Yes," Bastion moaned.

Marcus knelt beside René and yanked Bastion closer. Bastion re-situated so his legs hung off the bed. They splayed Bastion's legs wide, one on Marcus's shoulder, one on René's shoulder, and both kissed his thighs. Working their way up, they teased his balls with their mouths. René and Marcus angled their faces so they could lick up Bastion's shaft, meeting at the tip. René and Marcus kissed around Bastion's head, lips and tongues working at each other and Bastion's cock at the same time. Bastion called out, thrusting his hips.

Marcus gripped a handful of René's hair and pulled René's head away. He swallowed Bastion's cock in his mouth, and sucked up, withdrawing and pressing René's lips against Bastion's dick instead. He alternated between them, first with single bobs of their heads, then with longer intervals of sucking.

"Fuck!" Bastion grabbed Marcus's head, holding Marcus in place and fucking Marcus's mouth. "Fuck!" Bastion trembled and, a minute later, came. "Oh fuck!"

After Marcus swallowed, René cupped Marcus's chin and kissed him, running his tongue across Marcus's lips. They crawled into bed with Bastion and the three of them took turns kissing until they were ready to sleep.

RENÉ CRAWLED BENEATH the Christmas tree to water it. Bastion stood beside him.

"I bought something," he said after a few moments of silence.

"Okay." René nodded his head, attention focused on the tree. Two weeks before Christmas and it still lived, but René had to water it every day.

"It was a little expensive."

"Oh?" René raised an eyebrow, peeking up at Bastion from underneath pine boughs. "What'd you buy?"

"I'm not telling you." Bastion crossed his arms over his chest. "It was kinda two things. I couldn't decide between them. After shipping, I spent a little over a hundred dollars. Just don't look at your bill."

"Well, must be one fun board game." René already suspected what it was that Bastion bought, and the thought made him lick his lips.

"Marcus didn't tell you already, did he?"

"No. I promise he didn't."

Bastion snorted. "Don't open the packages when they're delivered. "

"I won't." René stood and kissed Bastion on the cheek. On the couch, Marcus yelled at the referee on the television screen. René and Bastion curled up on each side of him. René watched the game and Bastion toyed with the laptop.

"What cookies do you want for Christmas?" Bastion asked while scanning images of frosted sweets on the internet.

"I want sugar cookies shaped like ghosts," René said.

"Ha-ha." Bastion scowled at him.

"No. Bastion, I'm sorry. I didn't mean it to be facetious. May and I decorated our tree in cobwebs, bones, and plastic spider rings last year and baked ghost cookies."

"René, what the fuck is wrong with you?"

"What? Spooky things are my favorite."

"Commercial, Bastion." Marcus swatted at René and Bastion with a distracted hand.

"This game's already over. I told you at halftime." René glanced at the score. Their team trailed behind by seven points and didn't have the ball.

"They can still pull it off."

"They don't have enough time." René shook his head.

"Marcus, do you remember what happened last time you blew me off for a fucking football game?" Bastion glared at them.

"Gingerbread cookies shaped like cocks. Jesus Christ, Bastion, there's only two minutes left on the clock."

"Ghosts and dicks. Great, it's like my life on a cookie sheet." Bastion frowned at the laptop.

"What did May want when you messaged her?" René asked over Marcus's shoulder.

Marcus grabbed the remote and turned the volume higher.

"The kind with jelly in the middle."

"Then I want peanut brittle instead."

Bastion searched for a recipe as the clock wound down. Marcus screamed at the refs, the owners, the coach, and the players.

"I told you." René sighed.

"Well, if they'd gotten their heads out of their asses."

"That's what I said in the first quarter, but it never happened."

"Why'd I even have to pick out a cookie? It's not like I'm eating any of them." Marcus crossed his arms over his chest, glancing at Bastion and deciding to complain about something other than football.

"Because I fucking told you to."

"You can frost some white and use chocolate ganache to make the other ones black." René grinned.

"You don't seriously think I'd bake those, do you?"

"It's what he asked for. You have to bake them." René paused and then asked, "What did you do the last time Marcus ignored you for a football game?"

"Took his guitar and smashed it through the TV."

Chapter Fifteen

BASTION'S MYSTERY PACKAGES arrived one week before Christmas. René signed for them and placed them under the tree. He found Bastion in the kitchen. Bastion pulled a pan of gingerbread penises from the oven to cool.

"Hey, those packages came, and I left them in the living room. I'm going to take a shower. I'll be out in a few minutes."

"Okay, ask Marcus to open them for me before you go upstairs." Bastion shrugged as if he didn't care what René did.

"Sure."

Marcus practiced his guitar on the couch. René stood and listened for a moment while Marcus strummed through several cords.

"Hey, René." He looked up when he noticed René watching him.

"Hey, I put some packages under the tree. Bastion wanted you to open them. I'm going to take a shower real quick."

"Okay."

René rushed to his shower. He started the water and his stomach fluttered. He stepped beneath the hot water and scrubbed himself down. His heart refused to slow as René thought of what might be waiting for him once he finished. He suspected before, but now he knew the packages were for the bedroom by the nonchalant way Bastion ignored them.

After he cleaned and dried himself, he walked into his room wrapped in a towel. Marcus and Bastion stood in front of the bed.

"Early Christmas present," Marcus said.

"You're going to tie me up, aren't you?" René stared at his feet and played with his damp hair.

Bastion frowned at Marcus who held his hands in front of him as if to ward away Bastion's stare. "I did not fucking tell him so don't give me that look, Bastion."

"I knew what you were going to do the day you asked for Wi-Fi." René lifted his head.

"Then why didn't you just pick out your own restraints? We don't know what we're doing." Bastion crossed his arms over his chest.

"I wanted you to surprise me."

"They all looked gimmicky," Marcus said.

"I got a basic set." Bastion pulled the comforter away to reveal what he'd purchased. He pointed to a tangle of black straps with a blindfold and ball gag sitting in the middle of the pile. "But I was afraid it wouldn't be good enough, so I bought these things." He lifted up a spreader bar with leather loops attached to each end. One bar was shorter for arms, the other was longer to keep the legs pushed wide apart.

"René, you look awfully bashful." Marcus chuckled.

"Um, I'm excited. Usually when I say I'm curious about bondage, I get my wrists tied up with an old work tie. No one's ever bought me anything before."

"Well now you're in the presence of quality." Bastion winked at him.

"We looked on the internet to get ideas." Marcus frowned at the straps and bars.

"And we decided BDSM is boring." Bastion crossed his arms over his chest and rolled his eyes.

"He means structured."

"Boring."

Marcus shook his head. "It's very specific. You need to discuss scenes beforehand; both doms and subs have obligations in the relationship, and then there's aftercare."

"*Boring.*"

"Let it suffice to say Bastion has neither the sense of responsibility needed to be a dom, nor the obedience to be a sub."

"Oh, like you or René are responsible or obedient."

"So we gave up our delusions of being hardcore BDSM sex gods and just decided we were going to keep it casual."

"I just want to be tied up." René laughed. "And I already think you're sex gods."

"So then..." Marcus dug his fingers into René's shoulders. He wrenched René within his personal space and kissed along the shell of René's ear. "Are we going to stand here, or are we going to fuck your brains out?"

"What do you want us to do to you?" Bastion asked René. "We never made it past belts on our own."

"Well I never made it to belts, so you're more experienced than me." René scraped his teeth against his bottom lip and stared at the straps and bars.

Marcus snatched René's hair in his hand and shoved him on top of the bed and near the pile of straps. Marcus snatched a leather collar connected to a thin chain.

"We won't need this. After all, you're our roommate, not our pet." He tossed the collar into the trash bin near René's vanity. "Before we start, is there anything you don't want us to do?"

René laughed, the breathy, nervous chuckle he could never prevent when he flirted.

"Stop."

"Deal. Bastion, take his wrists."

Bastion pressed his nails into the soft undersides of René's wrists as he pulled René's arms out. "And if you do need to take a break or tell us something, you can hum 'Happy Birthday.'"

"Don't listen to him." Marcus pulled René's hair into a ponytail and stuffed the ball gag in René's mouth. He held a crimson silk scarf and glided it across René's neck. René tilted his head, exhaling as the silk caressed him. Marcus tucked one end in René's hand and tied the other end to Bastion's wrist. "One tug means yes or go on. Two tugs mean no or stop. Three tugs mean time-out. Do you understand?"

René tugged on the scarf once.

"I still think "Happy Birthday" would be more entertaining." Bastion strapped René's hands into the loops connected to the shorter bar, careful not to obstruct the scarf they needed to communicate while the gag kept René from speaking. Marcus dug through the pile of thinner bindings and found a chest piece with a metal ring in the center. As far as René could tell, the harness was for body decoration and not restriction, but Marcus tied the straps in a knot near the ring so they hung down like a mini cat of nine tails. He held the metal loop and smacked René's thighs with the leather strings.

"Do you want me to use this?"

René pulled on the silk once again. His cheeks burned as Bastion bound his ankles with the loops from the larger spreader bar. Marcus tied the blindfold around René's head. Black filled his sight and René's heart beat faster.

"Ready to start?" Bastion asked.

René tugged his scarf again.

Bastion slipped under the bottom bar, nestling in between René's legs to bite at his tender inner thighs.

Marcus rubbed René's shoulder with one hand and smacked René's side with the improv whip. The smacks were playful and not violent; however, each flick of the leather straps against René's skin made him jerk on reflex. The jolt caused the muscles in René's groin to twitch, but the ball gag muted his groan.

"Do you like this?" Marcus asked.

A single tug.

"You freak." Bastion teased René's balls with his cold fingertips while sucking on René's pale skin.

"He looks pretty hard. Bastion, suck his cock," Marcus ordered.

"You suck his cock," Bastion said.

"I told you to do it." Marcus chuckled. The bed shifted as they crawled closer.

"Who decided you could order me around?"

"Been doing it for years."

They kissed René's tip at the same time. René tossed his head back, hating how the gag muted his cry of pleasure. The nerves in his lower abdomen and groin ached with desire, and his cock throbbed beneath their lips. Bastion dropped low and tickled the delicate, pink skin around René's asshole with his tongue. He scored René's thighs with his fingernails as Marcus whipped René's chest. Marcus dotted René's chest with bites. He travelled to René's cock, sucked for a delirious, teasing minute, and smacked René's chest with the toy whip again.

"Bet you're ready to be fucked," Marcus growled in René's ear, the closest his voice ever got to sensual.

René nodded his head and jerked on the scarf. He wasn't sure if it was a question, but he figured it wouldn't hurt to express how he was still *very* into what they were doing. René tried to swallow, but the gag made it difficult.

"Too bad for you because we're not in any hurry." Marcus whipped him one last time. René heard the whip smack the wall as Marcus tossed it to the side. Next, Marcus planted kisses across René's chest, his fingers exploring René's torso with light touches. Bastion moaned against René's asshole. The vibrations tingled along René's nerves and his eyes rolled back. Bastion's fingers drew light patterns in the creases of René's thighs and scored his nails wherever he thought René was sensitive. Marcus licked around René's nipples, biting between licks.

René shook, a mix of want and cold. He bit the ball in his mouth, finding it hard to breathe. He considered pulling on his lifeline three times to ask them to remove the gag. At the same moment, Bastion grunted, climbed over Marcus, and eased the gag out of René's mouth.

"I don't like this. I want to hear you scream when I eat your ass." Bastion shimmied down to René's asshole, massaging and poking his tongue inside René's opening.

"Thanks, I was going to ask—oh god, your tongue feels good." René gasped and pulled deep breaths into his lungs. "Oh god, Bastion!"

They had his legs up in the air and his arms stretched over his head. He strained against the bindings, testing them. Bastion cycloned his tongue around René's rim, and René sputtered half-verbalized curses. He wanted to tangle his hands in their hair, but the restraints held tight, so he whimpered soft nonsense as they shifted their fingers and lips over his body. Marcus sat René upright, his legs still looped over Bastion, who kissed along René's Adonis Belt and used the pad of his thumb to stroke the underside of René's tip. Marcus pressed their mouths together.

"Rembrandt."

"Marcus." René sighed against Marcus's lips.

"Come here, Bastion." He crooked his finger to summon Bastion.

"What's up?" Bastion crawled close.

"Who do I fuck first?"

With the blindfold over his eyes, René could only hear the way their breath huffed and their bodies shuffled. Their legs jostled René, but he couldn't grope them with his wrists locked in the bar.

"Me." Bastion snorted.

"Isn't this René's Christmas present?"

"So what? I want you."

"You're so selfish." Marcus clicked his tongue.

Bastion laughed; the sound echoed off the walls. One of them took René's leg brace and flung it over and around Marcus, forcing René to first fall backward, and then sit up in Marcus's broad lap. René yelped in surprise, but Bastion only chuckled. He raised René's ass higher and shifted underneath him, also in Marcus's lap so that Marcus faced both Bastion and René.

"How's this?" Bastion asked once he had himself situated in Marcus's lap, and René trapped between Bastion's and Marcus's stomachs.

"This might be fun." Marcus purred next to René's ear.

René's legs splayed out on either side of Marcus. The spreader bar kept them angled in a wide V. Their bodies burned with cold, surrounding him in a blizzard of frozen limbs and chests. René inhaled the light, haunting scent of ozone that accompanied them.

"This works," he said.

"Good."

Bastion embraced René and leaned over his shoulder. Bastion and Marcus moaned. By the muffled sounds they made, René imagined them smashing their mouths together. He could hear them breathing roughly. Their fingers searched René's body. René squirmed, rubbing his body against theirs to get a sense of what they were doing to each other as they sandwiched around him.

"Marcus." Bastion gasped, struggling to breathe as he impaled himself on Marcus's cock and rolled his body forward and backward.

"*Ahh!*" René tossed his head back and gasped when Marcus's broad, coarse fingers squeezed René's cock and kneaded the hard flesh. Marcus stroked René as Bastion bounced onto Marcus's cock. They set up a rhythm, trapping René in the ebb and flow of their bodies. The breath shuddered from René's throat. He relaxed onto Marcus's chest and pressed his forehead against Marcus's cold, sweating skin. Bastion's hard cock rubbed René's ass as they rocked. Marcus locked his grip around René's shaft, stroking quickly. René bobbed up and down from Bastion and Marcus's lovemaking. He felt like a shipwreck survivor lost at sea, shaking from cold, teeth chattering, and wanting nothing more than to submit to the waves and sink into the cold waters forever.

"René, should we stop? You're shaking hard." Marcus touched René's burning face with his icy fingertips.

"I said don't stop," he whispered, "I want to come at the same time as Bastion."

"Whatever you want." Bastion curled his fingers over Marcus's. They both jerked his cock. René concentrated on the sensation of their hands. Every time he tried to move, the restraints reminded him he couldn't, and the thought sent an excited shiver through him. More than the bars, their bodies trapped him, *they* trapped him, and he never wanted to escape.

He balanced his forearms onto Marcus's shoulders, his breath labored. René thrust his cock into their grip, fast, fast, fast, groaning and tensing his body. René felt himself spasm at the same time Bastion called out. The sound of Bastion's orgasm intoxicated René, inciting his own climax and making him pant as his body spasmed. Their hands uncoiled from his spent shaft. Marcus grunted, pulling Bastion closer and crushing René between them. Bastion rode faster, growling and clinging to René as he rocked.

"Fuck, fuck, fuck!" Bastion wailed.

Marcus tensed, his muscles taut and his skin drenched with sweat. Marcus moaned and bit René's shoulder as he rode out his orgasm. They caught their breaths, sweat mingling between the three of them.

"Bastion, I love you," Marcus nearly purred the confession.

The breath caught in Bastion's throat. He didn't respond, stunned. It'd never been said before, not since René had known them nor in any of his visions. René also gasped. He felt like he was interrupting something between them and squirmed to distance himself from them, but he couldn't because of his bindings and the cage of their bodies. Marcus yanked René's hand bar closer instead.

"Don't slink away like you're not part of this. I love you, too, Rembrandt."

"Take the blindfold off." René shook his head. Bastion tore it away. René nodded in thanks and stared at Marcus, but he saw only a mirage-like shimmer in the air, and it made René ache. The pain throbbed from his chest to the tips of his fingers.

Part of René wanted—more than anything—to escape, but another stubborn, roguish part of René wanted—more than anything—to settle between them and acquiesce to the experience. It felt like the moment one died of exposure. The moment when the snow no longer stung the skin with cold and the victim could let go. He closed his eyes.

"I love you, too, Marcus," Bastion whispered.

"Say it again," Marcus growled, low and sultry.

"I love you." Bastion pressed his mouth against René's ear. "Rem, I love you too."

"Untie me, please. I want to touch you both."

Bastion untied René's hands while Marcus worked on his feet.

"Thank you." René twisted so he could kiss Bastion's mouth and card through Bastion's hair. He kneaded Marcus's shoulders, kissing him as well. René opened his mouth to return the words to them, but his voice cracked. Bastion chuckled, tugging the band out of René's hair and combing the loose strands. They settled onto the mattress. Bastion tucked the comforter around René for warmth, but René jerked the cover away.

"No, I don't want to feel blankets. I want to be held."

"Since when?" Marcus teased.

"Since now," René said. "I need it."

Bastion sighed, caressing René's brow. "René, you don't look well. I think your body temperature is too low."

"I don't care." It was true and he shook too hard to deny it. He felt light-headed and breathless. Gooseflesh puckered along the skin of his arms, but he needed to be held.

"Will you take a shower if we go with you?" Marcus cupped René's face, his touch ice against René's cheeks.

René closed his eyes and nodded, although he didn't want to get up to take a shower. He wanted to embrace them as he fell asleep shivering.

He forced himself up and walked to the shower. The scalding water hurt as it warmed his torso. Several minutes passed until his teeth stopped chattering and his limbs stopped quivering. Bastion stood in front of him and René leaned against his shoulder. Marcus stood behind him, rubbing René's back with a warm washcloth. René closed his eyes. He pretended they were alive, but he could only pretend.

Chapter Sixteen

MAY ARRIVED CHRISTMAS Eve morning. After hugs and tossing her things in a corner, she brandished a tall, paper-wrapped object covered in red and green ribbons.

"René, this is our Christmas present, and we're going to love it. Open it now."

"Shouldn't we wait?"

"No."

"Okay." René took the bottle—it was obviously a bottle—and tore the gold-colored paper from it. He pulled the two-foot bottle of Grey Goose from the wrapping and held it up to admire it.

"Cherry Noir. Just think, René, a foot of vodka for each of us."

"Good thing I cleaned the toilets before you came over. We might be spending a lot of time with them this Christmas."

"If we drink half tonight and half on New Year's we shouldn't get *too* sick."

"You haven't seen how many cookies Bastion baked."

"On my way." May strode to the kitchen. René lodged the bottle of vodka in the freezer to chill while May squealed in delight over the plates of cookies scattered across the table.

"I should have never taught him how to bake." René laughed.

"Chocolate-covered penis. Those are my favorite two things together in a cookie." May bit the tip off of a gingerbread cookie and moaned.

"Promise me you'll eat other food while you're here."

"I make no such promise unless vodka counts as food." May snatched two more cookies from different plates and walked back to the living room. She looked around. "Where are Marcus and Bastion, anyway? Usually you're talking to them."

"They're sleeping. We were up late last night."

"Mmm-hmmm, I bet."

"I wish I were still sleeping."

"Bah, you can take a nap later. Let's do something fun."

"There's nothing fun to do before seven p.m." René yawned. "Except sleep."

"Okay, I have to agree with you." May shrugged. "But we're not going to sleep, so let's watch cheesy, stop-motion Christmas movies."

"Only if we can have eggs for breakfast, instead of cookies." René laughed despite himself.

"Sure. We'll have the cookies for dessert."

"Only two cookies."

"Three."

"Deal. Find Rudolph and I'll cook breakfast."

They ate on the sofa. Near the end of the movie, Marcus led a groggy and cantankerous Bastion downstairs, in accordance to their standard morning tradition. Bastion sat on the arm of the couch and draped himself over René's shoulder.

"Whoever invented waking up should be shot."

"René's face just brightened. Good morning Bastion and Marcus." May snorted, a crooked grin decorating her face.

"Shut up, May," René murmured.

"You look so adorable when you're flustered, René."

"It's true." Marcus stood near the window and watched the empty street littered with snow drifts.

"Shut up, Marcus."

May shifted on the sofa so she could look at René. "You know what we haven't done in a long time? Look at Christmas lights."

"Yeah." René nodded. "The last couple of Christmases at least one of us had some wet-blanket Greg who refused to go, so we skipped it."

"You guys aren't wet blankets, right? You'll go with us?" May asked.

"We can't leave the house." Marcus spoke directly to her, although she couldn't hear him.

"They're stuck in the house," René translated.

"You said they can go around the block, right?" May shrugged. "This neighborhood has a lot of decorated houses. And come on, don't you want to get outside for a change?"

"Not really," Bastion muttered, more asleep than awake. "This house has a bed, and that's all I need to be happy."

"You're just saying that because you haven't woken up, yet." René waved away Bastion's words.

"Did May try any of my cookies?" Bastion asked.

René poked Bastion's shoulder. "Yeah, she's already eaten half a dozen, and when it's New Year's, and she gains ten pounds, I'm going to have her yell at you and not me."

"Wait." May narrowed her eyes at René. "Why the hell are you talking about me gaining weight? You can't talk about a girl's weight to ghosts right in front of her face when she can't hear what they're saying and defend herself."

"May, you know it's true."

May laughed. "He's right, you know. I probably will go ballistic after New Year's Eve. I have no self-control during the holidays, and then I always try some stupid, fad detox cleanse diet at the beginning of each year."

"Which ends with you wanting to binge again and me having to take your phone away so you don't order three large pizzas for dinner."

"Oh, that only happened once." May scowled.

"Twice."

"It was donuts and onion rings the other time. Totally different." May crossed her arms over her chest.

"You know, Marcus used to do the same thing every year." Bastion shook his head.

"Shut up, Bastion." Marcus scowled.

"Once, he even bought some diet pills because he wanted to 'improve his metabolism.'"

"I said shut the fuck up, Bastion."

"It got too quiet. What are they saying?" May asked.

"You're not the only one who's fallen prey to New Year's resolutions," René answered. "But since Marcus can't eat any of the cookies, I'm not worried about him. I think I'll wrap most of them and store them in the freezer. You'll have a secret stash when you spend the night for the next couple of months, May."

"I know it's for the best, but I was looking forward to getting trashed and eating two whole plates of cookies by myself before throwing up and yelling at you guys for letting me do it." May exhaled.

"I know. I've been your friend for a long time. That's why I'm going to put them away right now."

"Come on, René. We're going to casually walk around the block three times tonight. I'm sure that'll balance out the calories, right?" May combed her fingers through her hair, grinning.

René ignored her as he walked through the kitchen door, taking a clean plate from the cupboard and placing a mix of cookies on it. The others he stored in three freezer bags. He couldn't help but grab a large piece of peanut brittle on his way out.

MAY FUSSED OVER René's scarf, making sure he tied it tight around his neck. René fidgeted, but she smacked his shoulder and finished her knot.

"May, the cold doesn't bother me at all. Stop mothering me." He brushed her hands away.

"Exactly why I want to make sure your damn coat is on, and your scarf, and your gloves. Stop arguing with me."

"You better listen to her." Marcus crossed his arms over his chest. "Last thing we need is for you to get sick because you're a stupid masochist who gets hard from freezing his ass off."

"Only we get to make you cold. Can't waste body heat on the elements." Bastion winked.

"Agreed, save your heat for tonight when you're drunk and in our bed," Marcus said. He and Bastion completely phased out before they left the house.

"Let's go." René grabbed May's hand as best he could with them both wearing gloves. They stepped into the cold night. The lights from the other houses smeared colors over the icicles hanging from the eaves and the white snow capping the hedges.

"What?" Marcus asked. "Not going to hold our hand?"

He was teasing, but René stretched out his gloved fingers.

"No one will notice," he whispered.

"We've never looked at lights before." Bastion laced their fingers together. "It didn't seem like something cool rock musicians should do."

"Because it wasn't." Marcus snorted.

"I like it." Bastion squeezed René's hand. "I like how you and May make everything fun—even stupid things."

"That house is okay." May gestured with her free hand. The roof read *Noel* in red lights and multicolored strings snaked around the trees and shrubs in the yard. May stopped and stared a moment before moving on. "Too many people use all white lights these days."

"It's supposed to look more high-end." René shrugged.

"It looks boring," May said, nodding at the corner house. "Now *this* house. They know how to decorate. It looks like they got plastered, bought out the store on colored lights, and tossed them everywhere before falling asleep in the gutter."

"That's how we'd decorate."

"Next year. We're doing it." May nudged René with her shoulder.

"Even the part where we sleep in the gutter?"

"Marcus and Bastion can drag us back in the house after we pass out."

"Wouldn't be the first time I had to drag my drunken lover back into the house," Marcus said.

"Marcus says he's got us covered," René said.

"Good man, Marcus."

They continued around the block, stepping over cracks in the frosted concrete, walking the full perimeter of Marcus and Bastion's world. There was one house, across the street where they couldn't reach, that looked like Santa's workshop. They stopped and admired the house in silence for a few minutes.

"This one is cool," Marcus admitted.

René nodded, staring at the faux workshop. The rainbow of lights gleamed and blurred together in his vision. Bastion squeezed his hand again and René shifted his head slightly in Bastion's and Marcus's direction. Out of the corner of his eye, because of the blur of light and dark, René saw them—clearly. They stood side by side holding hands. Both looked soft and misty, but they weren't white outlines, simply translucent. René's first thought was they looked like ghosts, and he had to remind himself they were. He struggled to hold the image as long as he could, but his eyes watered, and when he blinked, their image folded back into the shadows. A loud sigh escaped René's throat.

"Is something wrong?" May asked.

"I-I saw you, for a second." It was an answer to May's question, although he spoke directly to Marcus and Bastion. "You know how you sometimes see something out of the corner of your eye, but when you blink, it's gone?"

"Neat. You can hear them now, so maybe in time, you'll be able to see them. I wish I had cool powers. René, what're the lotto numbers?" May teased.

René rolled his eyes. "I don't know."

"Seriously, though. We need to get a hot tub in the backyard ASAP, and we need gorgeous, Greek serving boys to pour champagne into our mouths." She held up her hand to silence René before he could speak. "And don't give me any crap about the serving boys. Just because you're tied down doesn't mean I have to drink my champagne from a glass. How barbaric."

"I wasn't going to say anything."

"Good, because I'm totally doing it. Drink like a peasant if you want, but I'm going do it right—straight from their mouths."

Marcus chuckled. "You should warn her about Bastion's bad habit of breaking glasses if she intends to use living men as champagne flutes."

"Hey, I've yet to break another man—not from lack of trying, mind you."

René laughed.

"What?" May asked.

"You shouldn't use people as glasses, because Bastion breaks them—glasses, I mean." They circled a second lap around the block.

"Don't touch my glasses, Bastion."

"Telling Bastion not to do something is the quickest way to get him to do it," René said. They stopped to look at the workshop again on their second pass. René kept skewing his vision at different angles, trying to recreate the effect of seeing Marcus and Bastion. When it didn't work, he grew frustrated.

After their third lap, May tugged at his shoulder. "Come on, René, let's go home and drink a foot of vodka each. I'm getting cold."

"Weren't we going to save some?"

"You should know better than to believe me on matters of restraint—I have absolutely none."

"We're going to get sick."

"Best. Christmas. Ever."

"This girl is crazier than me." Bastion flicked May's shoulder, and she swatted him away, missing his shoulder because she couldn't see him and accidentally smacking his face.

"Oops, sorry, I guess." She laughed when her hand connected to his cheek.

"Serves you right, Bastion." Marcus laughed.

When they reached the house, May peeled away layers of clothing, tossing everything near the door. René rolled his eyes and shimmied out of his hat, scarf, gloves, and jacket. He arranged the items on his coat rack and then scooped up May's things and added them beside his own.

"You're like a little child, May."

"This winter is so stupid cold. It wasn't this bad last year." May rested a warm hand on René's cheek. "Do you honestly not feel it anymore?"

"Kinda, but it doesn't bother me. Go by the fire."

"In a minute." May trotted to the kitchen. She returned with the cherry noir and four shot glasses.

"May, they can't drink. They'll vomit." René shook his head at the extra shot glasses.

"Then they'll fit right in." May winked. "No, I won't do that to you guys, don't worry. But you still have to drink with us. We'll play a drinking game, and you can shoot the empty glasses."

"What?" Bastion protested, "I'm not shooting an empty shot glass. That defeats the point."

René opened his mouth to say something, but May interrupted him.

"I may not be able to hear the voices of the dead, but I know your looks, René, and you can tell whoever—probably Bastion—to shut his mouth and drink from the empty shot glass. It's not my fault drinking vodka would make them sick. They still have to play."

"Hear that?" René raised an eyebrow in Bastion's direction.

"Come on. You know this will be more fun than sitting and watching." Marcus snuck behind Bastion. He roped his arms around Bastion's waist and nibbled his earlobe.

Bastion bit his lip to stifle his laughter. "I don't believe how low we've sunk. First we started using shot glasses instead of drinking from the bottle, and now we're using empty shot glasses."

"Hey, Bastion?" Marcus asked with a sweet tone in his voice.

"What?" Bastion's expression grew suspicious as he glanced over his shoulder.

"Try not to break the shot glass, okay?"

"I'll break it upside your head."

"That's still breaking it, love."

"What are we going to play?" René asked May.

"FUBAR. I'll get the cards." May arranged the shot glasses and vodka on the rug and rummaged through René's game closet, pulling out a deck of cards. "Does everyone know it?"

Marcus and Bastion nodded, so René nodded in turn to May to show they'd played before.

"Then I don't have to explain, but I wrote down the rules for each card since I tend to forget as the game goes on."

They took turns pulling cards and delegating shots per the rules. Communication wasn't much of a problem since Bastion and Marcus could hold up their cards for René and May to see. Still, René, kept the laptop open so May and Bastion could trash talk. Bastion drew the queen of diamonds and waved the card in May's face.

"That's right, bitch; take a shot."

"So what? Guess what card I got?" May fluttered the five of spades in the air. "I get to give five shots out, and you get them all, Bastion, because I know how much fun you're having taking imaginary shots."

"Damn, she's mean." Marcus chuckled.

Bastion rolled his eyes. His shot glass bobbed up and down in the air as he took his shots.

"Mmm, liquor. It tastes so good, like cherries." May sipped her solitary shot.

Bastion busted out laughing and dropped his shot glass. Had it hit the rug, it would have been fine, but he dropped it on René's knee, and it bounced, smacking the linoleum and cracking.

"Seriously?" May laughed loud, rolling, drunken laughter. "I thought they were joking about the glasses!"

"You're sober, completely fucking sober. How the fuck did you even manage to break it?" Marcus almost laughed as hard as May.

"Goddammit." Bastion swore.

At the same time as Bastion, René reached for the glass, amused and guilty since the shot glass had bounced off his knee. Their hands brushed together. René smiled and curled his fingers around Bastion's wrist.

"You know," he whispered, "maybe it's my fault you break so many glasses. You didn't have the problem when you were alive, did you?"

"Well, I don't have a glass, so I can't play anymore." Bastion grinned and tucked a lock of hair behind René's ear before disposing of the broken shot glass.

"Is Bastion disqualified?" Marcus typed on the keyboard.

"Yes. He is." May nodded with a grave expression.

"Disqualified my ass. I won since I took the most shots."

René raised the bottle and swished it side to side. They'd done a respectable job on it with a little over a quarter gone. "May, I know I'm going to sound like an old geezer, but I need to stop. My lips are numb. I can't taste the liquor anymore, just the cherries, and I couldn't stand if I had to."

"Guess I should have bought some beer to help us pace it." May slumped onto René's shoulder.

He closed his eyes and inhaled the mixed scents of the fireplace, the fir tree, and May's perfume, but he couldn't smell Marcus or Bastion—not the way he would have if they were alive. It was another barrier between them. They carried the faint smell of ozone, or the cold, clean smell of a forest covered in winter's first snow, and it was beautiful, but he wanted cologne, and sweat, and their natural musk. He wanted to taste salt on their skin, taste semen that wasn't ice water. Details René refused to address in his daily life snuck into his inebriated mind and refused to leave.

"René, are you falling asleep?" May asked.

"Maybe," René lied, wide awake and deep in thought.

"We need another game to play—one that doesn't involve vodka."

"Are we going to stay up until Santa brings us presents?"

"You know we're on the permanent naughty list." May snorted.

"Hell, this entire house is probably blacklisted from me and Bastion living here so long."

"Bet your sweet ass it is." Bastion elbowed Marcus.

"So let's keep the fire going in the fireplace and eat all Santa's cookies." May continued, unaware of Marcus's and Bastion's statements.

"Yeah, fuck white Coca-Cola-marketing Santa." René raised a drunk fist in the air. "We can buy our own presents."

"It's what we do anyway." May laughed.

"Let's play Jenga."

"René, I fucking love you."

Chapter Seventeen

THEY FELL ASLEEP at about four thirty. The four of them huddled in sleeping bags around the Christmas tree like a litter of puppies. They didn't need to exchange presents in the morning. Marcus and Bastion had already helped René break in his new straps and ties, and he and May already broke in the bottle of Grey Goose. They spent Christmas watching television, playing board games, eating poorly, and generally being lazy.

During the following days, May made it her mission to get René outside as much as possible. They avoided the main stores and postholiday shoppers, but drank coffee while walking around the park, saw two movies, and played pool at the Dive. With her vow to personally watch René, she managed to convince Marcus and Bastion to have another snowball fight—René was not allowed near the pool.

It pissed him off, them treating him fragilely, so he made it a point to wander near the pool every chance he got. After sneaking close one too many times, Marcus slung René over his shoulder and carried him back into the house. May and Bastion laughed behind him as he shouted curses at all of them. Marcus dropped him in front of the fireplace to thaw. René fought to escape the ridiculous prison of clothing May swaddled around him. May grabbed his hands as he pulled them free of their gloves.

"Jesus, René, your hands are freezing. Why are you so cold?"

"I can't see how I'm possibly any colder than you—you dressed me up like a three-year-old before you dragged me outside."

"I know, but you're freezing."

"I'm fine. You're overreacting."

"Maybe." May shrugged, but she looked worried. "I'll make cocoa."

May disappeared to the kitchen. Bastion used the opportunity to knead René's shoulders. The cold, shivering thrill of Bastion's tongue licked against the back of his neck. René bit his bottom lip to resist moaning. Marcus knelt in front of them, his back to the fire. He rested his left elbow on his left knee. As the firelight flickered around them, their images flickered into view. For a brief instant, René could see Marcus's hungry look simmering below his cool sage green eyes. The sight of Marcus made Bastion's licks and nibbles more enticing.

"You're gorgeous," René whispered.

Then René straightened himself upright because May reentered the room. "You didn't forget the marshmallows, did you?"

"Oh please, I'm not some amateur cocoa maker."

She handed René a mug to prove her point. Marshmallows and whipped cream and cinnamon all garnished the drink. René smiled. They sat in comfortable silence, content to drink cocoa and stare at the flames. When their mugs were empty, René went to the kitchen to wash them. This time, Marcus grabbed him from behind, pulling René's hair as only Marcus could and tracing his lips along the nape of René's neck. Bastion sat on the counter and watched.

"This is how all our cups break," René whispered, clutching the counter for support. "I know it's been awhile, but we have to suffer until the holidays are over. Tonight's New Year's Eve, and May will go home in three days."

"We won't wait that long." Bastion snorted, reaching out his bare foot to toy with René's chest. "And you can't wait that long. Your cheeks are burning."

René sighed because Bastion was right. He pushed himself away from them, in the stubborn, prudish way they loved because it made them feel like wolves on a hunt. In the living room, May lay curled on the sofa with a blanket over her and a pillow under her head.

"What do you think you're doing?" René poked her forehead.

"Taking a nap," May slurred her words, half asleep already. "If we're going to stay up late tonight, I need some beauty sleep."

"You don't need any beauty sleep." René snorted.

"Then I need some party sleep." May rolled over to face away from René.

"Okay, guess I'll go upstairs and get some party sleep as well."

May grunted, indifferent. René thanked providence for his luck and snuck up the stairs. He stripped to his boxers and slipped under the covers. Grinning, René closed his eyes and pretended to sleep. Marcus called his bluff by shoving Bastion onto the mattress near René's feet. René slit his eyes open so he could watch Marcus bite into Bastion's shoulders. Bastion tossed his head back and moaned with delight.

René grew stiff as Marcus continued to bite along Bastion's collarbone and knead at Bastion's shoulders with his broad hands. They struggled, rutting and grinding their bodies together. Bastion spread his legs. He grabbed Marcus's cock and lead it to his asshole. Marcus rammed his hard cock up Bastion's ass and Bastion, in a desperate grab for the bedsheets, squeezed René's ankle instead. Once he had a hold of René's leg, he scratched René's calf and muttered René's name. He stifled his moans into the mattress, a cute attempt to be courteous to May though she couldn't hear them. René sprung up, lunged to the foot of the bed, and stuck his tongue in Bastion's mouth, pulling louder, though still muffled, moans from his lover's throat.

Bastion held onto Marcus's forearm while his other hand clawed at René's shoulder. René snatched quick, hungry kisses from Bastion, and Marcus slammed into him. René slid his tongue as deep as he could stretch inside Bastion's mouth. Bastion tasted like a glass of ice water. When Bastion bucked his hips, René groped for Bastion's cock and stroked him until he came.

Next, René tore off his boxers and slammed Marcus onto Bastion's belly. He grabbed Bastion's hand and positioned Bastion's fingertips on the flesh of Marcus's asshole. Bastion didn't need instructions. He prepped Marcus while René bit into his broad shoulders and licked up the curve of Marcus's spine. When René entered Marcus, he paced himself to make sure Marcus could adjust to René's girth. Marcus exhaled stiff, lusty grunts as René thrust into him and Bastion stroked him. René bit his bottom lip, struggling not to call out, and nervous about the creaking of their mattress despite the fact that May wouldn't be able to hear them downstairs. He must have had a good angle, because Marcus's grunts shifted to a delicate whining, much more needful than anything René remembered hearing from him. Bastion licked from his neck to his nipples and back up again, drawing out Marcus's moans until they were frantic.

"You want to come inside me, don't you?" Bastion pressed his mouth against Marcus's ear.

Marcus gave a slight nod.

"Don't you?"

Marcus nodded hard while grunting in affirmation.

"Don't you, Marcus?" Bastion wasn't satisfied. He stopped stroking Marcus and grabbed his chin to force their faces close.

"Yes, dammit, yes."

Bastion wiggled onto his stomach so Marcus could re-enter him. René slowed his pace to accommodate for the change. Their posturing was odd, something from an amateur porn you'd see on the internet, but René tried his best to match Marcus's thrusts and it didn't take long before Marcus shuddered and came with his name in Bastion's mouth.

Their bodies were cold, so cold beneath René's skin. He shivered, but he was used to the combination of cold and arousal, and it didn't discourage his erection. He hissed; his nipples were hard and almost too sensitive as they brushed against Marcus's back.

Marcus bucked, pushing René away. Marcus and Bastion both tackled him onto the mattress. Bastion mounted René and rode him. René gasped, his fingers clawing at the sheets. Bastion always felt cold, but at the moment he was frigid from Marcus having finished inside him. René liked the idea, however, of all three of their sweat and saliva and semen mixed together. It was dirty and carnal, and that made it enticing. He wished he could smell them. The bed should be overwhelmed with the strong, humid, musky sweat of their bodies, but René only smelled ozone and snow—a beautiful smell, but not *them*.

Marcus cinched his fingers in René's hair and sucked on his neck. René moaned to keep his teeth from chattering. Despite his best efforts to disguise how cold he was, Marcus dragged the comforter out from under René's body and tucked it around him.

"Stop," René kicked the comforter. "I want to feel your bodies, not the blanket."

"René." Marcus finished swaddling René. "You need it."

René sighed and turned his head because he was too close to coming to want to argue. Marcus grabbed René's platinum hair and tugged it the way René loved, but Bastion looked sheepish as he rode René, guilty, like a teenager discovering masturbation for the first time. René shut his eyes to avoid their faces. He hovered a spasm away from orgasm but couldn't tip himself over. He knew they were worried, and René's skin puckered with thick, white gooseflesh from the chill of their bodies.

"Shower," Marcus stood up.

"No, I'm close, please don't stop," René begged because he was close, close, so close.

"Shower." Marcus grabbed Bastion's long, sable mane and yanked him off René.

"You heard him, René. Out of my hands." Bastion shrugged, playing coy.

"Damn you both," René whined, clawing at the blankets, balls aching from cold and need of release. René lay in bed a moment, shaking beneath his thick comforter. He didn't think he could walk; his limbs were too stiff with cold.

Marcus returned, lifted René, and carried him bridal style to the humid bathroom where they already had the shower running hot. The water burned as it thawed René's shaking limbs. Facing away from the water, he arched his back into the heat and pressed his hand against the wall for balance.

Bastion slipped between René and the wall, trying to kiss him. René turned away. He knew they were right, could feel his body temperature returning to normal as the water warmed him, but he was frustrated and upset from being denied his climax. He wanted to taste the salt of their sweat when they made love. He wanted to hold them without shivering.

"It's not fair," he choked out a whisper before he could stop himself.

They sandwiched him in their arms. René leaned onto Bastion's shoulder, still cold, but the water kept René from freezing. They wove their fingers over his body, trying to restore his half-lost erection. Marcus disappeared.

"Where are you—" René turned to figure out where he'd gone, but Bastion bit his lower lip. Bastion grabbed René's wrists and held him in place. René submitted, his anger washing down the drain and leaving him aching with need.

"Still not fair," René sighed into Bastion's mouth as he kissed him.

"I know." Bastion kissed him. "I know."

"It's not your fault," René whispered.

Marcus stood behind him again, digging his fingers into René's hips and pushing a dong inside him. René called out, much louder than he preferred. The toy was slick with lubrication and slid easily inside his body. He welcomed the distraction to his thoughts, holding onto Bastion as Marcus pushed the dong into him. René's thighs were taut as harp string—the only reason he didn't fall to his knees was because Bastion supported him.

"Better?" Marcus whispered in his ear.

"Shut up and fuck me, Marcus." René's words were barely a whisper in his mouth.

"Oooh, he's getting impudent with you." Bastion chuckled, toying with René's resurrected hard-on. "You should be nice, Rembrandt, or he might not continue."

"Then you'd be begging me, not sassing," Marcus added.

"Shut up. And. Fuck. Me."

"If that's what you want." Marcus readjusted his hold on René's hips.

"You're so pampered." Bastion nipped at René's neck.

"Bastion, stroke me faster." René panted.

"If that's what you want." Bastion repeated Marcus's line, squeezing René's cock before picking up his pace.

René hung onto Bastion. He pretended the warmth of the water was their bodies. Shutting his eyes, he blocked the foggy images of Bastion and Marcus from his mind and focused on the black behind his eyelids. Feeling them pressed against him, close and intimate with their skin touching, was what brought René to orgasm. When it was over, he twined his fingers with Bastion's and reached backward to do the same with Marcus with his left hand. René stood there, face buried in Bastion's chest, trying so hard to convince himself the water was their body heat.

Bastion glided his free hand across Marcus's hip as Marcus touched Bastion's cheek. They stood there, the three of them, a three-snaked Ouroboros. René's eyes stung. He blinked and told himself it was from the shower spray. Jerking away, he turned off the water

"Okay, I'm warm again. You can stop fussing over me." René wrapped a towel around himself.

Bastion disappeared and René stared where the ghost stood a moment before. He glanced at Marcus.

"Did I go too far saying that?"

"You know Bastion doesn't get offended. Not with us." Marcus sighed. He kissed René's forehead and tilted up René's face and kissed his lips.

Marcus disappeared and left René to dry himself and find a pair of pajama bottoms to wear before he searched for them. He found the couple in the guest bedroom. Bastion curled into a ball on the futon and Marcus knelt on the floor beside him. Bastion's face pressed against his knees, and he sniffled quiet, outraged tears with his hand covering his mouth to mute the sound.

"Don't...hide, okay?" René stumbled to the futon and dropped to his knees beside Marcus. He petted Bastion's hair. "I'm sorry. I'm a scumbag for snapping at you."

"Go away. I don't want you to see me crying." Bastion vanished, leaving only an imprint on the futon mattress.

"I'm sorry." Regret wrinkled René's brow.

"Asshole, you didn't do anything wrong." Bastion tried to laugh, but it didn't quite reach through the broken sobs.

"Then why are you sitting in the guest room when we should all be lying in bed together?"

René's words instigated fresh sobs from Bastion's chest, louder and higher pitched than before. René grabbed Bastion's shoulders, almost desperate.

"Please, Bastion, don't. I really am sorry. Please let me see you again."

"René, stop. I'm not pissed at you. I...just...I don't want to be dead. It was stupid. How fucking stupid is it to fall down the stairs? Christ, if we keep this up, we're going to hurt you." The fog coalesced into Bastion's shape once again. He fisted his hands, and he pressed both fists against his forehead.

"I'm sure it won't be so bad in summer when the weather's warmer, right?" René didn't want to acknowledge the truth in Bastion's words.

"It feels like there's a cloud between us when we make love. It was fun when we were just *roommates*, but now..." Bastion shook his head.

René understood. "What do I smell like?"

"Like, you, I guess, but it's like the scent's carried on the wind and not coming from your body."

"You smell like ozone."

All three of them sat on the futon without saying anything. The silence stretched out, a physical pressure clawing at René's chest.

"I think it's my fault I keep getting too cold. I want so badly to be close to you two..." René shook his head, refusing to finish the sentence.

Marcus nudged his shoulder. "In the shower from now on. At least until winter's over."

René nodded. He'd gladly let himself slip into the realm of ghosts to get closer to them if he could, but he could neither do it, nor argue the point to them. Bastion smeared the last tears away from his eyes.

"You don't want to start the year dressed like that." He sniffed. "Wear something better."

"All right, but only so you have some eye candy to stare at." René teased his thumb against Bastion's lips.

"You give in to him too easily. I'd never change. I'd let him bitch until he gave up." Marcus shook his head.

"I figured I'll be nice—since May's going to make you guys fake drink with us again tonight."

"I swear to God, if I break another shot glass, even May will hear me scream."

René paused. "Hey, Bastion?"

"What?"

"Will you, um...do that thing? With my eyes again?" René asked.

"Eyeliner?"

René nodded. His fingers twisted around strands of Bastion's hair.

"See? You spoil him." Marcus snorted. "Stop it before he expects me to indulge him like that."

"But it looked sexy on me, right?" René lidded his gaze at Marcus.

"It did." Marcus plucked a kiss from René's bottom lip.

"I'll go steal May's makeup kit." Bastion kissed René and Marcus before he left.

René changed in his room. He pinned up his hair and chose a dark-red top. On his pale body, the color reminded him of blood on snow. When he went back into the guest room, Marcus was kissing Bastion and whispering gentle, soothing words. Shoulders hunched and head bowed low, Bastion still looked miserable, and René still felt like an asshole. True, he couldn't help being alive any more than they could help being dead. Life—current or after—sucked. He cleared his throat to let them know he stood and watched them.

"I'm ready for my New Year's Eve date with you two."

"Not quite yet." Bastion flashed the tube of liquid eyeliner. René sat on the futon and endured the torture of Bastion pricking at his eyes with the liner wand.

"How do I look?" He asked when Bastion finished.

"You look good." Bastion smoothed his fingers along the collar of René's shirt.

"Let's start the party then." Marcus hooked his arms with theirs.

They escorted him down the stars. May snored on the couch, her hair a tousled mess. René laughed when he saw her. "She's going to be so pissed when she wakes up and sees I'm already dressed."

Chapter Eighteen

HOURS LATER RENÉ sprawled on the carpet, cartwheeling-on-a-tightrope-level drunk. "Is it...midnight yet? Because..." René laughed. "No, I seriously forgot where I was going with that whole sentence."

"René, is this how we beat the game?" May crawled to him with the empty Grey Goose Vodka bottle clutched in her fist. She flopped on her belly, holding up the bottle for display and approval.

"What game, exactly were you playing?" Marcus asked, unfortunately sober.

"The drinking game of drinking all the Vodka before midnight," René answered, a wise, drunken sage.

"You tell them that's goddamn right, René." May dropped the bottle to the rug and slung her arm around René's chest.

"Yes, you definitely won." Bastion laughed. He curled into Marcus's lap and toyed with his biceps.

"That's goddamn right," René answered as May instructed him to, again, total sage.

Marcus looked at the wall clock. "Two minutes."

"You'll have to tell me," René muttered. "If I sit up, I'll puke, and it would be bad luck to puke at midnight."

Bastion teased René's hair. May laughed when the pale blond wisps moved.

"Dude. It almost looks like they're moving on their own." She poked at the air until she found Bastion's hand and laughed.

"It's not hard to see them." René reached over his head and rubbed Marcus's knee. The jeans Marcus wore felt coarse against René's palm. If René closed his eyes and ignored the cold, he could pretend Marcus was sitting beside him— a living person instead of a ghost.

"I can hardly see them. You're just better at it," May argued.

"Are we going to countdown?" René asked.

"Nah, fuck it. Let's smooch." May rolled on top of René. He couldn't laugh because he had neither room nor air as May smothered his mouth.

"You taste like vodka," he said when she broke away. He didn't realize how drunk they were until they kissed. May usually pecked his cheek, though he'd bet money May was trying to make Marcus and Bastion jealous for the sake of riling them up, and it amused him.

"So do you." She dropped to the floor. "What do they taste like when you kiss them?"

"Cold. They taste...cold."

"What the fuck does cold taste like?"

"Like snow and ozone."

"Is it weird?"

"Kinda. It's nice, but...it'd be nice if they were warmer."

"I'm sorry it's hard. Shit, I knew we were special cases when it came to dating, but who would have thought it'd be this odd?" May hugged René.

"Maybe you need a ghost too. I'll keep my eyes open for any hot, single, straight male ghosts for you." René smiled and toyed with May's hair.

"You're my best friend ever, Rem. I tell you all time, right?"

"This is the first time this year."

"I'm surprised I haven't been kicked away from you so Bastion and Marcus can have their kiss."

"They haven't stopped kissing each other." René smiled at the sight of his lovers writhing against each other with their lips sealed together.

"Hey you jerks, kiss René too. I'm done with him."

"Maybe they think I have girl cooties."

"The vodka will disinfect it." They both laughed. May stumbled to her feet. "It's a good thing we don't have more vodka, because I would totally drink it." She wandered off to the bathroom.

Bastion's mane scattered around both he and Marcus and hid their faces. His wan fingers twisted and knotted into Marcus's shorter hair. Their breath sounded rough and it still confused René that they breathed at all, though he loved the sound of it.

Bastion separated his lips from Marcus enough to ask, "Not even a little jealous?"

"I'm having too much fun watching." René smiled, using the tip of his finger to trace the curves of Bastion's hair onto an imaginary canvas.

"We shouldn't have bedded him earlier, then he'd be needier," Marcus said.

"Or maybe I should dump some coffee over his head. It'll sober him up and make him take another shower."

"Aww, don't sober me up, Bastion. That's no fun."

"Bastion's jealous because he can't get drunk." Marcus laughed.

"You know what." René eyes lit up, and he smacked the rug in excitement. "I just remembered something I can use during sex that might help with the cold."

"What?" Bastion asked.

"Secret." René wagged his finger at them.

"When do we get to find out? When May leaves?" Marcus asked.

"Maybe a little after." René's smile grew wicked. "It'll be more fun if you just forget I mentioned it."

"How can we forget now?" Bastion crawled to René and kissed his mouth once, deliberate and sweet, though still like runoff from melting snow. Marcus followed suit, kissing René until vodka and cold numbed his lips.

When they paused, René blinked up at them. "Hasn't May been gone a long time?"

"Yes, actually. We should make sure she didn't drown in the toilet." Marcus started toward the bathroom.

"I don't want another roommate," René joked, but his face fell into a frown as soon as he said it

Marcus disappeared and reappeared a moment later, chuckling. "Guess where she is?"

"Bathroom floor?"

"Sleeping in the hallway."

"Let's move her to the couch." René struggled to his feet, using Marcus for balance.

"I'm not sure you'd make it that far." Bastion held René's hands and steadied him.

"Uh-huh." René pouted, swaying as he stood.

"Okay, keep up." Marcus walked toward the hallway.

René held his arms out for balance. He made it halfway across the living room as Bastion and Marcus half carried, half dragged May toward the sofa. They lay her on her side with a blanket over her midsection. Then Bastion shooed René toward the stairs.

"Bedtime. Go to bed."

"No, I have to watch her all night to make sure she doesn't get sick." René pouted.

"Don't worry, René. She's fine." Bastion teased his hair and nudged him toward the stairs again.

"Trust us. We're the experts," Marcus said.

AFTER THE HOLIDAYS, events fell back into a routine. René shopped and went to the Dive or movies with May. They met at the gym after work to work off Bastion's cookies. Otherwise, he stayed at home. He allowed them to take him in the shower for three weeks, until they all grew bored of it, before he searched his office for the space heater hidden inside a closet he used for storage. It was the *secret* he'd teased them about on New Year's Eve.

The house sat quiet and gray with dawn. Marcus and Bastion slept as René snuck downstairs with the space heater. He built the fire high and put the heater near the hearth. By the time René piled blankets around the fireplace, sweat had soaked through his shirt. He disrobed and waited in the middle of the nest of blankets and pillows.

"René?" Bastion called as he stumbled into the living room. Seeing Bastion awake without Marcus was rare and René smiled.

"Here," he called, voice thick and husky with want.

Bastion rubbed grit from his eyes. Why Bastion had grit in his eyes baffled René more than Bastion's and Marcus's breathing, but it was what it was. Bastion saw René kneeling naked and sweating near the flames. He started, jaw slack.

"Oh, shit yes." He ran up the stairs and returned a moment later, dragging a groggy Marcus behind him.

"What's so damn important—"

"Look, jackass."

René winked at him. Marcus's sleep-shrouded posture perked, and he and Bastion walked hand in hand to where René sat. René smiled at them.

"I've yet to say it back, haven't I?"

"Say what back?" Bastion ran his hands along René's naked chest before removing his own clothing. Watching the silhouetted striptease of them manually removing their clothing excited René. With the tips of his fingers, he explored Marcus's body first and then Bastion's.

"I love you. I love you both."

"Actually, you were the first to say it." Marcus held René's chin with thumb and finger.

"No. You said it first, Marcus." René shook his head.

"He doesn't remember. He was so fucked up, who can blame him?" Bastion snickered.

"What are you talking about?" René tilted his head to the left.

"You said it right here." Bastion gestured to the fireplace. "Long before Marcus said it."

"You said you loved us." Marcus nodded.

"And you called us boobs." Bastion chuckled.

"I kinda remember calling you boobs, because I wanted to bury myself between you."

They ran their fingers through René's hair, something they hadn't done in a while. René exhaled as they jostled him with their touches. His eyes widened.

"Oh God, I remember now. You were touching me, and I started rambling. It was the night May met you."

They nodded.

"It's so hot with the heater. Your fingers feel really good." René closed his eyes.

"Pretty brilliant idea," Bastion admitted.

"For you two, I'd confine myself to a life of sex in the shower, but I wanted more room."

"So we can lay you down?" Marcus dipped René to the blankets below them.

"Yes."

"So we can make love together?" Bastion asked René as he coiled his arm around Marcus's stomach and licked along the delicate curve of Marcus's ear.

"Yes." René swallowed, a broad drop of sweat rolled down his neck like a teardrop and settled in the hollow of his collarbone.

"How do we want this?" Marcus grabbed Bastion and pulled him close.

Bastion looked at René and then Marcus. "Any suggestions?"

René spread his legs wide and worked his hands down his thighs to make it harder for Bastion to think. Marcus smirked and pushed Bastion on top of René.

"This will work." Bastion rolled his eyes. "But we need—"

René held a bottle of lube he had stashed underneath one of the pillows.

"Ah, you had this planned out." Bastion grinned.

"For a while now, yes."

"Nice." Bastion coated his fingers and slipped two into René's ass. "Tell me when you're ready."

René's breath hitched every time Bastion intentionally brushed against his prostate. While Bastion fucked René with his fingers, Marcus held Bastion's hips and kissed up and down Bastion's spine.

"I'm good," René groaned. His cock twitched in anticipation.

Bastion slid inside him, and then Marcus slid into Bastion. René liked the position because he could look at both of them. In the dim, wavy firelight, he almost saw them in full detail. René overlapped his hands on top of Marcus's so they could both hold Bastion's waist. He propped himself on his shoulders so he could reach up and kiss Bastion's mouth while Marcus kissed Bastion's neck. René moved down to Bastion's neck and whispered their names.

"Marcus. Bastion. Marcus. Bastion. Mar-cus. Bas-ti-on. Damn!"

"René, you're so tight. Marcus, you're so thick. Fuck, oh fuck yes, fuck!" Bastion called out above the crackle of the fire.

René crashed to the floor, too close to keep himself upright. Marcus reached around Bastion and stroked René's cock. Bastion tried to help but his hand dropped to the ground near René's side. He was too caught up in his own moment to do anything but scream and arch his back. He rocked faster, and the quick, shallow thrusts made René's nerves ignite. René tensed, jaw tight as he came only a moment before Bastion pressed his head against René's chest. Marcus removed his hand from René and instead grabbed a fistful of Bastion's long, black hair, making him jerk his head back. René traced his fingers along Bastion's open mouth and smiled as Marcus took Bastion from behind. René mouthed *I love you* to them three times, but neither saw him—Bastion's head angled up and Marcus's eyes closed with the height of his orgasm. Afterward, they lay entangled and watched the red-gold flames. Bastion glanced at René.

"Are you cold?"

"Just a touch, nothing too bad." He nuzzled against Bastion's chest to show he didn't care about the cold. "I was scorching when we started."

"At least your lips aren't blue." Marcus smoothed his fingers down the jut of Bastion's hipbone. "I guess we can take you off shower duty for a while."

"So generous of you, warden." René snorted, half rolling his eyes. "I'll buy another heater to go near my feet."

He bought three more heaters so he could put one on each corner of his bed. May laughed when she saw the setup all neatly corded in a surge protector a week later, but it was worth being able to lay naked with his lovers touching skin to skin, instead of them swaddling him like a baby for fear of him going into hypothermia.

"I can't wait until spring," Marcus said, sitting near the window the next night. "I hate when the sky's gray."

"When I get my tax return this year, I'm going to buy a hot tub. Imagine what you two can do to me in July, outside in the hot water. Nothing will make me cold then," René said.

René thought that may have been a lie. The heaters helped, but more and more, touching Marcus and Bastion made the cold seep into the core of his body, especially when they came. He also wore sweaters inside the house more often, the chill clinging to his bones throughout the day even when they weren't touching him. René told himself it was the January weather and he was overreacting, but he knew better.

Bastion sang an old ballad René remembered from college. Bastion strolled to the center of the room, equally spaced between Marcus and René. While singing, Bastion toyed with the hem of his shirt or the button of his jeans. He undressed slowly, pacing himself. By the end of the song, he was fully naked. Marcus clapped three times, walking to Bastion and sweeping him up bridal style to carry him to the bed where René was waiting.

In bed, they took turns kissing each other's necks, each other's chests, each other's lips. Bastion straddled René's lap. He moved in quick, tight circles and René screamed to God. Afterward, he switched to Marcus's lap to do the same. Both spent, René and Marcus alternated as they sucked Bastion's cock until he clawed the quilts and came so hard they had to kiss giddy, happy tears away from the corners of his eyes.

THE NEXT MORNING René showered and ate oatmeal for breakfast, drinking coffee Bastion had brewed for him. He yawned and stretched, feeling relaxed. Little flashes of memory from the night before sent pleasant shivers down his spine. Bastion and Marcus, like night and day wrapped around him, and he was the world caught between them. The ice of their sweat and sleet of their breath nullified the heat blasting from each direction, and René had fallen asleep against Marcus's chest as Bastion sang. He smiled, rinsing his coffee cup and bowl in the sink before slipping on his coat and boots.

"Checking the mail," he called to his lovers as they argued over where the hot tub should be. It didn't matter how much they argued, René already told them it was going in the back corner of the yard, but they debated all the same.

"Want me to do it for you?" Bastion turned at the sound of René's voice.

"I know you think it's funny, but if anyone ever catches the mail floating through the air on video, my life is going to become a headache." René shook his head.

"You're no fun." Bastion snorted.

"Do you want teenage fucktard ghosthunters knocking on the door every Friday night?" Marcus asked. "Or worse, a real paranormal team. I'm sure René isn't the only person who can sense ghosts, and I don't want to hide in the closet for a week while assholes crawl all over with microphones and video recorders."

"I refuse to be an HBO special," René said.

"Yeah, yeah." Bastion sighed. "See if I ever offer to do something useful again."

"Thanks for the thought." Feeling playful, René stole a quick kiss from each of them before stepping outside. "I love you guys." He winked at them and then shut the door.

The snow crunched under his feet, and the breath puffed in front of his face. René rubbed his hands. He'd forgotten his gloves, but a trip to the mailbox wasn't worth him going back for them. He wanted to hurry to sit by the fire and finish reading *The Innkeeper's Song*. It was a little more fantasy than René usually ventured into, but who the fuck would say no to reading a Peter S. Beagle story?

The snow covered the curb and made it hard to see where the street ended and René's yard began, so he stood to the left of the mailbox instead of in front. Tugging the half-frozen metal door open, he gathered the pile of papers sure to be 90 percent junk mail.

René turned when he heard the squeal of tires. A *thunk* echoed in his ears. One second it was dark, the next Marcus and Bastion stood over him. Marcus hooked his arms around Bastion's chest to hold Bastion back as he lunged forward. René didn't understand why Bastion was screaming.

"Calm down. Bastion, calm down." Marcus spoke in a soft, restrained voice while he held Bastion.

"Fuck calm! That bitch broke our Rembrandt. I'll kill her! And her fucking shade of lipstick is hideous. Let go, Marcus; she deserves this."

"Nothing you can do now. Let's see how he's doing."

Looking beside them, René saw the car, an old 80s station wagon all but on top of him. He'd been hit. He wondered if he should move. Probably not. This was going to be another trip to the hospital if he wanted it or not, but he felt fine. In fact, he felt a little *too* good for someone who'd been knocked on his ass by a car. A large, graying woman with the most melted-crayon pink shade of Wet n' Wild lipstick ever to find its way to a dollar store clearance shelf squawked into her cell phone, something about the boy appearing out of nowhere.

"Bitch, I was standing on the *side* of the mailbox," René muttered, irritated with the woman's tacky, flower-print shirt as much as her bad driving.

René's words made Bastion and Marcus stop and kneel beside him. Marcus cupped René's face, and Bastion stroked his hair. They looked sad and it confused René.

"Hey," Bastion said.

"Hey," René said.

"How are you feeling?" Marcus asked.

"Good, oddly enough. I think I can stand." René held up his hands, and they lifted him to his feet. "Man, all that to be careful, and she still slid right into me. Please don't tell May. She'll freak out. Especially after the pool fiasco." René blinked, shielding the side of his face. "Why is it so bright?"

Bastion bit his bottom lip, looking away. Marcus held René's shoulders. René closed his eyes. There was something different, something wonderfully different, about Marcus he couldn't put his finger on, but whatever it was, it was too glorious a thing to remain a mystery.

"That's *the Light*, René," Marcus whispered. "It fades when you want it to, but it always returns if you need to see it. Sometimes...it's nice to look at it, although we never go near it."

René only half listened because, at that moment, he *could smell Marcus*. Not a cold, snow and ozone smell, but the smell of aftershave and musk, a rich, deep, manly smell, and how in God's earth did René ever live without experiencing it before?

"Fuck, you smell good," René whispered, leaning closer, but then opened his eyes. "What do you mean *the Light*?"

He looked to his right and looked back at the burst of light. It was warm and bright and so beautiful that it hurt to behold. It made René homesick for a place he couldn't remember. It also made René look down. His body lay pinned under the car. He quivered at the sight. René's hand poked out from the undercarriage, pale as the snow, but a spray of red soaked into the tire tracks, curling past René's mailbox and back to the road.

"Poor May" was all he could say or think about.

"I'm sorry." Bastion coiled his arms around René's neck. His arms shook as he held René. "I'm sorry. I'm so sorry. I'm sorry."

René barely heard him. Instead, he listened to Bastion's breathing and experienced, in a way he never could before, the sensation of Bastion's arms around him. Warmth soaked into him from Bastion's embrace, and Bastion's cologne smelled of fresh oak and woodsmoke. René combed his fingers through Bastion's hair, keeping a strand and staring at the dark, sable threads. Glancing over his shoulder, he gazed at Marcus. Sandy hair, gray-green eyes—the way they looked in René's visions, only this time, he wouldn't have to wake up from it.

"I can see you." René kissed him, tasting Bastion with his tongue. A warm and human taste and far from the wintry dreams of their past kisses. René couldn't stop moaning.

"René?"

"Oh God. Bastion, you're so warm, and I can smell you." He kissed him again. "And I can taste you." He grabbed Marcus and pulled him in for a kiss as well. "Both of you. I can taste both of you. Can we go upstairs? Right now? I want to touch you both. You're gorgeous, and you smell good, and you're *warm*."

"Rembrandt, you realize what's happened, right?" Marcus pushed the hair away from René's eyes.

"Well, yeah. I was confused for a moment, but that kinda cleared it up." René pointed at his physical body and the the bright crimson deflowering the snow. He looked at Bastion. "I'm sorry. I know you wanted me alive. I'm really sorry. I tried to stand on the curb to *specifically* avoid traffic, but it's done. After the cops and paramedics leave, May will be here screaming and crying, and I'll be crying with her, but before that, I just want to be with you two. I've never been able to taste you before now, and...I'm sorry, but I'm not sad at all. I'm excited."

"Maybe you shouldn't stay," Bastion whispered. "Look at it... It's so beautiful. I don't know exactly where *the Light* goes, but I don't want to keep you from it, René."

René sighed, shaking his head to disagree. "Honestly? Even if you two weren't here, I'd stay because of May. I'm her only real family, and I'd never leave her alone. So why wouldn't I stay with you two here to keep me company?" René kissed Bastion again as if to make sure he could still taste them and then whispered, "Please, please, oh god, please, let's go upstairs..."

Epilogue

MARCUS AND BASTION lay naked on the bed, and René stared at their bodies. For the first time, René could admire them with all his senses. He smiled, ridiculously happy for someone who'd died, but it felt too much like waking up instead of dying, like he'd never lived before, only existed. René crawled onto the bed to get closer. He began with small kisses, tasting their chests, their nipples, their necks. He inhaled their scent and listened to the melody of their combined breathing. René pressed his ear against Marcus's chest so he could listen to a heartbeat that shouldn't exist but did. René's own heart pounded from the thrill of truly touching his lovers for the first time. He exhaled a shuddering breath and inhaled the scent of their hair.

Bastion and Marcus smoothed their fingers through René's hair and across his ribs and down his stomach and up his thighs. Below them, cops photographed the accident and wrote reports. Below them, the world continued, measured by the ticks of clocks. The police probably wanted their shift to end so they could go home to eat dinner. To them, René's body was an item, something to be catalogued, stored in the morgue, and reduced to a passing mention in a conversation when their wives asked how their day went. But upstairs the clock's ticking served as background noise—not something to guide them, only another sensation to experience. They didn't have to worry about work, driving, dinner, the cold snow outside. René swallowed

Bastion's cock. His mouth watered at the first taste of Bastion's creamy, taut skin. Marcus positioned himself behind René.

The heat of Marcus's hands startled René when they gripped his sides, but he threw his head back and screamed in ecstasy when the warmth and wetness of Marcus's tongue flicked against his asshole. He enjoyed their previous rim jobs, in the same way one would enjoy foreplay with ice cubes, but feeling Marcus's licks like he was alive instead of a ghost made René's head spin. He lowered his mouth around Bastion's dick but continued to moan. The vibrations of his mouth forced Bastion to claw at the bedsheets.

"René!" Bastion screamed, his cock thick and twitching in René's mouth. "Oh, René!"

Hearing Bastion scream his name, *while* tasting him for the first time, sent jolts coursing through René's body. He relaxed his throat and took Bastion, bobbing his head with his lips sealed tightly around Bastion's shaft. René shoved his ass back. He rocked against Marcus's tongue and dropped to the base of Bastion's cock. Bastion wove his fingers in René's hair and tugged, thrusting himself farther into René's mouth and coming. René held his breath as he swallowed the initial burst of seed—hot, hot, gratefully hot, and not frozen—and licked away the aftershocks. Bastion gasped as René's tongue worked, face flushed and hair a mess from his heat and sweat. René drank in a breath, entranced by the sight. No, enraptured by it. Once they told René they sometimes forgot they were dead, and René realized how easy it'd be to forget when everything about them still lived. A flaw in the language, René thought. Dead should refer to bodies only, never people.

"You look really good," René whispered.

Bastion turned his head, laughing nervously. René noticed the subtle shift from flushed to blushing and grinned.

"Let me take you," Marcus begged.

"I need to taste you," René said. "I'll let you take me next time."

After a grunt of protest, Marcus lay on his back as Bastion moved behind René. As René swallowed Marcus's heated flesh, Bastion fingered René's ass while his free hand stroked René's cock. It took a moment to adjust. He'd grown used to icy fingers, so Bastion's warm digits milking his prostate had René's thighs trembling. René *wanted, wanted, wanted* them even as he took them. René sucked fast and hard, spurred on by Bastion's quick strokes. He dragged out the moment to last as long as he could, but Bastion knew René's body too well. With Bastion teasing his prostate and jerking him with a warm palm, René stopped his oral ministrations to curl his face against Marcus's thigh as he came. He gasped for air, but Bastion showed no mercy. He grabbed René's hair and situated René's mouth back over Marcus's cock. Bastion worked René's hair like marionette strings, helping René bob his head at Bastion's chosen pace.

"That's hot." Marcus perked his head up to watch, hitching his hips up in time with Bastion's movements. After two short minutes, Marcus arched his back. "I'm...close. I'm—*oh shit!*"

René relished his thick taste, but he especially enjoyed the heat. The semen warmed his mouth and his throat and René imagined it warmed his belly as well. Such a simple thing, warmth, but he'd never understood how much he needed it. René collapsed in between them, lost in the warmth of their bodies.

"No blankets. How do you like that?" Marcus asked.

"Yeah, and you're not shaking," Bastion added.

Sweat stuck their bodies together. His lovers smelled musky and sensual. René grinned, at first, but the more the thought about it, the more the heat tickled his skin, the happier he became. Until René could do nothing except lay in bed and laugh, hysterical and joyous.

HIS LAUGHTER BROKE into tears when May crashed on top of the sofa later that evening. Marcus and Bastion refused to go downstairs, leaving René alone with May. He hugged her as she swore and cursed and punched his shoulder.

"Asshole. You asshole. You selfish, selfish, stupid asshole."

"I'm sorry. I'm sorry," he whispered and petted her hair, knowing she could feel his hand but not hear his words.

May jerked away, dropped to the couch, and dried her eyes. The mascara bled down her cheeks and left trails no matter how many tissues she used to scrub her puffy face.

"I know it's not your fault. They charged the crazy old bat with vehicular manslaughter, but still—*still*, I can't help but feel you somehow did it on purpose to be with *them*."

René found the laptop. He frowned at the screen, thinking of how strange it was to need it to talk to May. *I tried to stay out of the road. She took the turn so fast I didn't even know why Bastion was upset when I woke up.* He couldn't think of a way to finish without upsetting May more, so he stopped writing.

"I *know*. I know that in my head." She grabbed another tissue. "I'm just saying. I'm still mad at you. It's still your fault, because yelling at you is my only coping mechanism at the moment."

René wanted to joke about the life insurance policy May probably didn't know about—she was about to inherit a lot of money. He wanted to joke about her buying a hot tub for the house, which she would also inherit, but knew jokes would make her cry harder so he rubbed her left shoulder and felt like an asshole, like he *did* do it on purpose. He felt so happy that afternoon as he slept between Bastion and Marcus without hot showers, heaters, or blankets, it seemed like he *was* to blame somehow.

"Oh, I don't know why I'm crying." May sniffed, trying her damnedest to smile. "Usually when people die, you never talk to them again, but you're right here." She patted the crown of his head, his cheek, his shoulder. "You're much easier to see than Marcus and Bastion. You look sort of like a cloud. A stupid, René-shaped cloud. Idiot. I should make you drink with me, even though I know you'd vomit."

René kept a bottle of Bailey's in the fridge for the occasional spiked coffee. He fetched two glasses and poured the drinks. He almost dropped the bottle, not used to manipulating physical objects as a ghost yet. René laughed and sniffed as a few tears trickled down his cheek. He promised to tell Bastion later so they could all laugh about it, but for the time being, he handed May her glass.

"I was joking, stupid." She smiled as she wiped fresh tears off her cheeks.

René typed on the laptop. *One last time. Serves me right. Bastion offered to check the mail for me. I should have let him.*

"Yeah, because watching the mail float through the air would have made the old goat drive *much* better." May snorted laughter into her tissue, but it became another sob.

René handed her a drink and wiped the tears off her cheek. He bit his lip to keep from jerking his hand away. May's face felt like ice.

"It's reversed," he muttered to himself since May couldn't hear.

"To you, asshole." She raised her glass in a toast before slamming the drink down in a single swallow.

René copied her. The drink reminded him of swallowing Bastion's or Marcus's seed before he died. Thick, cold, pleasant but otherworldly. The glass fell from his hand as soon as he finished swallowing. Nausea hit quicker than he imagined it would, and he ran to the toilet. He wasn't sure what he expected when he vomited—real puke that disappeared as soon as it hit the floor, slimy ectoplasm, the stuff seen in horror movies, but it was the Irish Cream that poured from his mouth. It looked unaltered from before he drank it. He heard May crying harder on the sofa. René curled in on himself, and he knelt on the tiled floor, sobbing.

The sounds of May's tears stopped. René crawled to the doorway. Marcus and Bastion sat on each side of her, taking turns typing on the laptop. May laughed at what they wrote, her normal laugh, and René exhaled because he knew it'd take time, but she'd be okay.

SPRING MELTED THE snow. The yard burst into green—dark-green hedges, crayon-green lawn. White and yellow daffodils grew along the fence line. As soon as the ice broke from the pool's surface outside, René started swimming. He poked his head up from the water and held onto the ledge. Marcus and Bastion relaxed on the grass and argued over a game of poker.

"I know you can't get hypothermia, but aren't you cold?" Bastion asked as he shuffled their cards.

"It feels like making love with you two before I died." René laughed.

"I don't think you're supposed to be this excited about being a ghost, René." Bastion shook his head.

"At least we don't have to worry about your dumb ass falling in and drowning anymore." Marcus shook his head.

"Always a bright side." René pulled himself from the water, dry as soon as he thought about being dry, but intentionally bare. René stretched his arms over his head, loving the way the sun felt on his nonexistent skin. "I think we have some time before May comes home from work."

"Oh?" Marcus grinned at him. "Were you thinking about going upstairs?"

"Perhaps."

"Anything to end this game." Bastion dropped his cards to the ground. "I don't see how I can be so bad at cards."

"You're so bad it's almost a talent." Marcus reorganized the deck.

"Yes, everything seems vogue when I do it—including sucking."

René and Marcus exchanged a look, asking each other who would say the obvious joke. Bastion sensed their amusement and distracted them by tugging the shirt over his head and arching his back on the grass in order to unzip his jeans.

"Why go upstairs? Take me here in the grass."

"You tell me I shouldn't be excited about being a ghost, but everything about this is amazing. No one can see us, or hear us, and we can have sex outside all day long—which is great. How can I not be excited?"

Bastion lay spread out naked with the sun heating his body and the grass tickling his legs. René dropped to the grass and climbed over Bastion to suck his bottom lip. After only a taste, Marcus yanked René's hair and pushed him off of Bastion.

"Who said you could kiss him?" Marcus teased, leaning over and replacing René's mouth with his own.

"I'll kiss you then." René tugged Marcus away from Bastion's lips.

He made good on his threat, relishing the taste of Marcus's mouth. No matter how many times he kissed them, how many times they made love in their bed—May inherited the house, but left René's room and the kitchen exactly the same—René never tired of the brush of their skin beneath his fingers, never tired of taste of their mouths, and never tired of the smell of their hair or the cologne they wore when they were alive, which still clung to them.

Bastion wedged himself between them. He kissed Marcus's chest and then sucked on René's left nipple. Back and forth, back and forth, and by the time he reached René's mouth, René tasted the shock of salt from their bodies off of Bastion's lips. Their petting grew fierce, heavier and heavier handed until Bastion raked his nails across whatever surface he could reach. Marcus growled. René knew the pain of Bastion's nails aggravated him but exhilarated him at the same time. Marcus grabbed Bastion's hips and situated him so he and René could both take Bastion at the same time.

They didn't need physical lubrication anymore, as with wet or dry, clothed or naked, the thought of it made it real. Another perk to being a ghost. Every day René discovered more and more reasons why he liked being a ghost better than he ever liked being a physical being. Perhaps they'd miss out on things: growing old, and arguing at the grocery store, and binge drinking with May, but René felt like William Butler Yeats at Innisfree. He couldn't mourn his own death, not when the sour heat of Bastion's breath blew on his cheek and the sweat of the three of them made his legs and stomach itch. Too happy, he was far too happy as a spirit, and he refused to stop enjoying himself.

Bastion clawed at the grass, cursing his men in his beautiful, lyrical way as Marcus snarled in passion and René whispered *please* with each breath. René soared toward orgasm, his thoughts lost somewhere between his lovers' bodies. One day they'd go into the light, all of them together, and whatever Heaven may wait for them—beyond the bright white aura—would have to be impressive indeed to supersede the current moment and call itself paradise.

About the Author

Sita Bethel loves writing fiction and hates writing biographies. Ya boi Sita feels like they all tend to sound the same when read out loud—like a bad gothic meme. Sita Bethel now suspects that author bios are actually bad gothic memes. No writer enjoys writing biographies, and yet still we write them. We have always been writing them. Sita Bethel has been writing this bio for over an hour now and will probably be writing another one by the time anyone sees these words.

Email: sitabethel@hotmail.com

Facebook: www.facebook.com/sitabethelfiction

Twitter: @sita_bethel

Website: www.sitabethel.com

Other books by this author

"Angels in Delaware" within *Beneath the Layers*
"Dressed in Wolf Skin" within *Into the Mystic, Vol. Two*
"Master Thief" within *Once Upon A Rainbow, Vol. Two*

Also Available from NineStar Press

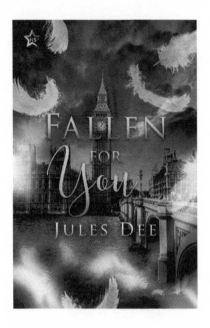

Connect with NineStar Press

Website: NineStarPress.com

Facebook: NineStarPress

Facebook Reader Group: NineStarNiche

Twitter: @ninestarpress

Tumblr: NineStarPress

CPSIA information can be obtained
at www.ICGtesting.com
Printed in the USA
LVHW091207310520
657057LV00002B/440